John Banim

The Peep o' Day; or, John Doe, the Last of the Guerillas

A Tale of the Whiteboys

John Banim

The Peep o' Day; or, John Doe, the Last of the Guerillas
A Tale of the Whiteboys

ISBN/EAN: 9783337073725

Printed in Europe, USA, Canada, Australia, Japan

Cover: Foto ©Andreas Hilbeck / pixelio.de

More available books at **www.hansebooks.com**

THE

PEEP. O' DAY;

OR,

JOHN DOE, THE LAST OF THE GUERILLAS.

A TALE OF THE WHITEBOYS.

BY

JOHN BANIM,

AUTHOR OF THE "NOLANS," "BOYNE WATER," "THE CROPPY," "THE CONFORMIST,"
ETC.

NEW YORK:

THE AMERICAN NEWS COMPANY,

115, 117, 119, 121 NASSAU STREET.

—

1876.

THE PEEP O'DAY;

OR,

JOHN DOE.

CHAPTER I.

THE old devotion to private skirmishing of the Irish peasantry is well known. Skirmishing would indeed be too mild a word to express the ferocious encounters that often took place among them—(we speak in the past tense, for, from a series of wretchednesses, the spirit has of late considerably decreased)—when parties, or, as they are locally termed, factions, of fifty or a hundred, met, by appointment, to wage determined war ; when blood profusely flowed, and, sometimes, lives were lost.

But, apart from the more important instances of the practice those pitched battles presented, accident, and the simplest occurrences of their lives—pleasure, rural exercise, sport, or even the sober occupation of conveying a neighbor to his last home—supplied, indifferently well, opportunities for an Irish row.

On festival days, when they met at a "pattern" (patron, perhaps) or merry-making, the lively dance of the girls, and the galloping jig-note of the bagpipes, usually gave place to the clattering of alpeens, and the whoops of onslaught. When one of them sold his pig, or, under Providence, his cow at the fair, the kicking up of a "scrimmage," or at least the plunging head foremost into one, was as much a matter of course as the long draughts of ale or whiskey that closed his mercantile transaction. At the village hurling-match, the "hurlet," or crooked stick with which they struck the ball, often changed its playful utility. Nay, at a funeral, the body was scarce laid in the grave when the voice of petty discord might be heard above the grave's silence.

These contentions, like all great events, generally arose from very trivial causes. A drunken fellow, for instance, was in a strange public-house; he could not content himself with the new faces near him, so struck at some three, six, or ten, as it might be, and, of course, got soundly drubbed. On his return home, he related his case of injury, exhibiting his closed eye, battered mouth, or remnant of nose; and, enlisting all his relatives, "kith-and-kin"—in fact, all his neighbors who liked "a bit of diversion," and they generally included the whole male population able to bear arms. At the head of his faction, he attended the next fair, or other place of resort, where he might expect to meet his foes. The noise of his muster went abroad, or he had sent a previous challenge: the opposite party had assembled in as much force as possible, never declining the encounter: one or other side was beaten, and tried to avenge its disgrace on the first opportunity. Defeat again followed, and again produced like efforts and results; and thus the solemn feud ran through a number of years and several generations.

A wicked, "devil-may-care" fellow, feverish for sport, would, at fair, pattern, or funeral, sometimes smite another without any provocation, merely to create a riot: the standers-by would take different sides, as their taste or connections inclined them, and the fray thus commencing, between two individuals who owed each other no ill-will, embroiled half the assembled concourse. Nay, a youth, in despair that so fine a multitude was likely to separate peaceably, would strip off his heavy outside coat, and trail it through the puddle, daring any of the lookers-on to tread upon it. Such defiance was rarely ineffectual; he knocked down, if possible, the invited offender; a general battle ensued, that soon spread like wild-fire, and every "alpeen" was at work in senseless clatter and unimaginable hostility.

The occurrence of the word "alpeen," here and elsewhere, seems to suggest a description of the weapon of which it is the name, and this can best be given in a piece of biographical anecdote.

Jack Mullally still lives in fame, though his valiant bones are dust. He was the landlord of a public-house in a mountain district; a chivalrous fellow, a righter of wrongs, the leader of a faction of desperate fighting men:—like Arthur, with his doughty knights—he was a match for any four among them, though each a hero: above all, he was the armorer of his department. In Jack's chimney-corner, hung bundles of sticks, suspended there for the purpose of being dried and seasoned. These were of two descriptions of warlike weapons,—shortish oaken cudgels, to be used as quarter-staves, or, *par excellence*, genuine shillelaghs ; and the alpeens themselves,—long wattles with heavy knobs at the ends, to be wielded with both hands, and competent, under good guidance, to the felling of an ox.

Jack and his subjects, Jack and his alpeens, were rarely absent from any fair within twenty miles, having always business on hand in the way of their association. When a skirmish took place, the side that could enlist in its interests Jack, his alpeens, and his merry men, was sure of victory. The patriarch was generally to be found seated by his kitchen fire. Business was beneath him ; he left all that to the " *vanithee ;*" and his hours lapsed, when matters of moment did not warn him to the field, either in wetting his sticks with a damp cloth, and then heating them over the turf blaze, to give them the proper curve ; or in teaching a pet starling to speak Irish, and whistle "*Shaun Buoy ;*" or, haply, in imbibing his own ale or whiskey, and smoking his short black pipe, or *doodheen* as he himself termed it. Here he gave audience to the numerous suitors and ambassadors who, day by day, came to seek his aid, preparatory to concerted engagements. His answer was never hastily rendered. He promised, at all events, to be, with his corps, at the appointed ground : then and there would he proclaim of which side he was the ally. This precautionary course became the more advisable as he was always sure of a request from both factions ; and time, forethought, and inquiry, were necessary to ascertain which side might prove the weaker. For to the weakest—the most aggrieved formed no part of his calculations—Jack invariably extended his patronage.

The vanithee, good woman, when she heard of an approaching fair or other popular meeting, immediately set about preparing plasters and ointments : this resulted from a thrifty forecast. For, were she to call in a doctor every time her husband's head wanted piecing, it would run away with the profits of her business. Jack, indeed, never forgot his dignity so far as to inform his wife that he intended being engaged on such occasions : but she always took it for granted, and, with the bustle of a good housewife, set about her preparations accordingly. Till at length a breach happened in his skull which set her art at defiance ; and ever since she lives the sole proprietor of the public-house where Jack oes reigned in glory. The poor widow has thriven since her

1*

husband's death ; and is now rich, not having lately had Jack's
assistance in spending (she never had it in earning). She re-
counts his exploits with modest spirit ; and one blessing, at least,
has resulted from her formerly matronly care of the good man :
she is the Lady Bountiful of her district ; a quack, it may be,
yet sufficiently skilful for the uncomplicated ailments of her
country customers.

Such ordinary facts as we have here glanced at, never fail to
strike with astonishment, if they do not greatly interest, the
English visitor to "the sister isle," when he is first made acquainted with them. In both ways were they regarded by two
young English officers quartered at a remote, though no very
remote period, in the inland town of Clonmel, before whom a
native acquaintance descanted on these traits of local character,
while he and his military friends sat over their evening bottle.
The bottle emptied, the Clonmel visitor gone, Lieutenants Howard
and Graham remained together, still occupied with the new and
extraordinary anecdotes they had heard. They separated for the
night, and continued to recur with interest to the information of
their friend. They were amazed, if not shocked : they could not
understand how such things could happen. In a civilized country,
indeed, a motive to the cool, scientific punishment that Spring
and Neat, or Spring and Langan bestow upon each other, was
easily comprehended : but they stared with utter consternation
at the mystery of an Irish fight, because it was discussed with
shillelaghs and alpeens, instead of fists and knuckles.

Next morning they met, after their early parade, at Graham's
private lodgings—for, at the time we speak of, the officers of a
regiment were afforded, even in considerable towns in Ireland,
but scanty accommodation in barracks. It was a hot, oppressive
forenoon in the close of July, promising a day of even more
relaxing influence, and ten hours of sunlight were before them,
to be spent in one way or other. To the man of business, or
to the professional man in London, to the needy author, the
toiling lawyer, nay, considering the various rounds of metropoli-
tan amusements, perhaps to the Cornet of the Guards himself,
this may seem no very embarrassing prospect ; but to the fashionable English lieutenant on country service in Ireland it might
well appear an endless vista, beset with doubt and fear, and all
the little fiends of apathy and idleness.

In their want of something to do, and while they again recurred
to the topics of the preceding night, the friends felt curious to

behold, as they had previously been surprised to hear of, an Irish row ; and—

"Oh, for a fight of alpeens !" said Graham, throwing up the window, as he rose from breakfast, and heaving one of those heavy sighs that denote the joint reign of heat and listlessness —" Howard, what is to become of us this ferocious day ?"

"There's nothing to be done with the fishing-rods," returned Howard : " Isaac Walton himself could not tempt to a bite any trout in his senses, till evening, at least. And I am tired of the two Misses O'Flaherty."

" And I of the three Miss Nicholsons, and of the four Miss Pattensons," said Graham ; " their prattle and tattle, their tastes and their raptures, are death to me. They have all been escorted through the streets, and on their public promenades, and to Church, Mass, or Meeting, by the poor ensigns of the last score of regiments quartered in their native town, saying the same fiddle-faddle things, and exhibiting to each set, successively and in vain, from time immemorial, the same faces and the same fascinations."

" Then their brothers and male cousins are such sots, asses, or puppies," continued Howard, in the same complimentary strain, towards people who thought themselves as the apple of his eye.

" And their mothers and maiden aunts such worriers," re-joined Graham in the same tone. " And the girls themselves, too, they walk so much, and they clack so fast, and they parade one so here and there, that a man had better be on a real forced march at once, than by their sides in such weather. But, suppose billiards ?"—

" Monstrous !"

" Then the racket-court ?"

" Terrible !"

" A cool hand at whist till mess-hour ?"

This proposal was also considered and declined. The friends having thus passed in review all the means of enjoyment suggested by their situation and ruling tastes, remained for some time hope-lessly silent, picking crumbs of bread off the breakfast-table, and gently filliping them out at the open window, until the entrance of their last night's guest gave a fresh and pleasing turn to their ideas. Renewing with him the conversation about Irish fights and merry-makings, they were cheered to find that a pattern was that day holden a few miles from Clonmel, where they might hope to become acquainted, at a civil distance, with the prowess of the Alpeen and Shillelagh.

A proposal from Mr. Burke, their Clonmel friend, to guide them to the spot, was immediately accepted; and, though the sun grew fierce in his strength, they resolved to proceed on foot, for he promised to lead them by a short cut through fields and meadows. The breeze of the open country was reviving, and they would saunter along, resting in the occasional shade, and by the side of clear cool brooks; no hurry was in the case; indeed it were better to come upon the scene of festivity towards evening. Altogether, everything was *now* practicable and delightful. So, sinking the military character in peaceful suits of clothes, a precaution prudently hinted by Mr. Burke, each gentleman, by his further advice, furnished himself with a respectable shillelagh, and the little expedition set out.

CHAPTER II.

AFTER a pleasant saunter through an open, interesting country, Howard and Graham, and their friend, gained the spacious plain on which the pattern was being held. For some time they rambled about amongst the people, looking on at their diversions, or occasionally joining in their mirth. Assuredly there was here a sufficient variety to engage attention. Some were employed at the wonders of the show-box, or listening with open mouths, and looks of respectful amazement, to the oratory of its accomplished exhibitor. Our gentlemen did not, themselves, refuse an approving laugh to one turn of the fellow's eloquence. He had in his hand, the knotted string, which guided the movements of a picture of a certain battle, celebrated in the annals of the Irish rebellion for a triumph over some regiments of Irish militia, by a mob of peasants, assisted by a part of the handful of French landed at Killala.

"Look to the right," quoth the showman, "and you shall see the Wicklow militia scampering off the ground, my Lord Monck at their head, on the gallant occasion. Small blame to his lordship, for the French are at his heels."

Passing from this group of rustic connaisseurs, our visitors next noticed a swarm of simple clowns, who stood, all their faculties of acuteness and comprehension brought to a focus, watching the coils of a strip of old hat, as the cunning knave, who professed this species of gambling, folded it up in good affectation of plain dealing : then, certain that they had kept an observant eye during the process, they proceeded, with hope almost raised to certainty, to stick a wooden peg in the proper loop. A half-penny was paid for the venture, and if successful they were to gain thrice the sum ; but, with all their sagacity, bitter disap-pointment was sure to follow. Many staked their money on the fascinating evolutions of the Wheel of Fortune ; and always with certain loss : others threw a stick at some wooden pins placed upright in the ground, ever filled with honest surprise that they could not hit any of them, though but a few yards distant. There were beggars with every boasted ailment under the sun, clamor-ously insisting on the charity of "the good Christians ;" and ballad-singers with cracked lungs, squeaking forth ditties of unique composition ; such as,—

"As I did ramble,
Down by a bramble," &c.

There were venders of cakes and of cheese, of apples and of gingerbread, all striving with incessant uproar to attract custom. But the principal diversion, and that to which the greater number were attached, was dancing on the green sod. As our trio stood a little elevated above the concourse, they counted ten pipers within ken, each surrounded by a crowd of " boys and girls," footing it away with every mark of utter glee and happiness. The manner in which a piper set up his establishment was simple enough. If he had a wife,—as which of them had not ?—she brought a stool, and, lacking that convenience, a stone served the purpose : he seated himself ; struck up a merry jig ; one or two friends patronized his muse, and presently he had a group around him, and was prosperous.

By the way, an occurrence noticed by our party, on their walk to the pattern, should here be mentioned. A few fields from the scene of festivity they perceived a young fellow, rakishly dressed in his holyday garb, stop, unconscious of observance, before one of those tall stones occasionally to be met with in the country parts of Ireland, but of which the use or meaning is unknown to us, notwithstanding that we have anxiously inquired after their tradition. The athletic fellow held his hat in his hand, bowed to the stone with all the air he could assume ; bowed again and again ; then replaced his hat, and began to dance rapidly before his stationary partner. He kept his eyes fixed on his feet, as if

to watch how they did their business ; and after some time, at
length seemingly pleased with his performance, he took off his
hat again ; again bowed profoundly to the stone, and with an
exulting shout, scampered off to the pattern. Here he was soon
recognized, using to a pretty girl, as he took her out to dance,
the same graceful ceremonies he had before lavished on an object
not so sensible of his fascinations.

"Tents," or booths, constructed in a very primitive manner,
were, to the number of forty or fifty, erected along the field.
Long, pliant wattles, stuck in the ground at regular distances,
and running some thirty feet, then meeting at top, and covered
with blankets, sacks, or such like awning, made up each tent.
A description of the interior of one, will give a proper idea
of the rest. A long deal table, or rather a succession of deal
tables, was placed nearly from end to end ; forms were ranged
at each side ; and on these sat a mixed company of old and
young. Here a youthful fellow was placed by a pretty girl, his
arm around her neck, while he whispered his best soft things, and
she smiled, and pouted, and coquetted : opposite sat two or three
old men discoursing on the weather, the crops, and the prices ;
the young folks no way bashful in their presence, and little reason
had they to be so ; for the ancients quaffed their liquor often and
heartily, taking not the least notice of what passed at the other
side. Here too was a piper, and the dance went on as vigorously
within as without. The landlord and landlady stationed near the
entrance were provided with a good store of ale and whiskey, at
the call of their customers, attended by a wench as comely as possible, eternally out of breath with running here and there, as the
incessant knocks of the empty quarts against the table challenged
her attention. It was her business to see that the same quart did
not thump a second time, and to be prepared with her best smile
and ready joke, and perhaps something else, equally ready and
desirable, for every customer who should choose to laugh or bandy
wit, or struggle for a stray favor, with the decently-coy Hebe.

Having walked everywhere their curiosity directed, without
observing any promise of an Irish row, our amateurs were, in some
disappointment, about to return home, when their unconscious acquaintance, whom they had seen bowing to the stone, made his
appearance from the aperture of a tent, his hat doffed, and leading
by the hand a blooming lass. It was evident he had seen the
party of gentlemen from within ; and now stopping and scraping
before them—" Gentlemen," said he, " here's a merry young girl

wants a partner for a dance." His fair charge whispered to him, and he continued, addressing himself to Graham—" Will you, sir, take a small dance wid the colleen dhass ?"

She sent, on her own part, a merry invitation from her black eye, and Graham's Clonmel friend answered : " This gentleman never said no to a pretty girl in his life." The girl curtsied, still looking to Graham, who, of course, repaid her with a bow. Whereupon she offered her hand, and rather led than was led by Graham into the tent, Howard, Burke, and the posture-master following.

Here they found themselves in the presence of fifty or sixty country people of both sexes and all ages ; some singing ; some spouting love ; some dancing, and some conversing vehemently, and with, at least, spirited gesticulation. But, though thus separately engaged in the detail, all were unanimous in one accompaniment, namely, the consumption of ale or whiskey, more or less ; their hearts wide open as their mouths and eyes, and their animal spirits ecstatic from the genial influence of the liquor.

With officious eagerness, they made room for the strangers, whose "health an' long life" was immediately toasted round from mouth to mouth ; and, according to the local usages of hospitality, Graham, Howard, and Burke, had to pledge every soul within view, each in his or her own magnum. This was more than an inconvenience ; but the visitors had determined to conform in everything to the taste of their circle, and, in the entire good-will of their neighbors, they found the benefit of their policy. For, when in turn they ordered some whiskey punch, and pushed it round, they had enlisted, for ever, the affection of every creature present.

" Arrah, thonomon-duoul, gintilmen, bud here's your hearty welcome among us ; here's long life an' glory to ye ! Upon my soul bud I loves the likes o' ye in the bottom o' my heart, that wouldn't be shy or afeard to sit down and take a drop wid the country-boys. Ye desarve the best in the tent, an' ye must have it as long as Paddy Flinn has a laffina in the 'varsal world— halloo, there !" and thump went the empty quart against the table. Mr. Patrick Flinn, the knight of the stone, had emptied his vessel at one draught, out of the good-will he bore them, and now pounded with a force that set all the other vessels dancing, while the tent echoed the sound.

During his delivery of this speech, Howard had time more closely to observe the face and probable character of their quon dam acquaintance. He seemed about twenty-three years of age, tall, wiry, and athletic : his features expressed rather shrewdness than openness ; the eyes grey and small ; the nose aquiline, and the mouth in a perpetual play of waggery and good-humor, which, perhaps, was as much a convenient affectation as a natural habit. His whole manner and dress, too, appeared ostentatiously disposed to claim notice for him as a queer, scapegrace-looking fellow. He now wore his hat on one side ; and the collar of his shirt being open, displayed a throat and neck red as scarlet, and rough as a cow's tongue.

While Howard made his observations, he was interrupted by a husky, gruff voice at his other side, saying : " Here's towd's yere good healths, gintilmin, an' that ye may thrive an' prosper, an' that I may live to see ye here again at the patthern this day twelve-months, I pray Gor."

The voice that pronounced these words was not in unison with them ; and when Howard fixed his eyes on the speaker, he felt, that neither in person or feature did they find a correspondence. The man was, in fact, of that outward description termed ill-looking. His face, large and gross, beamed with nothing kindly : in stature he was short and broad, but of Herculean symmetry : under a bushy black eyebrow lurked a deep, and, if not scowling, a watchful eye: the whole expression of his features was gravity of a disagreeable kind. At variance with the general costume around, he wore an ample, sailorly jacket, and a red handkerchief, that coiled like a cable round a throat unconscious of a shirt-collar. In other respects, his dress accorded with the usual one ; being composed of a nameless-colored shirt, breeches open at the knees, pale blue stockings, ungartered, and part of an old hat, tied with " suggaus," or hay ropes, about the small of each leg, and covering the tops of his brogues. His age might be forty-five.

But Howard was again diverted from his studies by—" Musha, yere healths, an' kindly welcome to the patthern a hinnies-machree,"—addressed to him and Burke by a sedate old matron, whose clothing, being of the most costly kind worn by the class to which she belonged, showed her to be " comfortable," and that she could well afford to spend a little on such occasions as the present. She had on a good blue rug cloak, the falling hood, lined with purple satin, and a large silver hook-and-eye to fasten it at her neck. A flaming silk handkerchief was tied on her head in the way peculiar to her country, the costly lace of her cap peeping from under it. There was a cordiality, an earnest ness of voice, and a soft benevolence of smile, accompanying her words, that formed a strong contrast to the last salutation.

" Healths a piece, genteels, all round—not forgetting you, sir," added a rosy lass, with a stammer, a smile, and a blush, and her eyes half raised over the vessel, as in the last words she addressea herself to Howard.   And in this strain arose the civilities of every individual in the booth : the phrase and sentiment varying with the age or character of the speaker.

In the mean time, Howard and Burke were lookers-on at the dance between Graham and his partner. When the jig was first about to be struck up, Graham, under the tutelage of Burke, requested to know the tune the lady wished. He was answered, according to invariable custom, with a set phrase—" What's your will is my pleasure, sir." But here the fair one proved over complaisant ; as, from his total ignorance of native music, Graham could name no tune likely to be understood. In this dilemma he had recourse to the piper, who sat with his instrument prepared, awaiting orders ; and in a whisper desired he would give his own favorite. But, before we proceed further, let us introduce more particularly Mr. Thadeus Fitzgereld, or—as he was called by his own friends—Thady Whigarald, the piper.

This popular votary of Apollo, was, if his physiognomy furnished proof, as happy in playing his pipes, as those they set a capering. He sat a good bulky personage, with a fat, pleasant orb of countenance, which, while he tuned his pipes, simpered like a joint of mutton in the dinner-pot : when at work his sightless eyeballs kept rolling about, as his head went backward and forward, and up and down, in unison with his own beloved strains ; while every other feature expressed correspondent applause and ecstasy. His rusty, broad-brimmed, hat was encircled by a small hay-rope instead of the ordinary band, and in this his pipe was stuck : the leaf turned up all round ; so that if Thady happened to be out in a shower, he must have a rivulet running round his head.

His grey frieze coat and waistcoat were much broken ; the knees of his breeches open as usual ; and his stockings so peculiarly tied below the fat knee, as to serve for convenient pockets. Into one he slipped the halfpence, the result of his professional skill ; and from the other occasionally extracted a quid of tobacco, which, with a dexterous jerk, he deposited in his mouth, scarcely ever allowing this digression to interfere with the progress of his music.   Thady was facetious withal ; from time to time encouraging the dancers, as good sportsmen cheer on their dogs. When he heard the feet beat loud time to his jig, which in his estimation was the beau-ideal of dancing,—"Whoo ! success attend you, my darling' !—Whoo ! ma colleen-beg ! That's id, à-vich-ma-chree !—Whoo ! Whoo ! that's your sort, Shaumus !"—these and similar ejaculations joyfully mingled with the notes of his instrument.

To Graham's request for his own favorite air Thady replied—" Why, thin, agra, becase your lavin' it to myself, I'll give you somethin' that's good : so here goes in the name o' God ;" and instantly he set his arm in motion to inflate his bag. Then volunteering a prefatorial shout, he struck up a jig, the rapid canter of which set Graham's extremities going at such a rate, as quickly to put him in a violent heat, and leave him panting for breath. Meanwhile, Graham's mountain-partner, possessing better lungs, or being more of an adept at the exercise, seemed little exhausted, and through common shame and gallantry he rallied his own spirits, and resolved to dance the battle out. But, notwithstanding the encouraging shouts of Thady, the lively and really mirth-inspiring air, and the importance which he could not fail to perceive was attached to durability—for at different intervals he was addressed by the spectators with—" That's id, your sowl ! hould on as long as Thady has a screech in the chanther !"—notwithstanding all this, Graham was at last compelled to make his bow, and retire to a seat, completely blown and crestfallen.

His partner, seemingly but just fresh for the sport, looked triumphant, and still timing the music, jigged towards Howard, with a rapid curtsey, and—" I dance to you, sir, i' you plase." Refusal was out of the question ; and, although he had his friend's fate before his eyes, up sprang the desperate man she had pitched upon. After some time Howard had the gratification to observe that his blooming adversary began in her turn to betray signs of fatigue ; and he was about to congratulate himself on a speedy victory, for he had fully entered into the spirit of competition he observed so prevalent, when another damsel bounced up, flung by her mantle with a jolly air, cocked and secured her coarse straw bonnet, assumed the place of the first, and set upon Howard with all her might. This reinforcement soon decided his fate. Burke took the hint from what had been done by the second girl ; Mr. Patrick Flinn relieved Burke. Other "country-boys" took part with the strangers, for it had now become a real contest between the sexes ; and the fun waxed uproarious. Thady blew with redoubled fury, and grew downright clamorous in his cries of encouragement. The excessive effort creating excessive heat, our military incognitos and friend indulged in frequent glasses of punch, to prevent bad consequences ; so that in a little time they joined in the loud mirth of their companions ; and unconsciously expressed their delight in the same manner as those around them. They turned their partners with a shout, and became *au fait* at the Irish screech. All in the tent felt flattered by the jocularity and heartiness with which they entered into the rustic mirth ; and they had to undergo exclamations of good will, shakes of the hand, and even hugs and kisses, from old and young. Every draught of ale and toss of whiskey went down freighted with " health and long life to the gintilmen, every inch o' them ;" and all declared their readiness, nay, anxiety, to die on the spot, if it could be of the least service to them.

CHAPTER III.

HOWARD, sitting down to rest during the progress of the dance, found himself again by the side of Paddy Flinn, who immediately addressed him.

" Musha, then, beggin' your pardon, sir, will you taste a dhrop of ale frum a poor boy ?" Howard tasted accordingly, and Paddy then caught his hand in an immense fist, hard as his own plough-handle, with a pressure that nearly caused the complimented person to shriek out.

" Sha-dhurth,"* Flinn continued—" upon my conscience, but I'd bear to be kilt stone-dead for you or any friend o' yours. Show me the man, standin' afore me, that 'ud say black is the white o' your eye !—whoo !"—(we have no better translation for the screech). " Whoo !—ma-hurp on duoul !—bud I'd batter his sowl to smithereens !" And, letting Howard's hand go, he smote the table with such might, at the same time emitting a tremendous yell, that the quart from which he was drinking jumped into his lap, and there emptied its contents. Paddy took it up very leisurely, and looking at it for a moment, while

* Your health.

his face assumed an expression of unique waggery, and lost the menacing appearance which a moment before it had worn, thus apostrophized the vessel.

"Why, then, fire to your sowl, an' ill end to you, for one quart, couldn't you be asy wid yourself, an' not to go spill a body's dhrop o' liquor ? Where do you think I'm to make out the maines o' fillin' you so often ?" He again thumped the table with it, however, and the smiling tapster appeared in a trice. "Here ma colleen dhass," he cried, "an' give us a quart the next time that wont be losin' the dhrink."

"A pretty girl, Paddy," observed Howard.

"Arrah, then, isn't she, sir ? an' all o' them, the craturs, considerin' sich as them, that lives on phatoes one an' twenty times in the week ?"* But here a sudden stop was put to the dialogue ; Howard, from what immediately, followed imagining the fellow had lost his wits. Paddy sprang up ; gave his hat a violent shove, that made it hang quite at one side of his head ; jumped across the table ; in his transit overset two old men who were talking Irish ; and, without waiting to apologize for his rudeness, brushed up to where the dance was going forward, and bellowed out, as he flourished a stick he had snatched in his progress—

"Show me the mother's son o' you that daare touch *that !* Whoo ! Dare *you* touch it ?"—whisking round, and playing the stick over the head of a young fellow near him.

"No !—bud I'd sthrike the man that would !—Whoo !" was the answer.

Paddy, after waiting for some time, hallowing and brandishing his weapon in defiance of the whole world, stooped down and raised a hat from the ground, which, with many professions of esteem and love, he presented to Graham, from whose head it had fallen in dancing, and who, in the full fling of the sport, had scarcely observed his loss. Paddy then moved quickly back to his place ; but Howard shifted his quarters, not choosing any longer the immediate proximity of so turbulent a spirit.

Perhaps Howard had another reason for this change of place. No intimate or cordial fellowship seemed to exist between Flinn and the short, dark man we have before described as attracting Howard's notice ; yet, on more than one occasion, he thought he observed a peculiar intelligence take place between them. It was interchanged slightly indeed, by the rapid elevation of an eye

---

* Three times a-day.

brow, the compression of the lips, a shrug, a faint smile, or even a stare; but these simple indications bespoke, in Howard's mind, a closer acquaintance than it was evident the parties wished to proclaim; and the mystery interested him.

Another circumstance, too, assisted the interest. At the very upper part of the tent sat a young man about twenty-four years of age, better dressed and of better air than most around him. From the moment our party came in he had occupied the same place, sleeping or appearing to sleep, through all the uproar, and the only person unconnected with it. He was booted and spurred, and soiled with travel; hence, perhaps, the weariness he could not, or would not cast off. Once, however, he was perfectly awake for a moment, and bending rather a stern eye upon Paddy, as he sat conversing with our friends, the young man called out : "Flinn !" in a commanding and quick tone. The word seemed to strike with equal effect upon Flinn and the gruff-looking man, for both rose, when Flinn said to the other, with a wave of his hand, "'tisn't you, but me, Jack Mullins," and proceeded alone to wait on the young person who had summoned him.

As they conversed rapidly and secretly together, Howard perceived, by the frequent recurrence to him and Graham of the stranger's keen blue eye, that he and his friend formed the subject of their discourse. Displeased, if not offended, his own brow and lip curled : he turned fully round in the direction where the young man sat, and challenged his attention. His manner was scarcely noticed by the person to whom it was addressed, except by a careless aversion of his glance, when, looking once more to Howard, their eyes encountered for an instant. Immediately after Flinn returned to his place, and the person with whom he had conversed turned his side to the company, crossed his legs, leaned his head on his hand, and relapsed into sleep or apathy.

Howard now took a seat beside Jack Mullins, as he had heard Flinn call the surly fellow, whose manner during the whole evening was taciturn in the extreme. For since he drank the stranger's health, upon their first appearance, he had never spoken to those near him, nor indeed, opened his lips, except to afford passage to the inundations of ale, against the influence of which he seemed completely proof, or to send forth a yell, his sole tribute to the general mirth. When Howard sat down by him, he turned his face slowly round, then, with a continued, stolid stare, moved his hand to a quart, and holding it before him, said : "sha dhurth, again, à-vich ;" drank and relapsed into silence.

Howard, from a variety of motives, wishing to draw him into dialogue, remarked : "My friend Paddy is a queer fellow, I believe."

"You may say that, à-roon."

"Then you know him ?"

"Anan ?"

Howard repeated the hypothetical question.

"Why, about us well as you know him yourself ; an' sure that's a raison for saying as much of him as you do, à-vich."

"Och, we all knows poor Paddy well enough," said a curious little old man, with a rusty buckle-wig, who, sitting opposite, overheard the conversation. "He's a boulamskeich iv a divil that never minds nothin' bud his divarsion. But for all that, he's us *good a boy* as any in the place, or the' next place to id, by Gor," and the old fellow's eyes twinkled, as he benevolently brought forward the virtues of Paddy's character.

"I'm glad to hear you say so," said Howard. "I perceive he is over fond of his 'drop o' drink,' as he calls it, and that temperance can scarcely be said to be amongst his good qualities. But I suppose he is an industrious lad ?"

"We never hard much to say fur him in the regard o' that," replied the old man.

"Well, then, he is a dutiful son ; supporting infirm parents perhaps ?"

A rude "ho ! ho !" here sounded from the throat of Mullins. But he corrected himself as Howard turned round ; and now presented a face of impenetrable indifference. The old commentator continued.

"Ulla-loo, à-vich-ma-chree, Paddy doesn't live with his father or mother. He's a stranger among us, like ; a laborin' boy that goes the country, doin' a start o' work for one body or another, just whin he wants the price of a gallon, comin' on a patthern, or a fair, or a thing that-a-way. Bud for all that, as I said afore, he's the *best boy* among us."

Howard, though easily comprehending that the willing expositor knew less of Paddy than Mullins, who professed to know nothing, was impelled to ask another question : "The best boy ! I should like to know what you mean. Paddy is good-natured, I suppose ; obliging, and willing to serve a friend or a neighbor ?"

"Why, a hinny, Paddy'ud be as dacent, an' as willin' as another to do a dacent thing. But sorrow a much has the poor gorçoon in his power, barrin' the one thing. An' maybe he'd do that as free fur fun as fur love. Yes, mostha ; he'd fight fur you till he was kilt, out-an'-out."

"Still you do not tell me how he is 'the best boy.'"

"Musha, God help you, an' beggin' your pardon, sir, à-vich, but I *did* tell you. A better boy nor my poor Pawdeen never walked a fair ;" and he looked affectionately at Flinn, who was, and for some time had been, dancing. "Divil a four o' the cleanest boys in the country bud he'd stretch with his alpeen, afore you could screech."

Their conversation was here interrupted by the hero himself who, as he sat down at some distance, commenced, in consequence of a general request, to exhibit as a singer. He sang in Irish, and Howard necessarily lost the literal sense of his verses ; but the air to which they ran had such a character of downright waggery, as could not for a moment be mistaken. Paddy prefaced each verse with a prose introduction, spoken in all the mock-seriousness of a finished exhibitor ; and the effect produced by the whole on the audience was most surprising. They seemed frantic with delight ; they jumped about, screamed, banged the table, and greeted the close of every verse with a general shout of extatic approbation. What would an applause-loving actor not give for such an audience ?

Howard, wishing to fathom the taste of his rustic friends, longed to be made acquainted with the nature of the composition, and for this purpose applied to a decent-looking man, who seemed more orderly in his demeanor than the others, and to whose opinion a universal respect was paid whenever he deigned to deliver himself, which was not often. In fact, this was the mountain schoolmaster, and Howard could not have applied to a better person. After some preliminary remarks, composed of the biggest and most obsolete words the pedagogue could recollect, he supplied a literal translation of one verse, which ran as follows :

> "Oh, whiskey, the delight and joy of my soul!
> You lay me stretched on the floor,
> You deprive me of sense and knowledge,
> And you fill me with a love of fighting ;
> My coat you have often torn from my back ;
> By you I lost my silken cravat ;
> But all shall be forgotten and forgiven,
> If you meet me after mass next Sunday."

The song passed away, and Howard again sought to penetrate the rhinoceros caution in which Mullins wrapped himself.

"An accomplished fellow every way," he said, turning to his neighbor.

"Ay, faith," was the reply.

"I saw him speaking to that strange young man, some time since," continued Howard.

"Did you ?" said Mullins, unmoved.

"And therefore conclude they are acquainted ?"

"Ay in troth ?" (asking rather than assenting).

"Well ?"

"Pray do you know that sleepy young man ?"

"Me ? —how could I ?"

"Why I thought when he spoke"—

"Harkee, à-vich," interrupted Mullins, with, for the first time, a slight approach to interest—"I know little of any body, and don't care how little any body knows of me : I never ax questions, for fear I'd be tould lies. Bud," he continued, changing his manner into an affectation of communicativeness, as he perceived Howard's displeasure—"sure we all know *that's* the farmer's son, that comes to hire us now an' then, to dig the phatoes, o' the likes o' that. An' sure Paddy Flinn, or any other laborin' boy of his kind, may know as much of him as another, an' no harm done."

Howard was here called on to take his place in the everlasting dance, and rose accordingly. The fame of the "gentilmen's" exploits had gone abroad, and the boys and girls poured in from the neighboring booths, totally abandoning the pipers without, to partake of the superior glee that was going on in the favored tent. The place became excessively heated by the throng, and, since dancing must be the order of the evening, it was proposed by Howard and his friends to substitute country dances for jigs, in order to do away with some of the monstrous labor of the occupation. The novelty of the thing made it highly acceptable, although, except the strangers, there were not, perhaps, two individuals present who understood the evolutions of a figure. Immediate preparations were, however, made for commencing. The gentlemen chose their partners amongst the very prettiest lasses ; took the upper places, in order that the others might study the figure before their turn came round : and, with an encouraging whoop from Thady Whigarald, at the same time that he struck up "Mrs. M'Cloud," set off in high spirits.

In a little time the lads and lasses began to understand the dance, and then wondering at and delighted with their own cleverness, the glee became deafening. Every soul in the tent was infected by the Imp of boisterous enjoyment. The dancers shouted as they bounded along : the piper drowned his own music in his own shouts. Children and old men and women shouted as the performers whisked by, and with gesticulation accompanied them in their career. Those who sat at the table beat time with their fists ; so that the quarts, pints, and tumblers went through the mazes of a figure of their own. And two urchins, bestriding an empty barrel, and kicking with their heels, provoked from it a sound that, while it assisted in the chorus, told equally well for the pocket of the landlord, and the guzzling capability of his guests.

In the midst of the sport, Howard, who had occasionally reconnoitred the upper part of the tent, where the persevering sleeper lay, observed that from time to time Mullins sidled his way in that direction, and was now within a few yards of the young man. The increasing puzzle had its effect on Howard, and he brought his mind to consent to a finesse, that under other circumstances he should certainly have rejected, no matter how urged on by curiosity or interest. Having danced to the bottom with his partner, he pleaded to her a slight illness, enjoining her not to make any remark ; left the party, bearing a glass of water in his hand, and stretched himself on a form nearly opposite Mullins, and about equidistant from him and the other person, who still seemed wrapt in sleep. To a gruff question from Mullins, he urged a bad head and stomach, and much fatigue, and then apparently composed himself to slumber, and in a short time gave natural symptoms of deep repose.

The *ruse* was successful. After a lapse of about ten minutes, Howard could hear Mullins move higher up on his seat, and then a quick whisper from the other—" No—no—stay as you are— no nearer. Do you think he sleeps ?"

" Like a top," answered Mullins in the same whisper,—" But let us step out, if you like, for a surety."

" Idiot !" said the other, " how can you propose *that* ? Don't you fear we are watched ?"

" Well, à-vich," answered Mullins, passively.

" Well or ill, listen to me. And dont turn round so, and gape at me. I see you with my side sight. Turn off, and look away from me, as I do from you. There, and now answer me in that position, but no louder than I question you. I have ridden hard at your appointment up from the harbor ; and a damned fag it is to one so long unused to it. Since I entered this tent and

2

saw you, I have suffered hell's torments, in not being able to ask you one question. *Is* he at the pattern?"

"I saw him on the road, an' he tould me he was for comin' here, as a good place to hire his men for the harvest."

"How long is this ago?"

"About five hours agone, I think."

"Are you sure he is to come alone?"

"Not the laste sure in the world; but all the other way. Didn't I tell you he guessed you were somewhere in the country? Didn't you say, yourself, this moment, he may be on the watch? An' sure he wouldn't come here widout a few alpeens, any way. The red divil himself can call his faction about him, an' so can *he.*"

"Well, how many of us are here?"

"Only myself an' Flinn, an' six boys more. But I often riz a good Faction in a worse place out o' nothin' at all bud good will for a scrimmage."

"You know you must not appear to him unless we are successful, out-and-out. The six other lads are abroad?"

"Yes; here an' there, an' over-an' hether. And Flinn, you see, for all his caperin' an' his divil's thricks, is watchin' the mouth o' the tent."

There was a pause, broken only by one or two impatient sighs that came from the younger person, who again resumed, in a hasty whisper :—

"Damnation!—if *this* fellow be only giving us the fox's sleep?"

"Avoch, don't fear him. 'Tisn't a soft omadhaun like him could think of any sich thing."

"But I saw him speaking to you?"

"Well, an' if you did? Sure I knew how to answer him : don't fear."

Another pause ensued, and the young man once more led the conversation.

"Mullins, now listen attentively to me."

"Well, à-vich."

"*His* life must be spared on this occasion. Let us first secure and get him down to the harbor. That's all I want for the present."

"An' that's little enough. I remembered you tould me so afore, an' sure I told Flinn, too, as you bid me. We'll all mind it."

"Again I warn *you* to keep out of his sight. The moment the game is up, take to the road, and wait for us a little way forward. If we fail, your continuing to live on good terms with the rascal is what we must mainly depend on for success another time. D'you hear me ?"

" Avoch, to be sure I do."

" Then move down from me, now, as easily as you can. I see another of these fools coming."

Mullins obeyed this order as Graham advanced in some anxiety to look after Howard. He found his friend seemingly asleep on the forms, and Howard allowed himself to be often called and shaken before he would acknowledge the restoration of his senses. At last jumping up he declared his illness to be quite gone. Wishing to communicate to Graham in private the strange conversation he had heard, he advanced towards the dancers, first observing that the young man had re-assumed his drowsy mask, and that Mullins had slid a good distance off, and was now looking at and cheering on the crowd, with as much affectation of enjoyment as his gross and lethargic features could assume.

" The very devil's in that fellow," said Graham pointing to Flinn, as they approached the revellers. " He has been continually out of place since you left us ; jostling and plunging, and setting every one astray. Expostulation was thrown away upon him ; I endeavored to give him some directions, and he listened pretty tamely for a moment, but as we spoke the precious piper emitted such a blast and shout, as were too much for him. Off he went like a shot, thump against another man's partner, who had not time to get out of his way, and brought her to the earth. But, without at all ceasing the motion of his feet, Paddy instantly caught her up, gave her a kiss, to which Petruchio's in the church was mere billing and cooing, and adding—' there alanna ! sure I'll kiss you an' cure you,' on he went as if nothing had happened."

Howard now made an effort to move through the crowd to the opening of the tent, beckoning Burke, and leading Graham. Considerable difficulty occurred in the very first step, as well from the good-natured officiousness of the people, as from their number and bustle. A moment after, other circumstances completely foiled any such intention.

Paddy Flinn was just about to lead down the dance. The last couple had just finished ; and at the entreaty of his partner he seemed endeavoring to bring his mind to a focus, and try to understand what he had to do, his face being turned to the entrance of the tent. Suddenly he sprang forward ; snatched an alpeen that lay quietly beside the piper ; and then, with a tremendous yell, upsetting every person and thing in his way,

flourished the weapon, and made a deadly blow at a gentlemanly-
dressed man who was just entering. The foremost of a considerable body of peasants who came in with this person, guarded
off the blow, and in turn struck at the aggressor. Their sticks
crossed and chattered ; but at last Paddy felled his man, crying out
at the same time, as the rest of the hostile party pressed upon
him—" Where are ye, my boys, abroad !—Come on for the right
cause !—Look afther Purcell !—he's goin' to escape !" Then
turning to the people in the tent—" Neighbors ! neighbors !—
neighbors an' all good Christhens !—stand up for honest men !
This is the divil's bird, Purcell !—stand up for the orphans he
made ! for the widow he kilt ! for the daughter he ruined ! and
the son that's far away !—Whoo !"

As he spoke, Howard looked with amazement at the sudden
and almost incredible change that in a moment was presented in
the face and manner of Flinn. His features lost every trait of
the levity and drollery that had hitherto appeared to be their
fixed character, and now bent and flashed with natural sternness
and ferocity. His figure became erect, firm and well-set. All
previous jauntiness and swagger were cast aside like a disguise :
his whole mien was that of a man made up to the accomplish-
ment of a desperate purpose, and seemingly incapable of a moment's trifling or good-humor.

The instant he concluded his speech, the shout was echoed from
abroad, and some six or seven, evidently the friends he had invoked, pressed upon the rear of Purcell's party, and gave the
greater number of them something to do. Flinn, after levelling
the foremost of the van, for some time singly engaged the remainder. And well did he uphold the character given of him to
Howard by the little old man in the buckle-wig. Within a few
minutes he had stretched four additional enemies by the side of
the first victim to his invincible arm and murderous alpeen. But
presently he was saved the trouble as well as the glory of a single
stand against shameful odds. Every male creature in the tent
flew to arms, and the greater proportion siding with Flinn, he
became the leader of the more numerous faction.

Now ensued a scene of truly astounding uproar. The tables,
on which the landlord had disposed his good things, were upset
in an instant : his jars and bottles went smash, and rivulets of
good ale and whiskey inundated the tent : bread and meat, and
cheese, were trodden under foot. Thady Whigarald was tumbled
from his seat, his pipes crushed to atoms ; and the last desperate

and expiring sob of the wind-bag, and scream of the chanter, mingled ludicrously enough with his own pathetic lamentations for the loss of his darling instrument. The landlord uselessly endeavored to harangue the combatants : in vain he pointed out the utter ruin hurled upon him. The girls and old women screamed, and tried to escape by the entrance ; but it was crowded with battle, and all chance of retreat, except with danger to limb and life, thereby rendered hopeless. So that after a time they flocked to the upper part of the tent, keeping shrill chorus to the war-whoops of the men of fight, to the frantic oratory of the landlord and landlady, to the clattering and clashing of alpeens, and the rapid and too audible blows that resulted from them.

But the worst is to be told. Arms were scarce ; and, woful to relate, the frail tenement that had hitherto afforded the combatants shelter and merriment was demolished in a twinkling, to supply the pressing want. The wattles on which the awning was suspended were torn up ; the blankets and sacks, that had formed the roof, pulled down and trampled to rags. Howard had, before now, seen a battle "in the tented field ;" Graham had long fondly imagined one, and both had speculated even upon an Irish row. But such an exhibition as the present neither had ever yet beheld or dreamt of.

They and their friends endeavored to make ,peace, counting upon the previous devotion expressed to their sweet persons. But such is the fickleness of all human influence and popularity, that broken pates were likely to be the only result of so ill-timed an assumption of superiority. No one, indeed, struck at them ; but they were shoved and shouldered aside, and sent helpless and unnoticed through the tide of battle, like bubbles dancing upon the war of ocean, or straws or atoms whisked through the conflict of the whirlwinds. Meantime the hand of chance alone shielded them from the promiscuous blows that were dealt around ; some of which they would, in all probability, have shared, had not a providential rescue occurred in their behalf.

An amazonian maiden, to whom Graham had been particularly "sweet," as she would herself say, in the course of the evening, observed his dangerous situation, and, with the energy and disinterestedness of a primitive heroine, plunged forward to snatch him from it. Dashing aside the waves of battle, she won her fearless way to Graham's side, clasped him in her arms, and, bearing him to the top of the tent, set him down on his legs amid the peaceable cohort of women who had there taken up their position. Some four or five, stimulated by her example, made the same exertions, and with the same success, in behalf of Howard and Burke ; and our three friends, being thus safely disengaged, the treble files closed upon them, clamorously refusing to afford further opportunity for peacemaking.

One of the first observations which Howard made, assured him that neither Mullins nor his drowsy companion remained where he had left them. In fact, they were nowhere to be seen ; and as, so far as he could recollect, they had not advanced to the belligerents, it was plain they must have retired through the space left after the demolition of the tent. Before he had been spirited away from the immediate scene of action, Howard could ascertain that Purcell, as he had heard Flinn call the gentleman who served as a provocative to the engagement, was also missing. And the yelling exclamations which now broke from Paddy, proved that he must have effectually baffled his foes, and escaped whole and uninjured, whatever fate had been alloted for him.

We have taken up some time in describing a scene, and the rapid succession of events, that in reality did not occupy above five minutes ; for, counting from the moment that Flinn gave his first blow, down to that during which Howard made the observations just attributed to him, not more time had certainly elapsed. As he concluded his reflections, Flinn, with a yell of mingled anguish and desperation, pressed his men through the opening of the tent to scour the plain abroad in search of the absconded foe. Purcell's party made feeble opposition to this movement, and presently the skeleton mouth of the booth, the only remnant of it that had existence, disgorged the throng of combatants, and our visitors were left, unmolested, with the crowd of women. These, too, soon disappeared, following, with screams of apprehension and terror, the fate of their "kith-and-kin," engaged in the sanguinary conflict. Some hasty and hearty kisses, and prayers for everlasting long life and good health, were, indeed, bestowed on the "gintilmin" before this final separation. But at last all withdrew, and Howard, Graham, and Burke were left alone, in the first twilight of a beautiful summer evening, to seek their way back to Clonmel, and congratulate themselves as well on their escape from, as upon their introduction to, the novelties and haps of an Irish skirmish.

They quickly struck out of the pattern-field, choosing, in the first instance a circuitous path, rather than exposure to the continued tumult that Flinn kept up all over the plain.

They conld, however, observe at some distance, as they retired, venders of all kinds of trumpery removing their stalls, and pipers' wives running off with a stool under one arm, and a blind husband under the other, in order to yield prudent way to the approaching stream of combatants. For a full half-hour too, the shouts of the field came on the evening breeze ; and they had gained a near view of Clonmel before distance completely divided them from all echo of the scene of struggle.

Howard, in talking over with his friends the conversation he had heard between Mullins and the stranger, felt pleasure in expressing his certainty that the proscribed victim had escaped their vengeance. His curiosity, indeed, continued excited to know the certain close of the matter, as well as the provocation to hostility, and all other circumstances of the case. But after some time he gave up the thought, and was content to regard the whole as "a mass of things" indistinctly seen, and never to be discriminated. He was, however, mistaken in the latter part of his conclusions.

CHAPTER IV.

A few days before the occurrences detailed in the last chapters, some of those rustic depredations, so utterly disgraceful to the country in which they take place, had been committed in the neighborhood of Clonmel, on a scale much inferior, however, to their late magnitude and atrocity. Howard and Graham had, among others, become acquainted with the rumors of such events, previous to their sortie to the pattern. But as their scene was laid in another and distant part of the county, and as they had yet assumed no very formidable aspect, nor created much sensation, they were not thought of sufficient consequence to interfere with the day's enjoyment.

In about a week after the era of the pattern, more alarming reports of continued outrage spread through Clonmel, and the public mind became considerably agitated. Bodies of nightly depredators, or terrifiers at least, traversed the county, attempting to enforce their own wild views in their own manner. These bands were, according to their private taste, variously designated;

the terms *shanavest* and *caraval*, invented by themselves, were adopted by the community at large in reference to them. Shanavest means "old waistcoats ;" caravat, "cravat ;" both words compounded of equal portions of bad English and bad Irish, and intended to describe the parts of dress by which the association chose to be distinguished. Without dwelling on strange words, it will be sufficient to say that the spirit of these combinations, one and all, was a resuscitation, in some shape or other, of the old spirit of Whiteboyism, concerning which we assure ourselves every reader has, by this time, the proper ideas.

It appeared that each body had a captain or leader, with a mock name, which was conferred at the pleasure of himself or his constituents, and also acceded to by the public. In recurring to these names, a singular feature of Irish character invites attention. It is remarkable, that in every act of proclaiming his real or imaginary wrongs, and committing himself to the black passions attendant on a course of ignorant self-assertion and unbridled revenge, the Irish peasant—the inheritor of misery and neglect, and sufficiently proving in the continuance of this turmoil his sense of so hard a lot—should evince a levity that can be supposed natural only to a body of men associated in the spirit of eccentric enjoyment. The president of a club of "queer fellows," might receive or assume such appellations as the most terrible leaders of Irish depredation invented, and promulgated for themselves. And in the exercise of his mock dignity, or while he humorously enforced his conventional pains and penalties, might affect about the same character that the Whiteboy captain put on at the very moment that he issued his ill-spelt manifestos of no sportive tendency, and while he was prepared and determined to exact the letter of their demands.

The local reformer of the mountain, the bog, or the desert ; the legislator for an almost uncultivated tract of impoverished country ; the desperate neck-or-nothing leader of a throng of desperate and sanguinary men, disguised his identity in a humorous ideal : wrote his threatening notices in the tone of an April-day hoax ; denounced a foe as one friend might promise to another a hit over the knuckles : talked of a midnight visit as the same friend might propose a pleasurable surprise to that other ; and performed his whole part as if he were Tom-fool to a corps of Christmas mummers. If this be the affectation of demoralized habits of thought and feeling, it is hideous and demoniacal ; something in the nature of the jeer and levity with which Goëthe has so startingly invested his Mephistopheles. But there is a bitter eccentricity often resulting from a long-cherished sense of wretchedness ; a kind of stubborn braving of ill-fate that ostentatiously shows itself in outward lightness and recklessness. There is a mockery of the heart by the heart itself ; a humor, in fact, which the inspired writings would seem beautifully to describe, when they declare, that " even in laughter the heart is sorrowful, and the end of that mirth is heaviness." There is this step between our conjectured opinion and the miserable creatures it would make tenfold more miserable, and all national distinctions apart, it leaves us a better sympathy than the first supposition could, with the common tendencies of human nature.

Craving pardon, according to the established custom of all ramblers, for this unintended digression, we resume, by proceeding to notice some of the names affected by these rustic Lycurguses. One called himself Capt. Starlight ; another, Capt. Moonshine ; a third, Jack Thrustout ; a fourth, Richard Roe ; and all who are familiar with rather recent Irish affairs will remember the doughty CAPTAIN JOHN DOE. This quaint title, as well as two others above-mentioned, originated from the fictitious names that the law, in its own roundabout and strange mystification, inserts in ejectments served on those whom it is gravely about to dispossess of their tenements. And it must have been curious enough to observe the incipient Shanavests or Caravats putting their heads together, spelling over the jocose piece of parchment, and making a variety of shrewd conjectures as to whom this Richard Roe or John Doe could really be, until, to their cost, they found him a very formidable personage, and, by some crude association in the recesses of their own minds, resolved, while they adopted his name, to be as farcical and as devastating as their merry prototype, in his best day.

Our hero was, indeed, of sufficient character to engage, almost as soon as he had announced his political existence, the attention of his Clonmel neighbors. Meetings were called to arrange a plan of warfare against him ; and proclamations of rewards, to a large amount, issued for his apprehension. In these official documents, his face, person, dress, and age, were, on good authority, set forth. And as the more peaceable inhabitants, together with the old ladies, servant-wenches, and little boys of Clonmel, read therein details of his swarthy complexion, stout figure, forbidding features, and wild attire, all belonging to a man of the stern age of forty-five years, great was the reverential panic

2*

inspired, and universal the abhorring homage paid to Captain
John Doe's grim person.

From week to week, from month to month, his fame spread
proportionably with his excesses. He at last approached pretty
near to Clonmel, and was said to hover about the town, now at
this side, and now at the other, from the adjacent heights of
Slievenamon and the Galteigh mountains. Parties of military
accordingly marched, from time to time, against him, but with
no material success. Captain Doe's adroitness, and uniform good
fortune in baffling a superior enemy, became as notorious as his
desperate resistance to, or triumph over, an equal or inferior one.
His hairbreath escapes, his rapid movements, and the various
disguises he could at pleasure assume, were the theme of every
tongue. In the vulgar apprehension, they equalled if they did
not surpass, the subtlety and wonderful finessee of the whole corps
of primitive Irish Rapparees, with Redmond O'Hanlon at their
head, and Cahier-na-Choppell bringing up the reserve.

Seven months after the pattern day, that is, in the end of the
succeeding February, Lieutenant Howard was ordered, with a
considerable party, from the head-quarters of his regiment at
Clonmel, to relieve another detachment which for some time had
been harassing John Doe among the mountains, about thirteen
Irish miles distant. Howard set off in good spirits. He was, as
we have observed, heartily tired of the refinements of the town ;
and was therefore excited and pleased with the prospect of seeing
more of the interior of the country, particularly on such a service.
He was, withal, confident in the strength of his party, and vain,
by anticipations, of the success which others had missed, and of
which he made no question. He had but one regret in under-
taking his little campaign, and this grew out of his separation
from Graham, between whom and Howard a sincere friendship
had long been cemented. To remove or alleviate this only disagreeable feature, it was arranged between them that Graham
should apply for an occasional leave of absence, and visit Howard
during his absence on this hill-duty, for a day or two at a time.
For the first leave he was immediately to apply ; and in order that
Graham might promptly commence the desired intercourse,
Howard was to write him an intimation of his quarters, as soon
as he took them up.

Three days after Howard's departure, a letter accordingly
reached his friend, but without proposing so immediate a meeting as had at first been contemplated. Howard mentioned, in

explanation, that he had scarcely gained his field of action. when the movements of Doe demanded his best measures. That he had since been marching and countermarching from point to point ; that after twice eluding his very grasp, Captain John. had now escaped all observation ; and that he, Howard neces- sarily proposed to scour the country- in search of him, and could not, therefore, name any place, nor indeed any day, for receiving Graham. He would, however, write from time to time, and anxiously hoped that the nature of his service might afford him a speedy pause, and thereby at once give opportunity for their seeing each other.

Subsequent letters continued to reach Graham, dated from the one spot, yet still declining to see him, on the grounds that the writer could not answer for his remaining one hour after another where he was. Doe's hiding place was still a mystery, although, night by night, some traces of him were left abroad : Howard had chosen his present quarters as the best point from which to take general observations, and originate, at a moment's notice, the most effectual sorties. And, while his sojourn in them was daily uncertain, there still arose a daily necessity for remaining stationary until circumstances, that an hour might produce, should call for a change of place and measures.

At last, Graham received a note, dated from new quarters, though only three miles from the last, which, on the strong probability that Howard should now, for a few days at least, occupy them, invited Graham to the long-planned meeting. It further hinted, that Howard's change of position was owing to a successful manœuvre against Doe, which, as he was thereby hemmed in, embarrassed that formidable captain, and, no doubt, would end in his destruction. The writer addressed his note from an Irish cabin, where he at present bivouacked, and to which his messenger would conduct Graham.

It was still moonlight when Graham, attended by the single soldier who had delivered Howard's letter, commenced his journey on the following morning. It was Sunday. The stars twinkled joyously throughout a deep blue sky, cleared by the influence of a frosty atmosphere : those brilliant hosts of light might, to minds of an imaginative tendency, seem shining forth in universal jubilee that their nightly course was run, and the relieving day at hand. As Graham and his follower gained the broad way that led on the outside of Clonmel, towards the recesses of Slievenamon mountain, and as the crisp frost crackled under his horse's

step, he felt all the buoyancy that to youthful hearts, such a morning, enjoyed in bounding liberty, could not fail to communicate.
. His attendant, a staid old soldier of sixty, systematic as a machine, grave as an owl, and commonplace as an old pinch-beck time-piece, was, however, a considerable drag on his happiness. This man rode a very indifferent hack; added to which, he had been some forty years out of the saddle, so that he could neither keep up with Graham's spirited animal, nor take much pleasure in the extra effort necessary in endeavoring to do so. Accordingly, it became his interest and policy to curb, by all prudent means, Graham's uncalculating career, for which purpose he more than once suggested to his "Honor," awkwardly essaying each time to carry one hand to his cap, the propriety of pushing on abreast, that his Honor might have the immediate service of an old soldier on a road by no means safe at such an early hour in the morning.

"Why, Evans," said Graham, at last pulling up, "I wonder what danger you can fear, man. Lieutenant Howard writes me word, and you confirm it, that this Doe is surrounded—almost taken prisoner, I may say. Besides, we are both well armed."

"Please your Honor," said Evans, slowly and gravely, "Doe, which they improperly call Captain, *may* be surrounded, or may *not* be surrounded."

"Pray what may that signify?" Graham demanded.

"Your Honor won't think I mean but that his Honor, Lieutenant Howard, is very sure he is surrounded," continued Evans, still more gravely, and with an additional shade of visage that might be called the shade mysterious. "But after all his escapes from our hands, when the oldest soldier didn't think it possible, and with all his disguises and outlandish tricks that were never equalled but in a play, played on the stage, in a play-house, it is hard to say—that is, to be very certain, that he is, at the present time—"

The speaker here interrupted himself with a "Hush!" and drew up his horse to listen, as the noise made by another horse approaching was distinctly heard in a side direction towards the main road, which was Graham's route, and which had lost much of its broad and level character since it had begun to turn amongst the first inequalities that flanked the main base of Slievenamon.

Graham also paused to listen, and, as audibly as his videt, heard the near approach of a horseman down a wild and narrow bridle-road, or boreen, about ten yards to the right of the way. He immediately took a pistol from his holster; Evans unslung his musket, which had hitherto dangled most awkwardly and inconveniently across his back; and both halted and sat up in their saddles observing profound silence, except that Evans whispered to his officer a respectful hope that the horse he bestrode might stand fire better than he knew how to trot.

In a moment they heard a noise accompanying that of the horse's feet—namely, a lusty, stentorian voice, sending forth, in measured and prolonged notes, some kind of a strain. It was too deep and serious for a song, unless a song of very severe and doleful character. At first Evans, taking the latter view of the case, thought he could recognize in it a generic likeness to his not quite distinct reminiscences of "The Death of Abercromby," or some of its interminable similitudes: but having vainly cocked his ear, while he cocked his musket, to catch a word of the old ditty; in fact, having ascertained that the singer gave utterance to a language that, whatever it was, was not English, Evans became assured that it must be Irish. Recollecting that among other curious things, Doe was much in the habit of carolling aloud his own rebellious songs, a conviction flashed upon him, which he communicated in another whisper to Graham, and both stood doubly prepared on the defensive.

The appearance, almost immediately, of a man, from the boreen, was not calculated, all circumstances of time, place, and prepossession considered, to allay the nerves of our travellers. He was well mounted on a strong, active, though not handsome horse: his figure seemed over large, and was enveloped from the chin to the boot-heels in a dark top-coat. On his head appeared a white mass of something, which the imperfect light did not allow Graham to distinguish or to assign to any known class of head-gear; and upon this again was placed a hat, with a remarkably broad brim, and a low, round crown. As he emerged on the main road, this apparition still continued its peculiar chaunt, and was only interrupted by the challenge—"Who goes there?—stand!"—of Graham, and its instant echo by the mechanical old soldier.

"Stand yourself, then," answered the stranger, in an easy, unembarrassed, but by no means hostile tone; and continuing rather jocosely, he repeated an old school-boy rhyme—

"If you're a man stand;
If you're a woman go;
If you're an evil spirit sink down, low."

"Did you say 'fire,' sir?" asked Evans, in an aside to Graham, and levelling his piece.

"No!" said Graham aloud. "Hold! And you, sir, I ask again, who and what are you? Friend or foe?"

"A friend to all honest men, and a foe, when I can help myself, to no man at all," was the reply.

"That's no answer," whispered Evans.

"You speak in untimely and silly riddles, sir," said Graham. "Advance and declare yourself."

"Begging your pardon," continued the stranger, still in a good-humored tone, "I see no prudent reason why I should advance at the invitation of two persons armed and unknown to me."

"We are, the King's soldiers," said Evans, rather precipitously.

"Silence, man," interrupted Graham—"I am an officer in the King's service, sir, and my attendant is a soldier."

"O ho!" quoth the stranger, "an officer, are you, but no soldier?"

"What sir!" exclaimed Graham, raising his pistol, while Evans had recourse to his musket.

"Hold! and for shame, gentlemen!" cried the other, seriously altering his tone—"What! on a defenceless and peaceable poor man, who has given you no provocation? Upon my life, now, but this is unceremonious treatment just at the end of one of my own boreens. In the King's name, forbear—if, indeed, ye are the King's soldiers, as you say, though I can discover no outward badges of it." For Graham rode in a plain dress, and Evans had disguised under his great coat all appearance of uniform, a foraging cap alone intimating, to an experienced eye, his military character.

"I pledge my honor to the fact," said Graham, in answer to the stranger's last observation, as he lowered his hand and was imitated by Evans, "and you will at least respect the word of a gentleman."

"'Tis my habit to do so, sir," said the strange man; "and in proof of what I say, I am willing now to advance to you, if you also pledge your honor not to be fingering your triggers, there."

"I do, sir—you may come on in perfect safety. But hold— I have also my terms to propose—are *you* armed?"

"Me? God help me, what have I to do with such matters?"

"But how am I to be assured?"

"Why, I'll tell you then," answered the other, resuming the

jocular tone—" You can easily see by the moonlight, and indeed by the daylight, too, which is just breaking on us, that in my two hands, at least, I have neither gun, blunderbuss, pistol, nor cutlass. See, I hold out both my arms in this manner."

"Stop!" roared Evans, as he saw the arms in motion, and suspecting a finesse, again levelled his musket.

"Recover arms!" cried Graham, impatiently. "Fall back, Evans, and keep yourself quiet."

"God bless you, sir, and do manage him now," the stranger said, as Evans obeyed orders—" I shall hold out my arms, I say, as they are at present, and we'll leave the rest to my horse. Come, Podhereen, right about face, and march."

The obedient animal moved accordingly, and a few paces brought his master and Graham face to face: "And now, sir," continued the stranger, "I suppose you are satisfied, and I may just lift the rein from the beast's neck as before."

To this Graham assented, rather because he saw no reasonable ground for refusal, than because he was perfectly satisfied. Though Evans, from behind, whispered: "Search him first, your honor; 'tis Doe, I'll take my oath of it, in one of his disguises. Look at him!"

Graham did look, and in truth, if his moral certainty was not so strong as Evans, he had his misgivings in common with the crafty old campaigner. The white protuberance on the stranger's head he could now ascertain to be some species of wig, bloated out over the ears, and the back of the neck, to an immoderate compass, and lying close to the brow and side of the face in a rigid, unbroken line, while it peaked down in the middle of the forehead—much like, in this respect, the professional head-disguise of the gentlemen of the long robe. The broad-leafed, round-topped thing on the pinnacle of this, still seemed to be a hat : the dark loose coat, with a small cape reaching between the shoulders, hid all detail of the figure. By his face the stranger was between forty and fifty ; exactly Doe's age. His heavy eyebrows, broad-backed nose, and expressive mouth, together with the self-assured twinkle of eyes that gleamed on Graham like illuminated jets, and a certain mixed character of severity and humor that ran through his whole visage, indicated a person of no ordinary cast.

Still Graham looked, at a loss what to make of a costume so outré, and, to his experience, unprecedented : till at last the subject of his scrutiny again broke silence.

"I suppose I may go my road without any further question, sir?"

'May I ask which road you travel, sir?" (Graham said, with obvious meaning.

"Tut, tut, now," said the other, "that's too Irish a way of answering a gentleman's question, on the King's high-road. Danger has often come of such odd answers. You see I am un-armed, and I see you have it in your power, that is, if you liked it, to strip me of my old wig and hat in a minute, and no friend of mine the wiser. In fact, sir, you now give me sufficient cause to look after my own personal safety. I have no wish to offend any gentleman, but you must excuse me for saying, I cannot be quite sure who or what *you* are. You may be Captain John, as well as any other captain, for aught I know."

This was said with perfect gravity; and Graham hastened, in some simplicity, to make the most solemn and earnest declara-tions of his loyalty and professional services and character.

"Well," continued the stranger, who had now turned the tables, and become catechist accordingly, "all this may be very true, and from your appearance and manner I am inclined to think the best of you. But if *you* are not he, how can I be so sure of that suspicious-looking person at your back?"

Evans, shocked to the bottom of his soul, as well as displeased, that under any circumstances he could be confounded with a rebel, traitor, and desperado, shouted out at this observation, and was with some difficulty restrained by Graham from taking instant vengeance for the insult. When he was restored to or-der, Graham assured the stranger, with emphasis equal to what he had used on his own account, of Evans's real character.

"Then pass on, gentlemen, and let me go about my lawful business," continued the man, drawing up at the road-side to allow them to pass. Graham accordingly put his horse in motion, and, followed by Evans, both still holding their arms, trotted by. Graham and the stranger touched hats to each other as they parted, but Evans only bent, on his now detected foe, a fero-cious look, which was returned in a burst of suppressed laughter.

"He's either Doe or the Devil, please your Honor," said Evans, when they had advanced a little forward. "And now why does he follow us?" he continued, as with some difficulty turning round in the saddle he saw the stranger trotting after them at about the distance of thirty yards.

"Never mind him, Evans," said Graham; "if he keeps that

fair distance, we can't hinder a peaceable man from pursuing his journey."

"But who is that coming down the hill-side before us?" asked Evans, pointing off the road to where the moon threw a shadow over the side of a declivity, which the day had not yet sufficient influence to relieve or dissipate.

Graham, looking in the direction to which Evans's hand pointed, saw a form in rapid motion down the hill ; and both, almost simultaneously, pealed out their usual " Who's there ?—stand !" but the form still continued to descend.

"Stand, on your life !" repeated Graham ; but no notice was taken of his threat. At this moment the horseman behind quickened the pace of his horse, and approached much nearer.

" We are surrounded, please your Honor !" said Evans.

" Fire, then !" said Graham aloud, and continued in a lower tone, " I will turn round to meet this other man."

" Nonsense !" cried the stranger from behind, who seemed to have heard Graham's orders to Evans—"Stop, man, stop ! don't fire !—'tis a harmless creature of my own !" But his words had little effect on Evans, the report of whose piece was almost instantly heard, succeeded by a loud bellow from the hill, and then the form continued to tumble down more rapidly than before, now evidently impelled by its own gravity, till at last it splashed through the thin ice into a little stream of water at the side of the road.

"There," continued the stranger, who had by this time come up ; "now you have done it. A brilliant affair it is for the King's men to boast of !"

" What do you mean, fellow," said Graham, confronting him ; "stand off, or take the consequences."

"Ulla-loo !—I'm not another calf to be treated in such a manner," replied the stranger ; " I tell you I'm no mark for such doughty knights. But stop—here's a second foe breaking the fence at the top of the hill—make ready—present—fire !"

" 'Twas a poor calf, of a certain, please your Honor," interrupted Evans, who had now returned from an investigation at the spot where the enemy remained stationary.

" A *poor* calf !" retorted the horseman. " 'Twas as thriving a calf as was ever seen at this side of the country ; and of all creatures in the world the very one I had my eye on for my next Christmas beef. And I must say, gentlemen, that if ye are what ye pretend to be, I take it rather ill of the King to train

up his soldiers in hostility to any poor man's meat. I thought
he had some other employment for them."

Evans's antipathy, now increased by a sense of shame, and a
growing apprehension of the stranger's ridicule, turned off in
dogged dudgeon, while Graham said—"This is all extremely
ridiculous, sir, but, perhaps, mostly owing to your own strange
and unsatisfactory conduct. As to the loss you have sustained,
if indeed the animal was yours, or, whether it was or not, here
is pecuniary recompense ; and so, good morning to you."

"Stop a moment, sir," answered the horseman, "I have no
claim on your money. 'Twas an accident, and must be arranged
as such : you will put it up, if you please :" with a wave of his
hand, an inclination of his head, and altogether the assumption,
for the first time, of an air, voice, and manner, that was impressive, if not gentlemanly and commanding. Graham mechanically
complied with the felt influence of this change of character, and
returned the money to his purse. The stranger continued :   .

"With respect to the other part of your implied terms, it
must be 'good morning,' or 'well met,' just as you insist on it."

"Good morning, then, if you please, sir," answered Graham,
and slightly bowing, again set off with Evans. Yet, he was
scarcely two minutes on his way, when he felt a kind of regret
at having so cavalierly rejected the stranger's half approach to
fellowship. In the improved light of the gradually expanding
morning this person's face had become more distinct, and more
pleasingly distinct during the last words he had spoken. Graham
now thought over the easy self-assertion with which he had re-
fused the money, and recollected that the language adopted in
his explanation was much more that of a gentleman than the
idiomatic turn of his previous discourse, while it also had less of
the brogue of his country. · In fact, Graham felt half sorry, and
half curious. He was getting deeper into the feeling, when the
object of it again diverted from himself this dawn of favorable
impression.

The noise of his horse's feet, in rapid motion, first awakened
Graham from his reverie ; and, looking behind them, our travellers saw the stranger nearer than they had reckoned, holding
out one arm, and crying, "Halt !—halt !"

Evans concluded that they were now in reality to be attacked ;
and Graham, impatient of so incorrigible an intruder, mended
his pace to avoid him.   ·

"Will your Honor please to leave me behind ?" asked Evans,

thumping his spurless heels against the sides of his hack, and applying the butt of his musket for a common purpose, as he vainly endeavored to keep up with Graham.

"Halt, I say!—your purse!—your purse!" cried the horseman, still closing them.

"I'll shoot you as dead as Abercromby first—blast my limbs, if I don't!" roared Evans, facing round.

"Why, you stupid and provoking fellow," said the pursuer slackening his speed, "won't you let me give your master his own?"

"Fall back, Evans," said Graham, advancing.

"Your purse, sir," continued the stranger, extending his arm; "it fell from you on the spot where we last halted. Again, good morning to you."

"I'm much obliged," said Graham, taking it. "And, now that we can all see each other better, suppose, sir, if our routes agree, that we push on together?"

"My way does not hold for more than a hundred yards further, along this main road," answered the stranger carelessly. "I must then turn off to the left."

"Please your Honor, that's exactly our route," whispered Evans.

"Then we are to be together, sir, if you have no objection," resumed Graham.

"None in the world," was the reply; and, much to the astonishment of Evans, Graham fell into line with the stranger, leaving the galled, and jaded, and fretted orderly to follow as he might.

The day was almost fully up. The thick vapor that had slept out the night on the bosom of Slievenamon, whitened in the returning light, and lazily obeying the summons of the breeze, began to crawl towards the peak of the mountain, and there once more deposit itself, as if to take another nap. Graham remarked on the picturesque effect: and his companion remarked, "Yes, it was odd enough that old Slievenamon should put on its nightcap just as all the rest of the world was throwing off that appendage."

Graham, too proper and systematic in the succession of his ideas to like this trope, did not notice it, but proceeded, with a little vanity of his travelled lore, to allude to the superiority of Italian over our island scenery.

"Superiority is a general word," said the stranger, "in the

way you use it. I presume you do not mean mere height, as
applied to such mountain scenery as surrounds us ; in other
respects, the Italian landscape, principally owing, of course, to
the influence of atmosphere, is more beautiful than the English
one ; and, from the scarcity of trees in Ireland, much more so
than the Irish one. But among the mist and shadow of our island
hills, as you call them, particularly in Kerry, I have always felt
a fuller sense of the sublime, at least, than I ever did in the
presence of continental scenery, either in Italy or in Spain.
Switzerland alone, to my eye, first equals us, and then surpasses
us."

This speech gave information of rather more acquaintance with
the distinctions, in a knowledge of which Graham took it for
granted he might shine, than it seemed practicable to turn to
advantage. He, therefore, avoided the general subject, and,
taking up only a minor division of it, protested he could not
understand why, unless it was attributable to the indolence of its
people, Ireland should be so "shamefully deficient in trees."

"Indeed !" his companion replied, in an indefinite tone ; then,
after a pause, adding, that "he thought so too ;" but Graham
did not notice the scrutinizing, and, afterwards, rather contemptuous look ; and, finally, the severe waggery of face, that filled
up the seeming hiatus.

So, having to his own mind hit on a fruitful theme, Graham
diverged into all the ramifications of Irish indolence. Obstinacy
was his next word : Irish indolence and obstinacy. They would
neither do, nor learn how to do, anything, he said ; they would
not even submit to be educated out of the very ignorance and bad
spirit that produced all this Whiteboyism. There was a national
establishment, he was well assured, in Dublin, with ample means,
that proposed the blessings of education on the most liberal
plan ; yet the very ministers of the religion of the country would
not suffer their ragged and benighted flock to take advantage of
so desirable an opportunity. The bigoted rustic pastors actually
forbade all parents to send their children to the schools of this
institution.

"Yes," the stranger said, "the parish priests—the bigoted
parish priests. And all because a certain course of reading was
prescribed in these schools."

"Precisely, sir," assented Graham.

"The bigotry of the priests is intolerable," said the stranger,
"and only equalled by its implacability. Nothing can bring

them to consent to the proposed terms, because, forsooth, they plead a conscientious scruple ; because they say their approval would be a breach of their religious duty. As if we had any thing to do with the private conscience and creed of such people."

" Or as if the body of respectable gentlemen, who framed the regulation, should accede, by rescinding their law, to the super stitious prejudices of such people," echoed Graham.

" Very true, sir. The Medes and Persians, I am given to understand, never repealed a law, and why should the gentlemen you speak of ?" Besides, there is so little necessity for the concession. The liberal and wise association can so easily accomplish its professed object without it."

" Pardon me, sir, there we differ : the object proposed is the education of the poor of this country ; and I cannot exactly see how they are to be educated, if—as is on all hands undeniable —the parish priests have sufficient influence to keep them, now and for ever, out of the school-houses."

" Oh, sir, nothing can be easier. But first let me see that we understand each other. You and I, suppose, are now riding to the same point. Well, a pit, an inundation, or a fallen mountain, occurs a little way on, rendering impassible the road we had conceived to be perfectly easy, so that we cannot gain our journey's end by this road. If you please, the place we want to reach shall stand for the education of the poor Irish, the object professed : *we* may personify the educating society, taking our own road, and the bigoted priests are represented by the monstrous impediment. Well, sir, we reach that insurmountable obstacle to our progress. Now, would it not be most humiliating and inconsistent, and all that is unworthy, if we did not instantly stop, and declare we would not proceed a foot further, by any other road, till our favorite one, that never can be cleared, *is* cleared for us ? So far I understand you."

" Then I protest it is an advantage I do not possess over you, sir," said Graham.

" All will be distinct in a moment," resumed his companion. " I say we are both exactly of opinion that the society should not, with ample means and professions, take a single step towards its end, unless by its own blockaded way. That, in dignified consistency, it should not vouchsafe to teach one chattering urchin how to read, or write, or cast up accounts, unless it can, at the same time, teach him theology. In other words, till it sees the mountain shoved aside, the deluge drained, or the bottomless pit filled up. In other words again, till the bigoted Popish priests consent to sacrifice their conscience, whatever it may be ; though, meantime, the swarming population remain innocent of any essential difference between B and a bull's foot, or between A and the gable-end of a cabin. We are agreed, I say, sir ?"

" Faith ! whatever may be your real drift, I must admit you have substantially defined, though in your own strange way, the very thing I but just now endeavored to distinguish. And, I must repeat, from what we have both said, that the main object of the society still seems shut out from attainment. This, however, was what you appeared to deny, I think. I should be glad to hear your remedy."

" We come to it at once, sir. By no means look out for another road, but try to get rid of the immovable barrier."

" I protest, you rather puzzle me."

" That's the way, sir," continued the stranger, running on in his wonted delight and bitterness. " No time can be lost, no common sense and consistency compromised in the hopeful experiment. That's the way."

" What, sir ? what do you mean ?"

" Convert the parish priests ; there is nothing easier."

" Pardon me, sir, but I begin to fear that you trifle with me," said Graham, mortified and displeased at having so long exhibited for the amusement of so strange a person.

" I should be sorry, young gentleman, to say any thing to offend you ; I am sure I have not intended to do so. But now farewell, Mr. Graham ; present my compliments to your friend Lieutenant Howard, and tell him he shall soon hear more of me. Farewell ! my road lies up against, or rather round the breast of this hill ; you will find your quarters two miles on. A good morning, sir :" and without more pause he turned off the by-road they had for some time pursued, into a rugged and narrow path, strewn with stones and rock ; and, after a few words of encouragement to Podhereen, his athlethic horse, disappeared among the curves and bends of encircling hills and inequalities.

Graham stared in consternation when he heard the stranger mention Howard's and his name. His rapid disappearance along so wild a path, together with what Graham now regarded as the uncommon assurance of his late manner, induced, more than ever, serious apprehensions as to his identity, in the formation of which he was abundantly assisted by Evans. Both seemed to think it was their policy to push forward to Howard's quarters with all possible speed ; and even Graham allowed the suspicion of an ambuscade to shadow his mind. Evans, accordingly, put his hack to the utmost stretch, now requiring but little accommodation from his officer, to keep him in view.

They gained, however, a near prospect of Howard's mountain quarters, without any further adventure. An untenanted cabin served for his bivouac. It was built in a desolate little valley, fronting the road over which Graham traveled, but considerably below its level, having one knoll of mountain at one side, another at the other, with an open background of flat and apparently marshy country. Before the door of the cabin, Graham recognized his friend, surrounded by the few soldiers who formed his immediate body-guard, and who, with the exception of a sentinel, seemed employed in furbishing their arms and accoutrements. About a quarter of a mile in the open ground beyond, the main force of his party was also discernible in a line round the marsh, standing to their arms.

Howard, almost at the same time, saw his friend's approach ; hastened to meet him ; and led him, laughing at his own means for hospitality, into the cabin. There, however, a good breakfast was prepared, and a bright furze-fire blazed in the ample chimney.

CHAPTER V.

DURING breakfast, Graham did not fail to mention to Howard his adventures on the road ; and the individual who, for a great part of the journey, had been his almost self-elected companion, became an object of equal interest to Howard as to himself. The fact of his seeming to know Graham's person, and the purpose of his route, with his parting allusion to Howard, which the friends now construed into a threat, won on their apprehension. Notwithstanding Howard's strong assurances that he could not be the man they almost feared to think, conjecture was still busy, and doubt uppermost.

After some time spent in discussing the matter, Howard recollected an engagement of importance which he wished to keep.

It was to meet, at the Roman Catholic place of worship of the mountain district, a Protestant clergyman, who was also a county magistrate, and with him a Roman Catholic priest of eminence, from whom they expected an address to the rude congregation, on their secret associations. This latter gentleman, Howard had already met, he said, at the house of a Roman Catholic proprietor in the neighborhood, where he had passed the last fortnight previous to the change to his present quarters. He proceeded to speak of him as a man who had gained much character by his writings and preachings to the common people. "Here," continued Howard, "are some of his pamphlets to the Whiteboys, which you will read and judge of for yourself. But I have to add of my good friend, Father O'Clery, that *he* is the friend of Flood, Grattan, Curran, Lord Avonmore, and other Irish stars, who have unanimously elected him a member of the festive body, quaintly denominated 'The Monks of St. Patrick.' Also, that he has officially received notice of the gratitude of government for his most useful, as well as talented exertions."

"The second fact I have mentioned, reminds me," pursued Howard, " of the facetious social character of O'Clery. Indeed, I have scarcely ever met a person of a rarer vein. Nature seems to have stamped him a wit and a satirist ; but he contrives, with peculiar good humor, to exercise her gifts in a harmless way. Then, every thing about him is, to me, eccentric. His swollen, old-fashioned, white wig ; his curious, round hat ; and the robust horse he rides, which he calls, I think *Podhereen*, or " Beads."

"Calls *what ?*" cried Graham.

"'Tis a curious name," answered Howard, "like every thing else in this curious country, and I do not wonder at your astonishment. Podhereen is the title borne by his horse, which, as I have translated it, means ' Beads :' hence the point of so calling a priest's horse, perhaps from the circumstance of the rider often saying his rosary on the animal, as he journeys from place to place."

"If Podhereen be indeed the creature's name," resumed Graham, "and if such a hat, and wig, and manner, as you describe, belong to O'Clery, then I have been on an ass, and the priest knows it, too, Howard."

"What !" cried Howard—"ah, I have it ! I have it !— O'Clery was this morning to have ridden from a friend's house

near Clonmel, to keep the appointment at the chapel, to which
his Protestant fellow-laborer, with whom he lives in some amity,
had also been invited. As I live by the sword, you met him on
t ie road, and lo ! your Captain John !"

" Nothing is more evident, I fear," replied Graham, rather
taken aback by the discovery.

" About two miles from where we sit," continued Howard,
" a straggling path diverges among the hills towards the friend's
residence, where I have met him, and where he had engaged to
breakfast. Lo, again, your mysterious disappearance ! He
knew you were coming hither,—I am to see him at the chapel,
and again and again, behold !"

"All too true, Howard," resumed Graham, shaking his head,
and laughing. "The worst is, I was goose enough to read him
a lecture on the bigotry of popish priests, in which the old
Jesuit seemed to join, till he had meshed me in a confusion of I
know not what ideas. But from all you say of the man's satirical
turn, I now clearly understand how I have been bamboozled."

" Exquisite !" cried Howard, " O'Clery will live on this forever and a day ! But come, you must see him in his true character. The hour of appointment is at hand, and we can scarcely
be in time at the chapel."

The friends accordingly proceeded across two or three uncultivated fields, to the mountain chapel of the district. It was
visible from a distance ; a low, almost squalid-looking building,
contrived, according to universal usage, in something of the
shape of a cross, with small narrow windows, many of which
were broken ; and thatched with straw, that in some places was
decayed and blackened by the weather. No " venerable yews"
shaded this less than humble conventicle. In fact, not a single
tree was in sight : no inclosure ran round it ; even the burial-
ground was exposed to all intruders.

"Can this be a Christian place of worship?" said Graham,
as they approached, " I rather thought we were going to yonder
smart-looking building, with blue slates and a steeple, at the
brow of the hill."

" To say truth," replied Howard, " being good and loyal
Protestants, that should be our destination. It is a Protestant
church, where the beneficed clergyman reads prayers, as Swift
often did, to one old lady who lives near, and,—if the roads be
good,—to two. Sometimes, indeed, as was also occasionally the
case with the humorist I have mentioned, the clergyman's clerk

3

represents, in a large and cold church, the imaginary congregation of the parish. Nay, O'Clery gravely asserts that, upon a particular occasion, even this parliamentary kind of representation ceased. His story is, that the old clerk died of a pleurisy, caught during a winter's attendance in the damp and deserted building, and that for three months, as there was no second Protestant of his rank in the parish, his office remained vacant. Some bungling endeavor at a schismatic substitute was, however, made. A young popish peasant, attracted by the salary, promised to attend ; but as the fear of a long penance, and, I believe, everlasting damnation to boot, forbade him to be present at heretical ceremonies, he contrived to reconcile his conscience to his interests, in the following manner. During service, the fellow walked outside the church, spelling the tombstones, or whistling an Irish ditty ; it was conceded that when the clergyman came to any part that required the response of a clerk, he should ejaculate, 'Hem !'—and at this signal the young man would run to the church door, thrust in his head, and having roared out—'Amen !'—return to his private amusements, and so get through the service."

After a laugh at this conceit, Graham expressed his surprise that a clergyman should be well paid for having nothing to do ; in fact, he could not even understand by whom, when he had no congregation. Howard answered, by the Roman Catholic landlords, farmers, and peasantry, of the country. An explanation which Graham thought odd, seeing how evident it was that those same persons could not afford, for the purposes of their own worship, a better edifice than the one now in view.

This conversation brought them to the entrance of the chapel, and Graham, from what he there saw, thought the matter still more singular. The body of the building was stuffed with people ; while, outside the door, hundreds continued to kneel in the open air many yards along the wet and miry approach to the chapel.

From the profound silence that reigned within and without, interrupted only by the monotonous voice of the priest, it was evident that prayers, or, technically speaking, mass had commenced. Whether habit or piety produced the effect, the visitors could not avoid noticing how deeply attentive even the outside congregation appeared to be. The old women and old men of the crowd held in their hands long black beads, or rosaries, to which as they slid down each bead, their lips moved in seemingly fervent prayer. A few young persons of both sexes had books ; some girls again had rosaries ; and even those who knelt unsupplied with any such clue to devotion, kept up the general appearance of an attentive feeling.

As Howard saw no means of entering the chapel through the crowd without disturbing their order, and as he knew of no other entrance but by this principal one, the strangers remained for some time disagreeably situated, particularly when they began to attract the notice of the people, and fear, if not consternation, seemed the result of the discovery. After standing still for about five minutes, with their heads uncovered, through a wish to conciliate the favorable opinion of those around, Graham pressed his friend's arm, and pointed to a side-face in the rustic assembly. There was no mistaking it, although several months had elapsed since the gentlemen had before beheld it. Its proprietor was the bowing knight, Mr. Patrick Flinn.

" I caught him watching us," whispered Graham ; " but, when my eye met his, he turned round with an affectation of unconsciousness, and assumed the deep abstraction of visage, and that rapid movement of the lips, you now perceive."

Immediately after, Flinn again looked towards his old friends. As if acting on a second thought, he bounced up at once, and with his old scrape and bow, and peculiar swagger, approached, and in an anxious whisper addressed them.

" Musha, long life an' honor to ye, gintlemen, and praise be to God for the day I see ye again. Won't ye come round to the sacristy where Father O'Clery, an' the ministher, good loock to him, an' Mr. Grace, *your* ould friend, Captain Howard, is waitin' fur you."

After due recognition, Paddy's offer was accepted, and Howard and Graham accompanied him round to the back of the chapel, where, by a small private door, he introduced them to what he had called the sacristy. Then, with repeated farewells and fervent prayers for their worldly and immortal happiness, he disappeared, leaving Howard not a little surprised at the intimate knowledge of his arrangements and acquaintances that the man's speech seemed to imply.

According to the usage of his superiors, Flinn was correct in the name he had given to the small apartment into which the visitors now entered ; as, even on the dwindled and sometimes wretched scale upon which the Roman Catholic religion is practised in Ire its professors fondly continue some shadow of its various

primitive accompaniments, of which the names, whether as applying to buildings or parts of buildings, to persons, ceremonies, or
the materials for ceremonies, had a different import in the olden
time.

The sacristy, then, was at the back of the altar: it was the
place where the priest put on his vestments previous to his appearing before the multitude to celebrate mass. Here, too, was
a confessional chair: the sacristy was also occasionally appro-
priated to the better order of parishioners, who might choose to
hear mass free from the pressure of the crowd. The floor was
earthen, the walls whitewashed, and perspiring with chill rather
than heat. Altogether, the place presented an aspect of little
comfort.

At the moment in which our friends entered, Mr. O'Clery, attended by the parish minister, issued from the sacristy by another
door, that led into a round, railed space before the altar, called the
sanctuary. Mr. Grace, the gentleman at whose house O'Clery
had breakfasted, and the common friend of Howard, was about
to follow, when, recognizing Howard, he turned back, and, in
profound silence, led him and Graham after the clergyman.
Graham remarked that as his friend passed out, he bowed with
a very fascinating smile to a young lady who stood veiled at the
door, and who, in spite of much abstraction and piety of manner,
as graciously returned the salute.

From the sanctuary, where seats were provided for them, the
visitors saw with amaze the immense surface of heads in the
body of the chapel, undulating like a sea, and thick and wedged
as paving-stones in the streets of a city. Some incidental pause
had occurred in the service, which afforded proper time for the
delivery of an exhortation. Of this the human mass seemed
aware; for there now arose a universal press forward, attended
with the scraping and clattering noise of hundreds of hob-nailed
brogues against the clay-floor of the chapel; and simultaneously,
the uproarious coughing, and blowing of noses, and hemming,
and sneezing, by which, as a matter of course, an Irish congregation prepares for a decorous attention to the harangue of its
preacher.

Mr. O'Clery was not of the parish to which on this day he
devoted his eloquence, having only been invited thither, as
Howard informed Graham, in consequence of his established
character. Mass had been celebrated by the parish priest,
who now stood with O'Clery on the altar, while the Protestant

clergyman remained on the side steps. Before the honorary
preacher could begin, the *bona fide* occupant thought it necessary to address his parishioners.

And he did so, good man, in a strain, and on a subject, and
with a manner, little eloquent. Advising them that Mr. O'Clery
was to follow in reference to their wicked associations, he contented himself with reprobating their general incorrectness in the
payment of his Christmas "dues." He protested that he had not
received a pound of their money since Easter : and how did they
think he was to live, and keep the poor horse, that morning, noon,
and night, was on the road in their service ? There again, his
horse : Mickie Delany had promised to send him in a grain of
oats ; and Tom Heffernan, a bundle of hay ; and Jack Hoolachun,
a whisp of straw ; but oats, hay, or straw, he had never seen since.
The very chapel above their heads, and above his head, they
would not cover. He had kept his bed for a week with the
rheumatism, imbibed from the droppings of the roof, as he said
mass on the last rainy Sunday. What did they intend at all ?
Was it their wish to remain in their ignorance, and their sins,
and their wickedness, like a drove of beasts, without priest to
give them the Word of God, or to christen for them, or to marry
for them, or to confess them of their abominations ? And then
to go, head foremost, out of the darkness of their life in this
world, into the eternal shadow of the next ?

This and much more the afflicted and really worthy man addressed to the gaping throng, who, whenever he gained a climax
of denunciations, sent up such a wail of singular pathos, as to
the uninitiated ear might promise a speedy arrangement of the
last Christmas "dues." Though we have never heard that,
eventually, it was of much benefit either to their own souls, or
to the bodies of the complainant and his horse.

At last Mr. O'Clery began his exhortation, in a style and
manner very different indeed. In setting out, he addressed
himself at once to the hearts of his hearers, ingeniously and
successfully endeavoring to insinuate himself into their affec-
tions and confidence. He called them his dear, though unhappy
children, grafting, as he went along, his disapprobation of their
crimes upon his sympathy with their misfortunes, and winning
them to become, in a sort, the judges and denouncers of their
own excesses. When he had sufficiently prepared his opportunity, the reverend gentleman did not withhold the broadest
statement of the atrocities that had been committed. Still he

kept his kind tone and manner, dwelling rather in sorrow than
in anger upon the national disgrace, and, to him, the personal
anguish of such a statement.   Presently he argued with his
audience upon the utter uselessness of their projects and acts ;
when disciplined forces were brought against them ; when they
were not countenanced by a single individual of their own religion, who from station and education might afford them counsel ; when the wisest heads in the country were leagued against
them ; and when they had the experience of the utter failure of
all their previous attempts.   After thus disheartening them, the
preacher next rapidly recurred to the moral delinquency of their
deeds.   Now, for the first time, he got in a view of their ille-
gality ; strengthening himself by giving the religion they professed as the rule of civil obedience ; fully defining the duties
that, according to it, they owed to their king and country, and
the deadly sin that followed a breach of those duties.   Here,
at last throwing aside the olive branch, and arraying himself
in all the sternness and terror of ecclesiastical power and authority, he called on the thunders of the Church to assist the
voice of the law, and uttered the deep threats at which the Irish
peasant has been in the habit of trembling, though recent events
prove to us a growing indifference towards them.   An evident
awe resulted from this ; and the speaker hastened to complete
his impression by once more touching the human feelings.   As
Irishmen, as Christians, as fathers, brothers, sons, and husbands,
he invoked them to adopt the course that would save their
country from opprobrium : that would save their little children,
their aged parents, their fond wives, from the ruin, and shame,
and sorrow, that must follow a perseverance in crime : that
would save themselves from shameful death here, and judgment
hereafter.   In conclusion, the preacher, in his own name and in
the name of all their priests, invoked them with tears upon his
cheeks.   Then falling on his knees, he prayed a merciful God to
give strength to his supplications.
    The final effect was decisive.   For some time an intense
silence had waited on Mr. O'Clery's peroration.   But, as he
rose to a climax, the weeping wail of women bore testimony to
its influence.   Some even shrieked in anticipated agony ; while
in the pause they left, sobs, "not loud but deep," intimated the
laborious working of grief and repentance in harder hearts.
Many a rough cheek, which since childhood had been dry, now
ran tears respondent to those shed by the reverend preacher

And, when he suddenly knelt, one mighty burst attended his unexpected movement ; every knee simultaneously sought the ground ; and, for a minute after, clasped hands and upturned eyes proclaimed the continuous sentiment and conviction.*

Indeed, to those who have never been present at such a scene as we describe, and who are unacquainted with the Irish character, this attempt to convey a true picture will, perhaps, appear exaggerated. Howard and Graham, taken by surprise, acknowledged, however, its immediate influence ; for they found themselves kneeling at the close, along with every other individual of the congregation. The Protestant clergyman did not withhold, even under a dissenting roof, the natural testimony that was only an admission of the sway of those broad Christian principles, which, in common with the preacher, he devoutly advocated.

It was now his turn to say a few sentences to the people. He was led up to the altar by the two Roman Catholic priests, and began, his eyes still moist, and his voice affected, to state, that it was under their permission he had ventured out of his place to speak a friendly word to his, as well as their common flock. After the powerful appeal that had been delivered, he would not, he said, hazard a single general observation. All he had to propose was peace and good-will, and, so far as in him lay, the measures to attain both. He then alluded to the difficult question of tithes ; volunteering concessions, and suggesting arrangements, by which he hoped, in his own person at least, to alleviate the hardship he was aware existed ; and promising for himself, to the utmost extent of his influence, not only pardon, but protection to such as would speedily give up their wicked courses and conform to the advice and precepts they had just heard.

His address seemed to produce, if not so powerful an effect as the last, certainly one more pleasing. The Mass was resumed under every appearance and hope of good results.

When it had concluded, and while the people were pouring out of the chapel, Howard and Graham gained the sacristy, where the first presented his friend to Mr. O'Clery, and to Mr. and Miss Grace, which lady, Graham recognized to be the same to whom Howard had bowed with such *empressement* on his way to the sanctuary. O'Clery, even so soon after an occasion and exertion that had intensely affected himself, let fly at Graham a

* The sketch of a usual scene.

few significant glances of his deep, black eye, while his lip curved
in a provoking smile. He shook him heartily by the hand,
however, and courteously expressed his pleasure in making the
acquaintance.

An invitation to dinner by Mr. Grace was declined by Howard,
on the plea of attending to his present duties. So, while O'Clery
and the Protestant clergyman, accepting it, accompanied Mr.
and Miss Grace to their house, the military gentlemen sought
their Irish cabin and casual camp-mess, loud in approbation of
the eloquence they had heard. ˙

CHAPTER VI.

"WELL, your prophecy holds," said Graham to his friend
after dinner, as he sipped a glass of genuine pottheen punch : "I
begin to like your smoky beverage better than I thought it
possible to have done."

"'Tis the only thing I can offer you in my wild quarters ; and
though, being both smoky and illicit, it goes against your palate
and my conscience, yet, necessity you know, Graham—"

"Has little to do with squeamish tastes or the parish gauger.
Pottheen you call it ?"

"Pottheen ; derivative, pot. Which utensil, with a crooked
tin tube, forms, I can learn, the whole distilling apparatus. The
natives, who ever mix up with abberrations of this kind a quaint
and singular humor, further term it 'Mountain Dew,' in allusion,
I believe, to the situation, and to the witching time of night, in
which it is generally manufactured."

"Well, Howard, I have now, for the first time, opportunity
to inquire after your romantic campaign here. You are sure
Doe is completely hemmed in ?"

"I am positive from the intelligence of my spies, that, at this moment, the formidable Doe, with part of his gang, surprised in their
retreat homeward, as usual, after a nightly depredation, lies, at
some concealed point, within a circle of three or four miles I have
formed round them. We repeatedly started and chased him during
the course of yesterday ; towards evening, however, he eluded us

Ever since the men stand to arms, where, at a distance, you have seen them. They and I are certain that he is within their lines, and that, if he does not appear, he must starve within them."

" Why not close in, and take him at once ?"

" You are unacquainted with the nature of the ground. He has retreated among the recesses of a bog, the area of which is some miles, and where regular soldiers, ignorant of the novel impediments and ambuscades of the place, cannot follow him. It would be madness, indeed almost sure destruction, if they did. You have only the aspect of the situation, softened by distance. In reality it abounds in alternate pools of deep water and marshy spots of soil ; while here and there huge clamps, as they are called, of turf, create hiding-places, and are, of course, dangerous impediments. No ; the advantage is mine, and I must not hastily forfeit it. He shall, as I have said, creep out to us, or rot where he is. The men are content to watch him, as on the edges of the bog, all around, they have, in turn, their occasional bivouacs, and, like myself, are in no want of rations."

" Are you aware of the number of the enemy ?"

" I believe they are rather numerous ; and, what is more, brave and desperate."

" Then all is not yet certain. Instead of crawling out to be hanged, they may break forth and escape, if they do not absolutely annoy you."

" It is possible. Though from our, at least, equal numbers, and commanding discipline, not probable."

" You have often seen this bravo ?"

" Never. That pleasure is in reserve for me. But I have often heard from him."

" Indeed ! in what way ?"

" In the shape of sundry written threats, directing me to draw off my men, and go quietly about my business, if I valued life or health."

" How did these notices reach you ? by what hand ?"

" I do not know. Sometimes, in the morning, I found them on my pillow ; sometimes nailed to the very door of my bivouac ; nay, I got one of them dangling at my sword-guard."

" In good earnest, now, what is the treason of these silly, as well as desperate men ?"

" If by treason you mean disloyalty to the person of our gracious king, I believe they are not guilty of that specific crime."

3*

" No ?"

" No. I have assured myself that their views do not involve the most distant aim at the throne. On the contrary, I believe they indulge a kind of wayward love and reverence for their present good sovereign. As to the Church, they take, in the way of resistance to tithes, or rates, or dues, almost as much liberty with their own as with ours."

" You surprise me. What *is* their object, then ?"

" They state it to be the lowering of rack-rents and tithes. This Captain Doe professes not to allow any person to set or take land, or pay tithes, but on his own terms. Upon any that trangress his orders, he wreaks, when he can, summary, and often horrible vengeance."

" Is the grievance real or imaginary ?"

" That is a question, Graham, that, if you had my duty to perform, you would scarcely wish to discuss. At all events, I believe we could not, as Englishmen, understand its naked merits. The great relative differences between landlord and tenant, and pastor and flock, in each country, must incapacitate our judgments till we are better informed."

" Be it so then. Of what rank and education may this Doe be ?"

" His excellency either does not know how to write, or else takes a new secretary at every turn. No two of the state papers he has done me the honor to address to me were written alike."

" Have you any of these precious documents to show ?"

Howard searched his pockets, and while thus employed—" By the way," his friend continued, " that was a pretty little Papist you smirked at to-day in the chapel. *You* thought so, evidently."

" I think I have some of these papers," said Howard, most properly replying to the first question, first—" Yes, here is one, predicting my annihilation in two short days if I do not forthwith return to headquarters." As he spoke, he looked towards the fire, his face emulating the color of his jacket.

" And not a word about the little devotee ? Well ; monopolize as you like. But let us see this other matter. Hollo !" continued Graham, laughing as he read, " what the deuce is all this ?" and he read aloud :

" ' Captain John Doe presents his compliments to Lieutenant Howard,'—oh, thou particular fellow ! (an interpolation by Graham) ' to Lieut. Howard, sending this private note to warn him, at the same time that he would do well to draw off his men ; that Lieut. Howard might also find it for the best to give up—' "

"Stop, Graham," interrupted Howard, in evident confusion, " I've made a mistake."

" ' To give up,' " continued Graham, still reading out, " ' all pretensions—' "

" I say 'tis a mistake—that's the wrong note—give it me ;" and Howard rose and advanced, but the other anticipating him, also started up, and holding Howard off with one hand, kept the note in the other, and went on.

" ' To give up all pretensions to the rich attorney's daughter,' —ha ! ha !—Finaud !—Love and War ?—eh ?"

"This is unlucky—ill-timed, I meant," mumbled Howard, his cheeks red as those of a blushing girl.

" ' For, by the moon and stars he reigns under,' " pursued Graham, still from the paper, " ' Captain John swears he can never permit purty Mary Grace '—what !—the little idolater ?— ' purty Mary Grace to be carried off from a gossip of his own, by an English red-coat. Signed, Doe,' and countersigned too ! —' Lieutenant Starlight, Serjeant Moonshine.' Why, Howard, how close and prudent you would be !—pretty Mary—no—*purty* Mary Grace, the rich attorney's daughter—ha ! ha ! ha !"

"Nay, Graham," said Howard, resuming his seat, and the least in the world sulky, "since you have at your pleasure possessed yourself of my secret—though I own I was just debating how I should best escape your cursed laugh in breaking it to you. But, since you have it, there is no need of that laugh, Graham. I'm not so ashamed of the matter."

" What ! Matrimony in good earnest ?" and Graham also sat down, returning the note.

" Really," answered Howard ; "a pretty girl, as Doe himself has defined her—"

" *Purty, purty ;* no perversion of text."

" A handsome girl, an amiable and sensible one, and a *dot* of five thousand, Graham. Though, for that matter, I would marry her without a penny. Laugh if you like ; but you know the proverb."

" Aye, they laugh that win. By Jove, hero of ours, let me congratulate you, rather. A fascinating little puss she must be. When did all this happen ? How could it ? You have made quick work—why, you are not yet a month on the service !"

"What need of a century? I had a pleasant billet at her father's house for a fortnight."

"Ah! necessity for remaining stationary; yet could not appoint to meet his friend, as he might be obliged to change quarters at a moment's notice, and so forth," said Graham, good-humoredly, alluding to the notes he had received from Howard, and of which we have before spoken. "But what will you do with the holy father?—purchase his dispensation? That will cost a world of money."

"Give him one, rather: that is, dispense with *him*: for I cannot see how he comes into the matter. You know, Graham, I have ever said I should not trouble myself about my wife's religion. Enough for me, if she has the spirit of any; and such I truly believe to be the case in the present instance."

"And of the disapprobation of his high mightiness, Captain John!"

"Oh, let to-morrow or next day settle that."

"Well—a bumper to your success in the rival fields of Mesdames Venus and Bellona. And now, Howard, 'tis time I were on the road."

"What! abandon us so soon?"

"Why, yes. After all our disappointments in meeting, when, each time I was prepared for a long visit, I could not, on the present occasion, get leave of absence longer than to-night. I must present myself in Clonmel to-morrow; but the next time shall be an age."

"Then you will have to travel all night?"

"Yes; but with old Tom Evans I shall not mind it."

"Take him. Though, indeed, I intended him for my own body-guard on a march I propose to steal across the country this evening."

"Humph—*purty* Mary Grace?"

"Perhaps you guess it. But no matter about Evans. The certainty I have that Doe is out of the way enables me to go alone, except, it may be, with a peasant for my guide, as my path is a cross one, almost unknown to me."

"How far?" asked Graham.

"Not more than three miles—Irish ones, though."

"Oh, doubtless you may venture it. Come."

"With you? But—Graham "—

"Well? Well?"—

"No need of remembering my little affair at headquarters, you know."

"Purty Mary and the rich attorney."

"Indeed, Graham, I must insist—"

"Ha ! ha !—fear nothing ;—I'm prudent." And the friends, after mutual farewells, separated on their different routes ; Howard and his guide towards Mr. Grace's house, and Graham—with Evans, grumbling in every aching joint of his body, at being again, and so soon, called upon to shake for thirteen miles, say sixteen English, in an uneasy saddle—towards Clonmel.

We are here obliged to close a very short chapter, in order to afford proper scope for the events now to be detailed.

CHAPTER VII.

AFTER conducting his old acquaintances to the sacristy, at the chapel, Flinn returned to his place among the kneeling crowd. Watching his time, till the service allowed, according to established form, general liberty to stand, he pushed on into the body of the chapel, and heard attentively the separate exhortations of his parish priest and of the Rev. Mr. O'Clery, together with the few words spoken by the Protestant clergyman.

When all was over, Flinn left the chapel with the rest of the people, but dallied near the place till he thought he might proceed, without their observation, to keep an appointment with a particular friend. With his hands plunged into his breeches' pockets, his hat hanging, as usual, on one side of his head, and while he whistled a lively air, Flinn turned down a by-path, which led from the chapel over a considerable declivity, towards a wretched little thatched hut called the "Forge." It was, in fact, the smithy of the district, erected distinct and far from any neighboring dwelling-house, and exclusively devoted by the proprietor, whose residence was a cabin at some distance, to the purposes of his trade. So that on a Sunday he made no use of, and claimed no right of possession over it. Furthermore, apprehending that little seduction to theft was held forth by the massive anvil or gigantic shattered bellows, the only available property left during the Sabbath on the premises, he had never gone to the expense of a door for the hovel, and it consequently gave an open, and, so far as in it lay, a hearty welcome, one day in each week, to all chance comers. And, the year round, the forge had—we are compelled to admit—almost systematically upon that day, its particular visitors. Some of the very lowest order of Irish peasants are passionately attached to card-playing, rather, it would seem, for the sake of amusement than in a gambling view. And of all convenient places in a neighborhood, the snug corner of a field, or the depths of a sand-pit not excepted, though both haunts are often resorted to for the same purposes, none surpass in attraction the deserted and isolated forge.

To the adjacent forge, then, our friend Paddy Flinn directed his steps. As he advanced, he met in succession two or three little boys, whom the party engaged in forbidden pastime had sent out and stationed as scouts, to give them timely notice of the probable visitation of their really good and zealous parish priest, from whom they had vainly heard repeated prohibitions against such breaches of the Sabbath, and who, failing in words, had often surprised them with his more convincing cudgel or horsewhip, while they were engaged in the fascinations of their game. The little urchins rapidly inquired of Flinn, as soon as he appeared, the destination of their dreaded pastor ; and having ascertained that, as he had gone to dine with Mr. Grace, no visit might this day be apprehended from him, they immediately abandoned their disagreeable posts, and separated to seek some more genial occupation.

As Flinn, pursuing his path, entered the forge, he found Jack Mullins, the friend he had appointed to meet, deeply absorbed with three others in the climax of a long-contested game. The anvil constituted a card-table for this rustic party, who sat round it on large stones piled one over another. They used cards which might baffle the discriminating faculties of more accomplished gamesters, as long fingering, and the hue and shape thereby left on each, confounded, to the uninitiated eye, all distinctions of number, color, and suit. Habit is everything, however. The present proprietors of these mysterious symbols appeared to recognize their fifty-two subtle subdivisions with as much ease as, in a more fashionable hell, gamblers of a higher order distinguish the difference of an unsoiled pack. Rumor adds, that here the means for arriving at such conclusions were not derived from much positive evidence of the marks originally stamped on the paste-board, but rather from subsidiary hieroglyphics that had gradually succeeded to the original signs, and as gradually become acknowledged, from month to month, nay, from year to year, by the persevering and watchful observers.

No notice was taken of Flinn's entrance, if we except a slight raising of the eyes, and an accompanying noise, like a grunt, directed to him by Mullins, and meant, we presume, for avowed recognition. The men pursued the critical turn of their game with all the abstraction of their caste, and with all the attendant symptoms of deep study ; that is to say, bent brows, protrusions and compressions of the lips, and occasional long pauses and unmeaning stares at the wall, or out of doors. Flinn, too, after his first unnoticed salutation, kept silence for some time, standing behind Mullins, and watching his play and hand. At last the interregnum of a deal allowed him a few words.

"Well," he said, "I was at mass, boys."

"You're all the better o' that, arn't you ?" said Mullins.

"To be sure I am, you gallows-bird, you," answered Flinn.

"An' wouldn't any thing, not to talk o' that, be better nor the prayers you get out o' the devil's horn-buke you hould in your hand there ?"

"Well, à-vich," said Mullins, tranquilly dealing the cards.

"What do you call well ?" cried Flinn. "I don't know what's well or ill mysef ; but I know the day that's in it is the day o' days. For, sayin' nothing o' the strange priest's sarmen, little did any of us think we'd live to see a Sassenach minister prachin' to us off o' the same altar wid our own soggarth, an' two red-coats kneelin' down by his side to pray the blessin' o' God on us, poor divils that we are, along wid Father O'Clery, good loock to every inch of him."

"They'd do any thing to sell us, betwixt 'em," said Mullins. "An' what rhaumaush did you hear from Father O'Clery ?"

"It was no rhaumaush,* you hell-hound," answered Flinn, "bud plenty o' good sense an' love for us, an' the right thing afther all, an' I'll stand by it."

"You'll stand by the gallows," said Mullins, in a jeering tone and manner.

"To see you swinging on it," retorted Flinn ; "when you'll

* Nonsense.

be afther walkin' in search of it, an' your own coffin followin' you,
two or three miles, of a market-day. I often tould you not to fear
the wather, Jack. Bud the short an' the loug is this. Father
O'Clery said nothin' bud God's truth this blessed day. There
wasn't a dry eye iu the place. An' if you can do any good,
Jack, by spakin' to any friend o' yours, or the likes o' that, it's
nothing but what 'd become you well. Aud so I'll tell the
farmer's sou, himself, when I see him next.''

"Let us play our play, a-hagar," said Mullins, " au' don't be
botherin' plain people wid what they know little about. Come.
Now all the loock is his that has the five fingers."*

"Aye, you'll play your own play, Jack. An' may be you'll
have the loock o' the five fingers too. The skibbecah's,† I mane,
while he's takin' your measure for the hemp cravat," observed
Fliun, as the gamblers now resumed their pursuit—"Bud stop,
for I think you'd betther," he continued, in au undertone, " au'
just turn round till you see who's lookin at you." With these
words Flinn escaped from the forge, hastily poiutiug to an orifice,
meant for the double uses of window and chimney, which was
situated in the wall of the hovel behind Mullins's back.

The men with whom Mullins was playing first took advantage
of Fliuu's hint, and, fixing their terrified eyes on this opening,
saw it almost entirely filled by the rouud, red face, and fat
shoulders of their parish priest, who, notwithstanding other engagements, could not conscientiously overlook, on this particular
Sunday, the chauces of the notorious forge, and had accordiug-
ly paid it a speculative visit.

"Ho-ho ! ye Sabbath-breakers !" roared the worthy man, pre-
cipitating himself into the forge, and, whip in hand, falling with
might aud main on the backs of his profane parishioners—" Have
I found you again !—have I found you again ! At the old work !
—at the old work !" Each iterated sentence was accompaniment
to a repeated lash, and Mullius's three gaming friends quickly, and
with ostentatiously loud screams, escaped through the open door-
way, while the priest turned round upon a whole nest of old and
young, who, we forgot to say, sat on the hobs of the forge fire, or
on the ground, anxious spectators of the ambitioned game. Among
these the zealous pastor also made impartial use of his horsewhip.
It was ludicrous to hear the cries and shouts of tall, rawbouned fellows,
of from six to seven feet high, as they quailed or jumped beueath

* Five of trumps.   † Hangman's.

the hand of a little round man, whose entire physical strength was not equal to that contained in one of their fingers, or who, at least, by the merest show of resistance, might have escaped his flagellation. But as the beasts of the forests all tremble at the lion's roar, so do the greater portion of Irish peasants shrink at the voice of their priests. We have seen a mob of some hundreds, even in the excitement of mutual passion and conflict, fly, forgetful of everything but the mortal terror of his presence, as the waters divide and splash when a heavy stone is dropped into them. On the present occasion, the flock of idlers in the forge bore testimony to a similar influence. In fact, the place was, in a few minutes, cleared of all except the clergyman and Mullins For Mullins would not run as the others did, but now stood doggedly, and, as well as he could, indifferently, his side turned to the parish priest, and his eyes fixed on the landscape abroad.

"And do *you* face me, you unfortunate sinner?" said the Priest, screaming at Mullins when he discovered him. "But I'll convert you—you as well as the rest—if there's virtue in whalebone and whipcord, I'll convert you one after the other;" and he wound a good lash at Mullins.

"Nonsense, soggarth, nonsense!" ejaculated the suffering party, when he had felt the smart of the whip. "Don't be doin' that agin, I advise you."

"I see you now, an' I know you now," said the reverend operator, somewhat daunted by the bad expression of the man's face. "You are one of those that have brought sin and trouble into my poor parish—you and your crony the jig-dancer"—Mr. Flinn, we presume, was meant. "But I disown ye—I renounce ye. Ye are two diseased sheep among my innocent flock, and two strangers that 'tis hard to speak about."

"Then don't speak about us at all, please your reverence," said Mullins. "An' if we're strangers, let us alone."

"Go, man, go," resumed the clergyman—"I know you not, and all I have to say is this. Come in next Saturday, to your Easter duty, and show your bad face at mass next Sunday, and behave yourself like a Christian creature in my parish. Or, if you don't, leave my parish. I won't give you my curse upon it —that's an awful thing to do—but I'll mark you, you Sabbathbreaker—I'll mark you!" And the virtuous, though, as we have seen in the chapel, scarcely accomplished pastor, hastily left the hovel, Mullins uttering an "Avoch!" as they parted.

He stood a few minutes after the clergyman's exit, apparently

in deep thought ; then suddenly turned to leave the hovel, when
he was met at the threshold by Flinn.

"Come wid me up by the side of this brook," said Flinn,
rapidly walking in the direction he pointed out. Let us get
among the hills before we spake anything more about it."

They accordingly continued their way until they had reached
the solitude of a wild little valley, and here Flinn again paused
and addressed his companion. "What are you goin' to do wid
Purcell ?" he suddenly asked, staring Mullins full in the face.

"Bad end to him, how do I know ?" said Mullins, "only he
asked me yesterday evenin' afther my work was done, to meet
him here, an' I said yes, because it was as good as to say no."

"You wouldn't, you curse-o'-God limb," resumed the other,
"you wouldn't be afther ˙sellin' the pass* on whatever poor
fellows you know any thing about—would you ?"

"Ho ! ho ! who are you spakin' to ?" replied Mullins.

"I don't well know, maybe," said Flinn. "Bud I know, an'
I think you know too, there would be neither honor nor glory,
gain nor saviu', in tellin' your thoughts to such a hound as Purcell, for all his magistrates' warrants an' the like. Though I
say agin, Jack, the strange priest tould us enough to-day to
make us to do our best in the fair cause."

"Hould your tongue," said Mullins, "I know nothing at all of
it. Don't be botherin' me for ever. What can you do bud spake,
spake, spake ? If you could do any thing else the evenin' o' the Patthern, I wouldn't had the trouble o' meetin' this black Protestan'
this blessed and holy night ; an' others 'ud be saved trouble too."

"'Twas none o' my fault, Jack. I done my best, if ever I
done it ; while you had only to look on wid your sailor's noose
in your pocket ; that, I say over an' over, you'll be outmated
at last. Bud how does Purcell trate you ?"

"Well enough, considerin' the likes of him ; an' the likes o'
me, too, that only works whin the fit is on me. He's always soft
wid me—maybe too soft, for all we know. Bud make off wid
yourself—I see him just turnin' into the glin—bad loock to him !
an' how 'ticlar he is, an' the evenin' only fallin'. Here, you

---

* "Selling the pass," a generally diffused proverb through Ireland,
is perhaps derived from the traditionary circumstance of an officer of
James's army, at the siege of Limerick, in 1690, having disclosed to
Ginkle, William's general, a favorable part of the Shannon, by means
of which, it is said, Ginkle put an end by treaty to the long-contested
siege of the city.

scapegrace, get behind this big stone, an' lie quiet if you can, an'
say your prayers if you remember any o' them. I'll soon send
him off."

Flinn obeyed the instructions of his companion, completely
hiding himself behind a tall rock that sloped from the path
against some adjoining masses of stone that skirted the valley,
and which was also partially surrounded by brushwood, as if to
add to its present usefulness. When he had squatted in his am-
bush, Mullins walked slowly away from the spot, and then up and
down at a little distance, while he awaited the approach of Mr.
Purcell, the gentleman in whose employment, as a garden laborer,
he now was, and the same who had given rise to the fray at the
pattern some seven months before.

"I am glad you are punctual, Mullins," said Mr. Purcell, as
he came up. "But are we alone?"

"Din't you see we are?" answered Mullins.

"I thought I saw another by your side, when I first entered
the valley."

"You thought wrong, then, Mr. Purcell, unless it was *who
you know*, keepin' me company, for your sake, till you came
yourself."

"Whom do you mean?" said Purcell, half guessing from the
nature of the man, as well as from a recollection of the confidence he had given him, the probable allusion.

"Hauld your ear an' I'll tell you. The *old bouchal*, Mr.
Purcell," answered Mullins, very calmly; "an' I'd make little
wonder if you thought right, after all."

"Tut, tut, Mullins," said Purcell, laughing, yet, perhaps,
somewhat disagreeably affected. "No more of that folly. Indeed 'tis worse than folly in such a place."

A pause ensued, during which it would seem that Purcell
wished Mullins to say something; but whether or not such was
his intention, he was himself compelled to continue.

"I have trusted you very freely on this matter, Mullins, because
I think I may have faith in you. Besides, the more you know
of it, the better you can serve me."

"Maybe so, Mr. Purcell."

"Mullins, I have loved Mary Grace for years; I have tried
to win her for years."

"I know that. You tould me the like afore."

"At first, as I said, she slighted me, on account of that unfortunate young lad, Kavanagh. But when he was put out of the way,

that is, when his own doings put him out of the way, then I
found favor with her."

"Are you sure, Mr. Purcell ?"

"No doubt of it ; I had no fear of success till this English
interloper came between us. Do you think I would propose to
force a woman who had not given me the first encouragment ?
Not I, Mullins ; you know I would not. But you see, as I said
over and over, all is owing to this English subaltern."

"Aye ; the red-coat Sassenagh. Well, à-roon ?"

"Don't you think it a shame and a pity, now, Mullins, that
the girl and the money should leave the country with a red rag
like him, when I offer to keep her as she ought to be kept, and
make her an Irish lady on my own estate ?"

"Thonomon-duoul, yes ! The grounds you took over poor
Kavanagh's head are as good as an estate to you."

"Come, come, Mullins, nothing of that."

"An' the blood-money you got for huntin' him to the black
north made a gintilman o' you."

"What has this to do with the business, Mullins ?"

"An' sure, you're a justice o' the peace, too."

"Do you mean to insult me ?"

"Avoch, no ; only you see how it is."

"Well, then, to business. You will assist me ?" continued
Purcell, thrusting a bank-note of some value into Mullins's hand.

"Try me, à-vich," answered Mullins, crumpling the note hard,
after he had looked close at it, and then buttoning it up in his
pocket.

"I believe you're a steady fellow, Jack ; and the rest of the
lads are ready."

"Are they ? Who's to head 'em ?"

"Why, myself, Mullins !"

"Yourself !—ho ! ho !"

"Why do you laugh ? Yes, disguised as Doe, and under his
name, I will this night carry her off."

"Will you ? Curp-on-duoul ! That's a bright thought."

"But Mullins, one uncomfortable thing has happened. You
know, we thought Howard was to stay away from the house for
some time, and that all would, therefore, be snug."

"Well ; an' isn't he to stay away ?"

"No ; I have just discovered he is to set out for Mr. Grace's
in an hour."

"Well ?"

"If he comes we are bedevilled and ruined."

" Well ?"

" Isn't there any way to prevent him ?"

" I don't know, faith, Mr. Purcell."

" Suppose ——" and Purcell paused a moment, then resumed quickly, " Couldn't *you* prevent him ?"

" How is that ?" demurred Mullins.

" He is a worm in my path, Mullins ; you know he is. He has crossed me at the very moment of hope."

" Aye ; so he has. Well ?"

" I ask you, now—leaving yourself to guess it—how many journeys more ought he to take ? I think, but one," and Purcell slid another note into Mullins's hand.

" An' that one—is"—said Mullins, slowly, as he put up the second bribe.

" From this world to the next !" interrupted Purcell, in a whisper, yet of so sharp and audible a kind, that the banks and rocks around indistinctly repeated it.

" Whist, man !" replied Mullins, seizing Purcell by the arm, while his tongue, though deep and hollow, was less revealing than Purcell's whisper—" How do you know what ear the stones may be tellin' it to."

Even in the imperfect light Purcell stood visibly pale and trembling, and this hint increased his nervousness almost to a paroxysm.

" Have you deceived me, you scoundrel ?" he asked, drawing a pistol, and stepping back.

" Me ?—for what or for why ?—put up your barker, Mr. Purcell, or give it to myself for Howard. Sure I meant nothin' at all. I was just as frightened as yourself, about it ; only I don't look so white, an' shake, afther a manner. Yourself knows walls have ears, an' walls are made o' stones like the stones near us." During this harangue, Mullins had contrived, without giving any suspicious appearance, to stand directly between Purcell and the rock under which Flinn lay concealed.

" I must continue to trust you now, however," resumed Purcell, after a pause, and as he returned the pistol to his pocket.

" Well ?" said Mullins, coming back from this digression, and assuming an earnest air.

" I have bribed another friend to *guide* him to Grace's house," continued Purcell. "Howard thinks the man is loyal to himself, because Mr. Grace pointed him out as a proper person for such services. But he's mistaken, maybe."

" Then, what use o' the likes o' me ?" asked Mullins.

" Much, Mullins, much. My other friend might miss the thing ; may be overpowered ; for Howard is bold and active. You can follow them."

" So I can ; an' I see it now, Mr. Purcell."

" Mullins—there is a pass a little way on, between the wood and the river ; they will get into that. 'Tis crossed by the mountain stream, that stream is deep and headlong, and, at last, it meets the river." A pause succeeded.

" Aye," Mullins at length resumed—" when once in, we needn't fear he'll rise again."

" Right ; or you know well how to prevent it, if you like, Jack. Weren't you taught how to make a basket to put a stone in, when you were a man-o'-war's man ?"

" I could thry, I think ; never fear, Mr. Purcell."

" You know how little *we* can be suspected. It is just the time and place for an English officer to be looked for by such a man as Doe, or some of his people. Then, I'm a loyal person, and a magistrate, and you're in my employment, Mullins."

" Aye, faith : sure I understand it entirely, Mr. Purcell."

" Come, now. But stay—we must not walk together towards my house."

" No ; an' you'd better go home to the colleen that's expectin' you, Mr. Purcell. What 'ill you do wid poor Cauth, I wonder ?"

" Oh, d—n her, Jack, let her go her ways," answered Purcell, his brow and eye darkened by this sudden question : " I'm long tired of her."

"An' so let her, sure enough," said Mullins ; " 'tis good enough for any of her sort. An' yet, Mr. Purcell, she was a clane, likely girl when you saw her first ; an' now her best days are over. Faith she has few 'ud give her a welcome, I'm thinking. Still, if we get Mary Grace for you, Cauthleen must take the dour, anyhow."

" Good-by, Mullins," said Purcell, evading further explanation on this last point. He walked a few steps away, then returned, and again spoke.

" When it is done, and well done, come to my house by the back way. You'll find me in the parlor ; and then we can prepare for the other business."

" I will," responded Mullins. Purcell stood a moment silent, and again turned off, with a " good-by."

" Good-by," then," echoed his companion.

"Stay an instant here, 'till I'm out of sight," Purcell continued. " You remember every thing, and mark me ?"

"I do," said Mullins, and Purcell rapidly walked away.

"Or," muttered the other, when he was out of hearing, "if I didn't, the Devil has marked you, an' that's enough for us both. Flinn!"—and Mr. Flinn accordingly appeared.

"The false thief!" pursued Mullins—"the bloody informer! —wid his acres around him that he schamed an' swore out o' the hands of honest people! ,An' he thinks he can buy me up? An' he thinks to do what he likes without our lave? Where's he farmer's son, Paddy?"

"At hand, I'm thinkin'," said Flinn. "Bud *what bolg is on you* * now, black Jack? I didn't see you in a right kind of a passion afore, since the day the ministher offered to lave the oats on your field if you went to church next Sunday. What was Purcell sayin' to you at all, at all?"

"Go tell the farmer's son," Mullins condescended to explain, "that Purcell, the Rapparee, is goin' to take off purty Mary Grace."

"Musha, Jack, was that all the Omadhaun wanted wid you? —an' did he cross your fist?"

"Did he gi' me a bribe, is it? Avoch, bad loock to the lafina he offered me; an' if he did, d'you think I'd touch it, Paddy, frum the likes of him?"

"Maybe not, Jack, à-roon; bud I'll tell you what I was considerin' while you both left me to get could under the stone, there. Faith, I was thinkin' that there was no raison in the wide world why we couldd't manage Purcell where he stood, an' so get over, quietly and han'somely, the little obligation we are owin' him this long time, for another man's sake."

"Maybe I was thinkin' o' the like myself," said Mullins; "it was so new a thing to see him from home without his red-coats about him. But all for the best, Paddy. It's a long lane has no turnin'. Let us go tell the farmer's son what he wants to do in the regard o' Mary Grace."

"The farmer's son knows it already. But for the night that's in it, he can't help it, poor fellow."

"Curp-on-duoul! an' why so, man?"

"I thought you could tell the raison, of your own accord, Jack. All his tenants on the spot are doin' somethin', an' the rest too far off to be here in time."

"That's thrue enough—bud no matter—he's at home?"

"Where else 'ud he be?"

"We must spake to him, thin, about another small matter

* What is the matter.

that Purcell has on hands.   D'you know, Paddy, a-vich, he
wants to have the Red-Coat to himself ?"

"Musha, how, Jack ?" asked Flinn.

" He wants just to stretch him in the glin, below there.   An'
I'm to help him you know."

"Och, sure I know," said Flinn, laughing.

"Ho ! ho !" echoed Mullins ; "for the matter o' that, I'd
have little objections to make a hole in a red jacket, any day ;
bud we must hear what the farmer's son says about id.   Come,
there's no time to be lost.   Howard is on the road by this time."
And the two friends went on their errand.

Meantime, Purcell approached, by another path, his own house,
deeply and sternly revolving a purpose that for some months
had occupied his mind, and that now, bent as he was on making
Miss Grace his wife, and so near the time of his attempt, too,
engaged every bad energy of his soul.   The poor creature to
whom Mullins had just directed his attention, and whom he described as expecting Purcell at his home, was the object of Purcell's thoughts.   She sat, indeed, expecting him ; him—her sole
earthly protector : the self-elected substitute for every other ;
her heart's early and only love, for whom she had sinfully abandoned the world and the world's smile, to keep, in friendless and
otherwise cheerless solitude, a constant place at his side.   Alas !
she did not think what a requital he contemplated for her.

Purcell had not found the destruction of this now helpless creature an easy exploit.   She had withstood his smiles, his oaths, and
his ardors—his gold she at once spurned—until, in the fervency of
passion, the constitutionally calm villain had given her, in writing,
a solemn promise of marriage.   Then she fell, and with her all her
influence, attraction, and hopes.   Years passed over without any
disposition on Purcell's part to perform his contract.   The victim
could at first only weep, and kneel to him for mercy and justice ;
and then, when she gradually saw the nature of the man to whom
she had abandoned herself, and felt in words and acts the effect of
that nature in reply to her supplications, the wretched girl could
only mourn in silence.   If she did speak, it was in the tone of a
poor slave abjectly begging a favor, rather than in the voice of
conscious right demanding the fulfilment of an obligation.   She
could compel Purcell to nothing, even if her weak and self-accusing
heart dared to meditate a severity towards the master that, even
with knowledge of what he was, it still worshipped.   The forlorn
girl had no friends to advocate her cause : her crime, along with

other things, had scattered them over the earth, or sunk them in its bosom. Since her ruin, too, Purcell had, by all available means, thriven in the world ; and fortune thus added another link to the mean as well as guilty chain that bound her to him. Increasing wealth lent him increase of sway ; and while her love remained unabated, her awe increased, and abject subjection followed.

Yet, though she did not continue to plead her own cause, she still had Purcell in her power, and he knew it. Cauthleen held his written promise of marriage, nor could lures or entreaties prevail on her to thrust it for a moment into his hands. Purcell had lately expressed some slight curiosity to see it, but Cauthleen had never attended to his wish. The man's designs on Miss Grace prompted him in this instance. As he himself truly stated to Mullins, his long and strenuous endeavors had been directed to a union with that young lady ; and among many other firm objections urged as well by her father as by the high-spirited girl herself, the written engagement to Cauthleen which was generally talked of, met him at every step. Purcell, therefore, determined to remove that obstacle, even though the unhappy Cauthleen should become still more a victim.

In truth he had now for some time brought himself to contemplate with indifference the expulsion of Cauthleen, from his house, and her subsequent wandering alone, and in shame, through the world. It cannot even be said that his passion for Miss Grace had caused a disgust of his unfortunate mistress. Purcell bent his ambition, not on the person of the lady, but on the alliance with her father's wealth ; to which, as she was an only child, he would, in the event of becoming her husband, also become heir ; and his new-sprung name and pretensions must thus gain strength and countenance in the country. No ; he had not even the poor pretext of alienated and ungovernable passion to urge for his neglect of the wretched girl, whom, having made so, he should never have abandoned. He knew but one plea for his disgust—for his hatred : he had tired of her. And perhaps, with lengthened investigation, we could not advance a better reason, duly considering the character of the man.

With a breast and brow made up to the prompt execution of his purposes, Purcell now gained his own door. Poor Cauthleen' herself answered his knock. It was her constant practice to anticipate the servants in doing so, when, by the fond fidelity of ear that can distinguish the step, nay the breathing, even at

4

a distance, of one beloved, she had learned to interpret this signal of Purcell's approach.

She smiled faintly as Purcell entered. He only returned her mute welcome with a ruffianly gathering of the brow ; then, slapping the door, and hastily passing her, he flew into a brawling passion against the servants for neglect of their duty, in not attending to his knock. A foul purpose will seek to nerve itself in preparatory and cowardly excitement, as men, not over sure of their own mettle, have recourse to dram-drinking before they enter the ring.

With drooping head, Cauthleen slowly and silently followed Purcell to the parlor, vainly endeavoring to stem the tears that had flowed plentifully in his absence, and, only dried up at his approach, that again sought vent under this fresh sorrow. Her seducer flung himself rudely into a chair : as she timidly took an opposite seat, her tears became evident, and he instantly seized on this as a new theme for dastardly reproach and outrage, exclaiming in the idiom of a vulgar ruffian :

"Damnation ! am I, forever and forever, to be met in this manner ? Nothing but cry, cry, cry, from morning to night ? What do you wish me to do ?—have I left you in any way unprovided for ? Is there a lady—a married lady in the land—who has more of the comforts of life—who is more her own mistress ? Why don't you speak to me ?—what is the matter with you ?"

Cauthleen only wept on.

"You won't answer me, then ?—I advise you, speak. By the great Lord, if you do not speak, I'll make you repent it, Cauthleen !" He had now wrought himself up to a climax of actual rage, and he uttered the last words with a violent knock on the table, while his teeth set and his eyes flashed savagely upon her.

"My dear Stephen," Cauthleen said at last, trembling with terror, " indeed it is not obstinacy ; only I couldn't answer you in a moment. And—I—I cried first because you were away from me—and now, I believe, because you are come home to me—and indeed I did not mean to vex you, and I will cry no more—there. If 'tis my poor smile you want instead, there it is for you, Stephen, from my heart, too—from the bottom of my heart.—Don't, don't be angry with your Cauthleen, Stephen—don't frighten her in such a way."

Nature, even in the bosom of a scoundrel, asserted her sympathy to this appeal, and Purcell, turning his face to the fire, remained silent a moment.

"Cauthleen," he then continued, "you can be a good girl when you like. Have you since found that little paper? You'll let me look at it to-night, won't you?

"Indeed, Stephen, some other time. But to-night I'm too—too—"

"Too what?" interrupted Purcell, resuming his boisterous tone—"are you sick? or too stupid? or too insolent? Or why can you not oblige me?"

"I can never be too anything not to oblige you, Stephen. But that unfortunate paper—"

"Where is it? Cauthleen, I must see that cursed scribble, for your own sake. I have a particular reason. Go for it. 'Tis in your room, isn't it?—Why don't you go?—Then I'll go myself—and—drawer, box, or press, shall not keep it from me. I'll break them into splinters sooner than let it escape me"—and he rose and took a candle.

"Stay, Stephen," said Cauthleen, also rising—"It would be useless—quite useless—indeed it would. That paper is not in any room in the house—I declare solemnly it is not."

A startling apprehension crossed Purcell's mind at those words, and, resuming his seat, he said:

"Then you have sent it to the attorney?—What! is that the way you would treat me?"

The reproach, the insult, the voice and manner completely overpowered Cauthleen, and she sank into her chair convulsed with tears.

"Answer!—have you sent it away? have you put it out of your hands?—answer, I say!" and he shook her violently by the shoulder.

"Spare me, spare me, Stephen," cried Cauthleen, falling on her knees—"I have not sent it out of the house to any one—I could never send it where you say—indeed I could not."

"Where is it then, woman?" he asked, stamping, and holding out his clenched hands. At this moment Cauthleen drew a handkerchief from her pocket, and a crumpled slip of paper fell on the carpet. One glance of Purcell's eye recognized the long-sought document, and he was stooping to pick it up, but Cauthleen hastily anticipated him, snatched it, and placed it in her bosom.

"I'll have it, by heaven!" exclaimed Purcell, stooping to-

wards her ; but Cauthleen, starting up, rushed into a corner,
and there again, kneeling, addressed him :

"Do not, do not, Purcell?" she said : "I'll give it to you
when you hear me—to-morrow, when you hear me calmly, I'll
give it to you. Do not," raising her voice, and wringing her
hands as he approached—"For the love of that heaven, whose
love we have both missed !"

"So," resumed Purcell, now standing over her, "you had it
about you, at the very time I asked for it, and you would not
let me see it ?"

"You should not be angry with me for that, Stephen. I'll
tell you about it. When you are away from me, and that I am
quite alone in the world, I draw out that paper, and read it
over and over, and kiss it, and cry over it, and lay it on my
heart. 'Tis my only hope—and, if there be any, my only shadow
of excuse to myself and before God !"

"Nonsense !—trash !—folly ! Give it into my hand this
moment !"—and he caught her by the wrists.

"And sometimes, Stephen," she sobbed, out of breath, blinded
in tears, still feebly struggling with him—

"Sometimes I steal up to the cradle, where our last and only
boy is sleeping. The rest were taken from us, one by one, for
a judgment—we deserved that curse. And there I kneel down
by the poor baby's side, and ask him, in a voice that would not
waken a bird, to look at it, and understand it, and see that he is
not entirely the child of shame, and that his mother is not entirely the guilty creature they will tell him she is. Oh, Stephen,
have mercy on me !"

"Come, Cauthleen," interrupted Purcell, bending on one knee,
and using more force—"give it me, if you have any fears for
yourself." But, in the paroxysms of passion that Cauthleen felt,
he encountered more resistance than he had expected ; and, ex-
asperated to the utmost by her continued struggling, the mean
and cowardly ruffian raised his clenched hand—it fell—the girl
fell under it—and Purcell got possession of the paper, and instantly approached the fire. Cauthleen, though stunned and
stupefied, wildly understood his movement, and screamed and
tottered after him. But she was too late ; Purcell cast it into
the flame, and with—"There—since we have so often quarrelled
about it, that's the only way to end disputes," he sank into his
seat.

Cauthleen, with clasped hands, her tears now dried up by in-

tensity of anguish, looked with agony at the shriveled film in
the fire, and then, in the hollow tones of despair, said, as she
turned away :

" And now you can wive with Mary Grace, to-morrow !"

Purcell, at first startled, turned quickly round. But his features only wore a bitter mockery, while he asked :

" Who told you that fine story, Cauthleen ?"

" Never ask me, Purcell, but answer me !" she exclaimed, in
a manner the very opposite to her late meekness and timidity—
" Is it true ?—am I not to be your wife indeed ?—after all your
oaths—the oaths that stole me from my mother's side, and then
broke my mother's heart. Will you take Mary Grace to yourself, and leave shame as well as sorrow on Cauthleen ?"

" Fear nothing ; I'll provide for you."

" It *is* true, then ?—this, at last, is to be the lot of Cauthleen
Kavanagh ?—And at your hands ?—Whose ?—The hands that
brought ruin on all of her name !"

" Silence, Cauthleen—or—"

" Or what ?—you'll make me ?—how ?—kill me ? Do !—I
wish it—ask for it—expect it. Yes, Purcell, I expect it—the
robber, the perjurer, and the murderer, need not disappoint
me !"

" Fool ! take care what words you speak—and listen to me
in patience. I courted and won you, because I loved you.
Listen to me ! I can love you no longer—and why should we
live in hatred together ?"

" Cursed be the hour I saw you, Purcell !"—the maddened
creature cried—" accursed the false words that drew me, from
virtue and happiness, under your betraying roof—your roof,
that I now pray God may fall on us as we stand here damning
each other ! Oh ! I am punished ! I trusted the plunderer of
my family, and the murderer of my mother and brother, and I
am punished !"

" I told you to have a care, Cauthleen," said Purcell, starting from his seat, pale, haggard, and trembling with rage—" I
warned you to weigh your words, and you will not ;" and his
distended eye glanced on a fowling-piece that hung over the
chimney.

" I know what you mean, Purcell !" the girl shrieked in a
still wilder frenzy, " I saw where your eye struck—and,
knowing and seeing this, I say again, robber and murderer,
do it !"

"By the Holy Saints—then!" he exclaimed, snatching at the weapon of death.

"Aye, by the Saints and all! the murderer will not want an oath—pull your trigger, man! But, stop a moment!—first hear that!"

Purcell had the piece in his hand, and was raising it, when the faint cry of an infant reached them from an inside room. His face grew black: he flung the weapon on the ground, and turned away.

"Leave my house," he added, after a moment's pause—"you and your brat together—leave it this instant!"

"I will," muttered Cauthleen—"I would not stay here now. She rushed through a door, and returned with the infant on her arm.

"The night draws on, Purcell," the wretched girl said. "It was just in such a night you sent my mother from our own old home, that, in her agony and sickness, the cold blast might deal on her. I leave you, praying that it may so deal on me! My mother cursed you as she went: I pray to have that curse remembered. And I add mine! Take both, Purcell—the mother's first—the daughter's last—may they cling to you!"

Having spoken these words, Cauthleen caught closer in her arms the wretch they encircled, and, bareheaded and unmantled, rushed out of the house of crime. After an instant's lapse, Purcell heard her frenzied, and already distant scream, mingling with the wail of her baby, and the bitter gust of the winter night.

CHAPTER VIII.

WHILE the last events were occurring, Howard was on his way to Mr. Grace's house. The guide, for whose honesty, as Purcell had stated, Mr. Grace gave a guarantee, was a man of unusually large stature; in height above six feet, broad, well-set, and muscular in proportion. So that he appeared a good subject to inspire Howard with confidence or apprehension, according to the degree of trust his presence induced.

Had Howard taken the main road to his friend's house, no

guide would have been necessary. But he did not choose to expose himself to the too frequent observation of all passengers, and therefore adopted a by-way, which was shorter than the approach by the road. It first led, after crossing the road from Howard's bivouac, over two or three marshy fields in which a path was scarcely distinguishable, and then continued through a wood, which, with the exception of a few old nut-trees, was recently planted, and therefore, from the slightness of the stems, and the want of brushwood, together with the total absence of foliage, afforded no facilities for an ambuscade.

We should say that this wood clothed the side of a declivity : consequently, as Howard followed his guide along a winding path, he sank, step by step, from the level of the road they had crossed. After leaving the wood, without danger, or any symptom of it, they entered on a flat sward, through which, at about ten yards' distance, a mountain-stream hurried along. To gain Mr. Grace's residence, it was necessary to pass this impediment : and Howard was preparing to make the attempt, when his guide warned him of probable hazard at that point, and said, that a little way on, by keeping the course of the water, they should meet with an easy crossing. This was all well, and Howard followed in the man's steps.

He followed, without any positive misgiving, and yet with little confidence in his guide. The fellow had from the outset resisted Howard's efforts to draw him into conversation, and exhibited none of the native-good-humor or heartiness, that the young man had been accustomed to, since his first acquaintance with the Irish peasantry. Absolutely rude, indeed, he was not ; yet his short, and apparently abstracted answers, and the deep tone in which they were given, fell, unpleasantly enough, on the ear of the intended victim.

Pursuing their way, they had left the wood behind them, but still were coursing the long ridge of hill, on part of which it grew, and which now presented a rough termination of broken bank and rock to the level ground, that Howard and his guide walked over. The moon rose on them, and began more distinctly to bring out such rugged features of the path as we have just noticed. In passing a particular spot, where an unusual group of rock formed a considerable recess on the side of the hill, the guide, who was some yards before Howard, suddenly started back, and at the same moment Howard thought he observed a figure glide into the recess. After a moment, however, the man continued his way, seemingly unembarrassed ; and Howard asked :

"Whom have you spoken with ?—what man was it that crossed you ?" for he fancied that he had heard a hasty whisper as the fellow paused.

"Me ! spake, sir ? Who could I spake to ?—No one crossed me ; an' 'tis only some shadow has frightened you in this lonesome place."

"Very likely," Howard replied. But, with sword in hand, having gained the rocky recess, he thrust his head into it, and looked around : so far as he could distinguish no one appeared, and they continued their route.

The stream now made a sudden bend, widely deviating from the line of the hill to which it had hitherto run almost parallel ; and exactly at the apex of the angle it formed, the guide paused, and, pointing to a tree that was flung over the water, told Howard that in this place they must cross.

"It is a slippery and dangerous passage, over," said Howard, "and the water is much deeper and wider than it was above. I would rather have ventured the leap when we got out of the wood."

"Och, musha, it's very safe, sir," replied the man ; "sure I know it well this many a day."

"Lead on, then. What—are you fearful ? Why do you step back ?"

"Troth an' I'm not afeard," said the fellow, "only I can do the best fur you, by followin' close."

"Take your hand out of your breast, you scoundrel, or I'll run you through the body !"—cried Howard. "Pass on—and quickly."

"Hoght mille duoul ! Go on yourself, then !" replied the man—go on !"—and with his left hand he shoved Howard, as if he had been only a child, within a few paces of the stream, while with the other he presented a pistol.

Howard, recovering from the push, darted on the assassin like a wildcat. Ere they closed, the pistol had been snapped, but it only burned priming ; and, as Howard pressed on, he with a desperate pass ran the fellow through the thigh. In an instant he was in the ruffian's giant clutch ; and, after a few unavailing struggles, was dashed on the ground, and then felt himself dragged towards the stream. In vain did he resist and cry out ; the strength that tugged him along was almost superhuman. The verging prospect of his terrible fate had almost made him insensible to his continual progress towards it, when the startling whiz of a bullet by his ear, and the immediate report of a pistol, called back his powers of observation. Instantly he was free, for his colossal antagonist had fallen, scarcely with a groan. The bullet had gone through his brain.

" He's quiet now, I believe," said a voice by Howard's side, while he was at the same time assisted to rise by an unseen hand. When he had gained his legs, he beheld, close by him, a young man of rather slight figure, buttoned to the chin in a tight grey surtout, and wearing on his legs leather gaiters, also closely buttoned.

" Dead by heavens !"—said Howard, in reply to the stranger's remark. "Sir, for this timely aid I must ever be your debtor—if indeed "—he added, in an undecided tone—" the bullet has hit its true mark."

" I don't know well what you mean, sir," said the young man, proudly drawing himself up ; " I fired at this fellow to save your life."

" I really believe it, sir," rejoined Howard. " But we were so close, 'twas rather nice shooting."

" Bah !" said the other, " it was nothing at all to talk of. I could do it as well if you both stood cheek by jowl."

" Then, sir, I must cordially repeat my thanks and gratitude."

" Oh, no thanks. What is it but what one gentleman should do for another? I only wish you had been with me half an hour ago on the road ; you might then have conferred the first obligation.

" I may ask to what you allude ?" said Howard.

" Why, yes," replied the lad (for he was little more), with indifference, " I have just been stopped and plundered by Doe, and three of his men."

" What do you tell me, sir ?" asked Howard in consternation : " I thought I had left him pretty securely guarded ?"

" He's out, Mr. Howard, I assure you."

" Perhaps, some other ?"

" No, no, no—I saw the fellow, face to face."

" You know his person, then ?—have you seen him often ?"

" Often."

" They plundered you, you say ?"

" They did—I said so."

" Of what, pray.

4*

"Of what ! Of my money and arms, to be sure."

" Your arms ?"—repeated Howard, glancing at the pistol the stranger had just discharged, and which he still held in his hand. Immediately after, Howard fixing his eyes on his face, thought he could recollect to have seen it before.

" Oh—aye—this little pistol," the young man answered ; " I found it on the hill after them, and you are just as welcome to it as to the slight service it has done you ;" offering it as he spoke.

" Thanks—but you see I have my sword. Will you allow me to ask if ever we have met before, sir ?"—continued Howard, again glancing at the pale, handsome features of his companion.

" Upon my soul, not that I know of," was the answer.

" But you seem to know my person well," resumed Howard.

" You have been pointed out to me, to be sure," said the other, " and I have often been looking at you, when you little thought it—that's all."

" Pray, what sort of man is this Doe ?"

" Something of your own height, I think," said the stranger, surveying Howard from head to foot—" or mine ; as I believe you and I stand about the same height in our shoes. But he is much stouter than either of us, and, perhaps, twice as old."

" About forty-five, then ?"

" Let me see—yes. About forty and five."

" Well-favored ?"

" No. Black complexion, black hair, strong, rough features, a lowering brow, a haughty, cruel mouth. Altogether a face of much ferocity."

" Thus I have heard him described by all. But I, too, shall see him, perhaps."

" Perhaps," echoed the stranger, drily ; or as if, joining the opinion of the outlaw's cleverness, he slighted Howard's pretensions to out-manœuvre him. The tone fell disagreeably on Howard's ear ; nor, indebted to him as he was, could he well relish the easy kind of swagger that ran through every word, look, and action, of his new acquaintance. So that he now turned rather sharply round with a peculiar—" sir ?"

" Let me exhort you, Mr. Howard," said the young man, without at all seeming to notice this change of manner, " to return with speed to your corps, who must now, I think, require your presence. Pardon my freedom."

" You have purchased a right to use it, sir. May I beg to know to whom I am so much indebted ?"

"My name is Sullivan ; I live at my father's house some miles up the country. I went to a fair near Clonmel to sell cattle, and was this evening returning with the money, when Doe stopped me. Curse the fellow, these are new tricks, that he might better let alone."

"You are farmers, then ?—you and your father ?"

"Farmers in a small way, sir : we had been better off, but rents and tithe-proctors now leave us little by the trade. If you think of returning to your men," Sullivan continued, in a manner that had all the appearance of interest, though it still wore a feature of something like dictation—"I shall be very happy to lend you my company ; 'tis a bit out of my road—but no matter."

Howard, rather conciliated by this proof of attention, and overlooking the dash with which it was conveyed, and which he now began to attribute to the manner of the country, rather than to the individual, answered :

"I thank you. I had intended to proceed further, to Mr. Grace's house ; but your information, and, indeed, this accident, have determined me to return, and a brave friend like you may be useful."

"Very possible," Sullivan replied.

"Before we proceed further," Howard continued, "I shall trouble you to accompany me to the nearest place, to dispatch a messenger with a note of apology to Mr. Grace."

"First of all," said Sullivan, turning on his heel to where the dead body lay, "let us quietly dispose of this fellow's prodigious carcass. Bon Dieu !—what a Goliah !—and what a pretty little David am I that gave him his lullaby, just by the edge of the brook, too. Upon my conscience, I thought I should have split with laughing, when I saw the damned queer figure you cut, dangling after him, like a calf tied to an ox's tail."

"It was very ridiculous, no doubt, sir," replied Howard, rather offended, "and, perhaps, more than ridiculous to one of the actors, though not to the spectator. But, pray," he continued, in a changed tone, "what are your views towards this wretched carrion ?"

"Why, to begin," answered Sullivan, kneeling, "I claim the well-known right which every honest man who can shoot a robber possesses over him. I beg to see what kind of lining he has got in his pockets. If I don't mistake, the inquiry will be worth our while ;" and he engaged at once in his investigation.

"Worth *your* while, I presume you mean, sir," observed Howard.

"Thank you," said Sullivan, half jeeringly, "that's blunt and kind, and what I expected from you. Another poor subaltern in your place would be crying halves, or quarters, at least. But you remember my loss on the road, just now, and so leave me all the luck. And see, here it is, by holy Saint Patrick, crosier and mitre to boot—here it is—one—two—three—four—four one-pound notes, and almost another pound in silver. He drank a drop since he got the big five-pound slip whole and entire. Well ; I believe I know who I may thank for my good fortune to-night."

While Sullivan was speaking, he extracted from the most secret pocket on the person of the dead man a small piece of old rag, carefully tied up, and from this, again, the bank-notes and silver he had enumerated. Throwing away the envelope, he now very coolly deposited the money in his own pocket, and jumping up, continued :

"And the next thing I intend to do, Mr. Howard, is to drop him in the very spot he had an eye on for yourself. Come, my lad, it's all one to you now, you know." He stooped to move the body, but was interrupted by Howard, who, during the entire last scene, had felt disgusted at the levity and hardiness of the young man's manner and proceedings.

"I protest, I cannot see," said Howard, "why this should be done. Even for our own sakes we ought to leave the wretch where he has had the misfortune to fall."

"Nonsense, man," replied Sullivan, in an impatient voice. " I know what I am about : just leave me to myself. I commit no crime, I believe ? And let me assure you, Mr. Howard, 'tis the best thing for *yourself*, too ; indeed, what concern of mine is it at all ? There may be visitors· here in an hour or two, perhaps in half an hour, perhaps in a moment, who will expect anything but to find him in your place ; and you might not be the safer of the discovery for the whole night after. Just let me have my own way, I say."

"You will do as you please, then, sir," said Howard, turning off, and walking from the spot. As he proceeded, he could distinctly hear the noise caused by the trailing of the body over the crisp soil, and, a moment after, the heavy plunge in the water In another moment, Sullivan was by his side.

"And now, about your note of apology to Mr. Grace," he said, as he came up, still speaking in an unembarrassed tone.

"I shall have to ask admission into some house to write it," said Howard. "Whose house is that yonder ?"

"A black villain's !" answered Sullivan, his voice suddenly altered to a subdued, hissing cadence.

"What is the name of the proprietor ?"

"Purcell."

"Let us try to get in there," said Howard.

"Never !" cried Sullivan, almost in a scream, and while he stamped his heel into the sward.

"And why so, sir ?" asked Howard, coolly ; for he began to tire of the whimsical impatience of the young man's manner.

Sullivan, changing rapidly into a deeper tone, and almost speaking through his clenched teeth, went on, with passionate vehemence : "Never, I say, but in defiance, shall my foot rest on his threshold. Never shall I darken his door, but when I come as the shadow of death and destruction might come, to darken it for ever. To your quarters—or, stay; here are pen and ink"— and he produced a small tin case containing both—"and here is a scrap of paper, and yonder I see a light in a cabin. Write the line there, and I will faithfully carry it—'tis on my way."

Howard assented, and they rapidly bent their steps towards the cabin. Meantime, his curiosity awakened by the sudden and uncontrollable passion of his previously *nonchalante* companion, he said :

"This Purcell must indeed be a villain, or your prejudice against him is strong."

"Ma Foi ! but you have just said the truth twice over," replied Sullivan ; "he *is* a hell-born villain, and I hate him worse than I hate hell—or fear it, either."

"He has deeply injured you, then ?" inwardly speculating how it might be that now and again these French expletives slipped from his farmer-friend.

"Injured me !—ha ! ha !"—and he laughed a bitter laugh ; but whether the emanation of a sense of wrong, or in mockery of Howard's question, could not easily be distinguished. After a moment, however, he checked himself, and then added, in a calmer voice : "*Me*, sir ? No, not *me*, but his doings to others mark him for the detestation of every honest man."

This was not well carried ; but Howard contented himself with, "Who or what is he ?"

"What he is now, and for years has been, everybody knows. What he exactly sprang from, no one can tell. At least I cannot. But he first appeared here the follower of a nobleman we never saw ; some kind of collector, I believe. Soon after, he became a tithe-proctor ; then a fire-brand ; and, at last, a bloody traitor and informer. Then, of course, a land-jobber, gentleman at large, and county magistrate."

" Pray, explain," said Howard, much interested, and completely astonished.

" The particulars would be a long story. Privately he stirred up the wretched and ignorant people around him to resist rack-rents, that he throve by as privately exacting. When he got them involved by his agents, he informed against them, running their blood into money. Those who held lands on reasonable terms, he thus contrived to turn adrift on this world, or launch into the next, bidding for the vacant land himself, and then letting it, at tenfold its value, to starving creatures, who, though they sweated like the beasts of the field—which they do—could not meet their rent-day. There was one family in particular—but come, let us push on to the light ; I delay you."

" By no means ; you have deeply interested me. There was, you say, a particular family ?"

" There was. A mother and a son, a daughter and old grand-father—the father was long dead. Purcell, by his underhand practices, ensnared the son, a lad of eighteen or nineteen, in nightly combinations. Then he arraigned him before the landlord ; and then—for their lease was expired—son and all were turned out of their home—the old man and all. All, except the daughter."

" And what became of her ?"

" Villain—eternally damned villain !" exclaimed the boy, in another burst, and while his youthful face and figure took a stern and formidable appearance—" what became of her ? He had trodden her down beforehand—seduced her—and she went with him into his house. She left her sick mother, and her old grandfather, on the field before their own door, and turned to the menial hearth of him who—pardon me !—the night wears—we walk too slowly."

" Pray, continue. What of the rest of this poor family ?"

The narrator, touched, perhaps, as well by Howard's evident sympathy, as by the subject he was about to enter on, answered, in a broken voice :

" The mother, as I said, was ill ; she could get no further than the ridge that gave her a last look of her old cottage. She sat there till night came on—'twas a bad night—and—she died in it," he added, with a voice scarcely audible.

" My God ! And the son ?"

" The wretched son was not then at home. He returned with an oath to revenge his poor mother. Purcell gained information of his purpose, and at the head of a body of soldiers hunted him through the country. In the north the boy escaped him, and there, it is believed, took shipping for America."

" It is, indeed, a shocking story," Howard said, much moved ; " and I will not press you to enter the house of such a man. But, since you are so kind as to offer it, I can write my note in the cabin, which, when we have got over this hedge, I presume we shall have gained."

The impediment to be surmounted was a fence of earth and stones running straight across their path, with, here and there, a bunch of furze or of dwarf-thorn shooting out on the top and at the sides. As they prepared to clamber over it, their attention was caught by the sound of low and continuous moaning, which arose from the opposite side. Howard, first gaining the top of the hedge, saw on looking across, a young and beautiful woman, who was seated on a large stone, her hair hanging loose about her, her face pale as marble, and an infant resting on her lap. The moon flared fully in her front, and as she was not above two or three yards distant, developed into a sort of statuesque clearness her face, figure, and drapery. Her head was turned and inclined over her shoulder with an expression of utter woe and helplessness ; thick sighs every moment interrupted her lament, and distended her white bosom. Her infant seemed to have just dropped asleep, and now lay back, along the beautiful arm that tenderly enclasped him, his little knees slightly drawn up, his half-open hands approaching his mouth, in that infantine attitude of repose which Westmacott has so well and so touchingly reproduced.

Howard saw, in deep surprise and interest, the mother and her infant, and was silently continuing his gaze, when Sullivan, who soon stood by him, suddenly seized his arm, and uttered a deep curse, the tone of which indicated the utmost consternation and astonishment. His exclamation reached the woman's ear ; for she turned her head, ceased her perhaps unconscious wail, and, fixing her eyes for a moment on Sullivan's face, screamed and rushed into the cabin, which was only some yards distant.

" Don't follow me !" exclaimed Sullivan. " This is my affair —I shall be with you in a moment ;" and he leaped from the top of the hedge, and rapidly pursued the girl into the cabin.

When he entered, she was crouching down, with her face

hidden on the knees of au old man, who sat by the hearth. One
arm hung at her side, the other still pressed her now complaining
child, and in reply to the old man's repeated—" whisht ! whisht !
á-vourneen," she panted, " His ghost !—his ghost ! come over the
waters and the mountains to punish me ! Hide me, grandfather !
hide me !"—

"Ghost or no ghost, Cauthleen, speak no word to me yet,"
said Sullivan, who now stood at her back. "There is an account
to settle for you, before we can ever—if we ever do—look
straight into each other's faces." But it was useless for Sullivan
to have given this warning : at the very first sound of his voice,
the girl had fainted at the old man's knees ; her infant still held,
however, to her bosom.

"And is this the way so soon ?" continued Sullivan, speaking
to the old man—" could he not wait for me a little, but add this
last, this very last wrong to all the rest ? When did he turn her
out, dha-dhu ?"*

"This is the first I heard of it, á-vich," said the old man ; " I
did not think of seein' her to-night, till after you called upon
him yourself."

"Hush !"—said Sullivan, pointing out to the door—" Did you
tell her I was in the country ?" in a lower voice.

"How could I, when you bid me not ?" returned the old man.
"Though last night, as I spoke to her out of her window, and
scalded her heart with the story of Purcell's courting of Mary
Grace, I was nigh comfortin' her, poor soul, on the head of it."

"Bring her to the barn, dha-dhu, as fast as you can," rejoined
Sullivan—" and stay—we want you in other matters. You must
instantly mount and away to the elm-trees—you know for what ?"
the old man bent his eyes blankly on the ground—" You remember, don't you ?"—continued Sullivan, as, from a suspicion of the
old man's occasional weakness of intellect, he began to doubt his
energy and correctness in the business he wished him to undertake.

"Do I remember, is it ?" asked the other, as, recovering from
his abstraction, he raised Cauthleen in his arms, and stood upright,
with the vigor that in one of his great age was surprising ; while
a strong color spread over his cheek, and his grey eyes sparkled
insanely—" Do I remember your biddin' ? And why it is to
be done ? With this load in my arms, and you standin' before
me, you ask do I remember it ?—Do I remember anything ?—

* Grandfather.

Do I remember the day that once was, and the day that is, the day that is to come ? And if old age, and the heart-break strove to make me forget, *could* I ? Where, then, would be my dreams on the hill-side, and in the rushes and the long grass by the water's brink, when, night after night, I dreamt it ?—When the moanin' came on the hill-breeze, and the cracklin' and the roarin' of the blaze was in the reeds that covered my old head ?—When the mountains fell back, and the sky grew clear, and the wide waters were no hindrance to me, and I saw you through them all, afar off, with the sword in your hand, and *him*, twinin' like a red worm at your feet ?"—

" Hush ! hush ! dha-dhu," again interrupted Sullivan, " there is one abroad must not hear or know : you had better call on God to strengthen you, and make you clear, and watchful, and prudent. And now, go your ways to the barn, first, and then to the elm-trees—this lost creature is in a long fit, and we have nothing here to serve her. Go, she seems coming to, a little. Go, now, without a word. Rest with her, abroad in the air, and then she'll walk with you. And now—yet one other word —is Flinn gone to get Father O'Clery out of the way, and to talk to him about the work ?"

" 'Tis an hour since he went," answered the old man, " and he'll scheme him to the barn, as you told us."

" Then, don't lose another moment," said Sullivan ; " or, just wait where you are, while I step out with this rush-light." He took the niggard taper, and approached Howard, who still remained on the hedge, his curiosity excited to the utmost, his fears stirring on account of Sullivan's statement as to the escape of Doe, and feeling, as a neglect of duty, every moment that kept him from his men.

" We can't do it in the cabin," said Sullivan, as he stood under Howard, at the bottom of the hedge ; " but come down, and I'll hold the light while you scribble on this stone. The wind is low, and won't hinder you."

Howard accordingly descended, and, using the materials with which Sullivan supplied him, wrote his note to Mr. Grace, and handed it, unsealed, to Sullivan.

" I'll deliver it punctually," said Sullivan, " within as much time as it will take me to walk and run to the house. And now, Mr. Howard, good night, and make haste to your soldiers. Don't mind walking among these hills, with people you are a stranger to, for all the pretty faces about Slievnamon—but we shall talk more of that, maybe, when I have the pleasure to see you next. "Good-night, sir ;" and he turned again into the cabin.

Great as was Howard's anxiety to get to his quarters, he could not withstand the temptation of concealing himself a moment behind the hedge, in order to watch some continuance of the interesting scene, to the opening of which he had been a witness. So he recrossed the mound, and stooped his head under it, at the side turned from the cabin.

In a few moments he heard Sullivan's voice, wishing some one good luck and speed. Almost immediately after, he saw him leap the stream, of which the course continued so far as the cabin, and Howard watched him running across the low ground at the other side, in the direction of Mr. Grace's house. His curiosity was next bent to catch a glimpse of the woman and child, and, looking cautiously over the hedge, he saw her, leaning on the old man, walk from the cabin towards the place where he stood concealed. They did not, however, directly pass him, but, continuing their way by the other side of the hedge, issued through it at a gap about twenty yards distant, and then, turning to the left, began to ascend a broken and uncultivated declivity.

Howard argued that this declivity must be a continuation of the ridge over which he had descended with his traitorous guide, when he first left the road that commanded his quarters ; and he concluded, that if he also mounted the hill, in the footsteps of the old man and his charge, it must lead him again to the road, some little distance from the point he wished to regain. So, mistrustful of traveling any longer in by-paths that had proved sufficiently dangerous, and also prompted perhaps by anxiety to track the young woman, Howard followed at a distance.

After gaining the brow of the ridge, the old man and his companion disappeared from Howard's view. He also hastened, therefore, to win it. When he had done so, he looked out, and discovered them still walking in a direct line across a wide waste of marshy ground, bounded at some distance by a low wall, on which the moon shone clear and white, distinguishing even the stones of which it was composed. He felt surprised that, having passed the hill, so considerable a space should still remain between him and the road. But, assured that the wall he now saw was its boundary, he continued to follow the two figures.

They again disappeared over the wall, and Howard, mending his pace, crossed the low barrier, which he perceived to be formed of loose stones, and, in increased surprise, saw another stretch of open ground before him, over which the figures still moved. The lines of the road and the hill, he thought, must have suddenly departed from their parallel ; but it was, meantime, impossible that he should miscalculate his route, and so he persevered in it.

This second wild tract of moor proved nearly twice as extensive as the first ; yet it was at length terminated by another loose wall, which was successively passed by the old man, the girl, and Howard. The amazement of our military friend changed into a disagreeable misgiving when he now found himself at the base of a growing ascent, round which, as he gained the other side of the second barrier, his unconscious guides were just winding. In a moment they had entirely eluded him ; and, vexed and impatient, he hurried after them to inquire his way to the road, even yet positive he could not be far astray.

As he rapidly turned the bend of the hill, and looked forward for those he supposed before him, they were not to be seen ; but the wailing of a female voice, and the shrill cadence of the old man, as if speaking in comfort, guided him in his course. He followed till he found himself at the mouth of a pass, where the hill divided it, and afforded entrance to its own recesses. Up this way, Howard turned to the right, and soon saw the female and old mau, the one sitting, the other, with the infant in his arms, standing over her, both continuing to converse in their mixed tones of anguish and feebleness. He hastened on to join them. All were now wrapt in the shadow of the hill, and, as Howard precipitately advanced, he stumbled over some fragments of rock and fell. The woman and her aged protector, with cries of terror, ran in a contrary direction. Howard rose, not materially hurt, and called loudly after them ; but this appearing only to increase their fright and speed, he exerted his own legs in pursuit. They fled, for some distance, along the pass he had last entered, and then turned into another which struck off almost at right angles. He once more missed his guides, till he arrived at the point they had doubled. But he then marked them in the stretch of moonlight, which the sudden turn afforded, flitting over the side of the divided hill, and apparently bent on gaining its top. Still he held chase.

Pausing on the verge of the ascent, he saw them hastening over a wide spread of sloping country, at the extremity of which a huge peak of mountain took its rise. In fact, he had not understood, that all this while, ever since he left the cabin, he had, across moors and all, been rapidly, though imperceptibly ascend-

ing towards the bleak and craggy summit of Slievenamon. He
gazed about, confounded and almost terrified, and shouted louder
than before after his mysterious seducers into this maze of danger.
They less than ever heeded his appeal ; and when, resuming
once more his efforts to overtake them, he endeavored to keep
them in his eye, the two figures suddenly sank from view, and
left him completely at fault.

He ran on in the direction they had taken, until, gaining the
verge of the moor, he found himself altogether impeded in his
progress by a deep gully, that, like a trench before a stronghold,
seemed to guard the base of the mountain. As the weather had
lately been very dry, scarcely any water now sought its way
through this natural canal ; and, advancing cautiously to recon-
noitre, Howard could perceive that the gully was deep and abrupt,
and lined, at either side, and at the bottom, with sharp, project-
ing fragments of rock. His next investigation was to discover
in what part of the pass the old man and his companion lay concealed, for he could not suppose they had been able to cross it ;
nor could he otherwise account for their sudden disappearance,
than by concluding they had descended into it. No trace of them
appeared, however. He had paused in much embarrassment, una-
able to form any plan of proceeding, when they abruptly reap-
peared at the opposite side of the watercourse, moving towards a
broad, flat stone, that, supported at one end by two props, also
of stone, was raised in that direction from the ground, while the
other end, that nearest to Howard, seemed buried in the soil.
He looked, without knowing its traditional nature, at the ruins
of an old Druidical altar. But had he been a thorough antiqua-
rian, and ever so well acquainted with all that has been said and
written on the subject of this rude relic, little interest would it
have had for him at the moment. His notice was solely directed
to the two figures, who hurried towards it ; and he hallooed
lustily and long in hopes of fixing their attention.

All in vain, however. The figures continued, in speed and
silence, to near the stone ; and when they had gained it, and
while Howard exalted his voice into the shrillest possible key,
they became once again, and finally, invisible. But, as if not to
allow him to waste his lungs for nothing, scarcely had he emitted
the last bellow, when it was caught up in a contrary direction,
and prolonged and repeated rather beyond his wishes. He
paused a moment, supposing he might have heard an echo ;
but, when too much time had elapsed, to permit, according to

natural laws, of possible iteration, the shouting was again renewed, by more than one person, now sounding nearer, and awak-
ing the deep voices of the outspread moors and desolate hills.
Our adventurer, though no poltroon, felt a disagreeable qualm at
heart, as these wild signals of approaching strangers, and to him,
foes, closed right and left upon him. He stood one moment in
something not unlike consternation, and then the strongest in-
stinct of nature lent him lightning thought, and, as will be seen,
scarcely less than thunderbolt execution. Behind the flat stone
the figures had found a hiding-place ; behind it he, too, would
seek safety. He measured the gully with his eye—it was at
least four yards over—perhaps more—no matter. Howard drew
back for a good run—sprang across the chasm like a chamois-
hunter—and lighted on his feet in the shelving sward at the opposite side. But this was only the first consequence of his leap ;
for, after striking his heels into the soft ground, he next sank
through it, and fell, with a chaos about his ears, and a hellish
uproar ringing in them, down—down—he knew not where, into
the bowels and mysteries of the mountain.

CHAPTER IX.

Now, could we, at our pleasure, and not in violation of the
known and admitted privilege of story-tellers, change the scene
of our narrative some miles away from Lieutenant Howard, and
leave the reader in a consequent agony of suspense as to the issue
of his adventure. But we scorn such petty tyranny over the
minds of those millions whom it is our wish, in perfect disinterestedness, to treat in the best manner : therefore, we proceed
straight forward in our tale.

The first perception of Howard's restored senses brought him
the intelligence of his being in the midst of an almost insuffer-
able atmosphere, oppressive, as it was strange and unusual. He
breathed with difficulty, and coughed and sneezed himself very
nearly back again into the state of unconsciousness, out of which,
it would seem, coughing and sneezing had just roused him ; for
he gained his senses while performing such operations as are

understood by these words. When a reasonable pause occurred,
and that reflection had time to come into play, Howard wondered
whether he was alive or dead, and whether or no he felt pain.
Due consideration having ensued, he was able to assure himself
that, so far as he could judge, he lived, and without much pain
of any kind into the bargain. Next, he tried to stir himself;
but here he was unsuccessful.' Some unseen power paralyzed
his legs and arms, feet and hands. He lay, it was evident, upon
his back, and the surface he pressed seemed soft and genial enough.
While in this position, he looked straight upward. The stars,
and a patch of deep blue sky, twinkled and smiled upon him,
through a hole in a low, squalid roof, overhead. This was a help.
He remembered having fallen in through the slope of the hill,
and, as an aperture must have been the consequence, or the
cause of his descent, he ventured to argue accordingly. He had
intruded, it would rather seem, upon the private concerns of some
person or persons, who, from motives unknown to him, chose to
reside in a subterraneous retreat among the very sublimities of
Slievenamon. Here the strange scent again filled his nostrils
with overpowering effect. There was some part of it he thought
he could, or ought, to recollect having before experienced, and
he sniffed once or twice, with the hope of becoming satisfied. But
a fresh, and, he conceived, a different effluvia, thereupon rushed
up into his head, and down his throat, and he had again to
sneeze and cough his way into a better comprehension.

When Howard was, in this second effort, successful, he observed
that he dwelt not in absolute darkness. A pandemonium kind
of light dismally glared around him, clouded by a dense fog of
he knew not what color or consistency. Was he alone? He
listened attentively. The melancholy female voice that he had
heard lamenting at the cabin, and among the hills, came on his
ear, though it was now poured forth in a subdued cadence. Still
he listened, and a hissing of whispers floated at every side, accompanied by the noise of a fire rapidly blazing, together with
an intermittent explosion that very much resembled a human
snore.

Again he strove to rise or turn, but could not. " I will just
move my head round, at all events," thought he. He did so, very
slowly, and his eyes fixed upon those of Jack Mullins, who, bent
on one knee at his side, held his left arm tightly down with one
hand, while with the other he presented a heavy horseman's
pistol. Howard, little cheered by this comforter, turned his head

us slowly in the other direction, and encountered the full stare of another ruffianly visage, while, with both hands of his attendant, he was at this side pinioned. Two other men secured his feet.

" Where am I ? and why do you hold me ? and how did all this happen ?"—asked Howard, as he began to comprehend his situation.

" Hould your tongue, and be quiet," said Mullins.

" I know *you* well, Jack Mullins," resumed Howard. " 'Tis some time since we met at the pattern, but I know your voice and face perfectly well."

" Nonsense," said Mullins. Hould your pace, I tell you.

" You surely would not take away my life for nothing. And it can be no offence to ask you why you hold me down in this strange manner."

" Bother, man. Say your prayers, an' don't vex me."

" Mullins, I have drunk with you out of the same cup, and clasped your hand in good fellowship ; and I desire you for the sake of old acquaintance to let me sit up and look about me. I never did you any injury, nor intended one."

" I don't know how that is," observed Mullins.

" Never, by my soul !" repeated Howard with energy. " This unhappy intrusion, whatever place I may have got into, was an accident : I missed my way among the hills, and wandered here unconsciously. Let me up, Mullins, and you shall have a handsome recompense."

" The divil a laffina you have about you," said Mullins.— " Don't be talkin'."

" As you have *found* my purse, then," rejoined Howard, easily suspecting what had happened, " You are most welcome to it, so you release me for a moment."

" An' who, do you think, is to pay us for the roof of our good, snug house you have tattered down on our heads this blessed night ?"—asked Mullins.

" I will to be sure," replied Howard—" who else should ? Come, Mullins, bid these men let me go, and you'll never be sorry for it. Is this the way Irishmen treat an old friend ?"

" For the sake o' that evening we had together at the pattern, you may get up—that is, sit up, an' bless yourself. Let him go, men, bud watch the ladder."

The three other men instantly obeyed Mullins's orders, and, Jack himself loosening his dead gripe, Howard was at last free to sit up.

"Now, never mind what you see," he continued. "An', in troth, the less you look about you, at all, at all, so much the betther, I'm thinkin'." And Mullins sat down opposite his prisoner, still holding the cocked pistol on his arm.

This caution seemed in the first instance altogether useless ; for Howard could observe nothing through the dense vapor around him, except, now and then, the blank and wavering outline of a human figure, flitting in the remote parts of the recess. The whispers, however, had deepened into rather loud tones ; but here he was as much at a loss as ever, for the persons of the drama spoke together in Irish. At length he gained a hint to the mystery. A young man, stripped, as if for some laborious work, approaching Mullins, said, somewhat precipitately : "Musha, Jack, the *run* 'ull go far nothin' this time, unless you come down an' put your own hand to the still."

Here, then, from all he had previously heard, and could now see, smell, and conceive, Howard found himself in the presence of illicit distillation, at work, though it was Sunday, in all its vigor and glory. He snuffed again, and wondered at his own stupidity and indeed ingratitude, that he should not at once have recognized the odor of the pottheen atmosphere—a mixture of the effluvia of the liquor and the thick volumes of pent-up smoke, in which for some time he had, under Providence, lived and breathed.

When the young man addressed to Mullins the words we have just recorded, that person's ill boding face assumed a cast of more dangerous malignity, and, after a ferocious scowl at the speaker, he said with much vehemence : "Upon my conscience, Tim, a-gra, you're just afther spakin' the most foolish words that your mother's son ever spoke : an' I don't know what bad blood you have to the sassenach officer, here, that you couldn't lave him a chance for his life, when it was likely he had id. Musha, evil end to you, Tim, seed, breed, an' generation !—mahnrp-on-duonl ! What matther was it if the whole *shot* went to ould Nick this blessed evenin', providin' we didn't let strangers into our sacrets ? Couldn't you let him sit here a while in pace ?—But since the murther's out, take this, you ballour* o' the divil," —giving the pistol,—"while I go down to the pot. An', Tim— lave well enough alone now, an' if you can't mend what's done, try not to do any more. Don't be talkin' at all, I say ; you

* Babbler.

needn't pull the trigger on him for spakin' a little, if it isn't too much entirely. Bud take care o' your own self, Tim, an' hould your gab 'till I come to you agin."

After this speech, the longest that Mullins was ever known to deliver, he strode away from Howard's side towards the most remote end of the place, where the fire was blazing. Howard comprehending that Jack's indignation was aroused, because of the revealing summons of the young man, and that his own life might probably be sacrificed to his innocent advancement in knowledge, very prudently resolved to avail himself of the hints contained in the harangue he had heard, by observing, in Mullins's absence, the most religious silence, and withal the most natural unconsciousness. The latter part of his resolve was, however, soon rendered superfluous and unavailing. The wind rose high, abroad, and entering at the recent aperture, attributable to Howard, took an angry circuit round the cavern, agitated the mass of smoke that filled it, and compelled the greater portion to evaporate through another vent at the opposite side. In about five minutes, therefore, the whole details of the apartment became visible to any observer, nor could Howard refuse to his curiosity the easy investigation thus afforded. And what he saw is now to be written.

The place was evidently an excavation scooped in the side of the hill, and then, as Howard could remember from his observations abroad, added to his present survey, roofed over with trunks and branches of trees, and covered with sods level with the contiguous soil. Into this den one entrance was now visible; for, looking across, Howard saw the rude ladder, of which Mullins had spoken, guarded by the three fellows he had ordered to that point. Against the sides of the cavern, almost all the way round, turf, furze, or well-filled sacks were piled. One end appeared to be dedicated to the purposes of a barn, for it was stuffed with sheaves of corn at one side and straw at the other, while on the ground lay two flails, half hidden amid a litter of a compound description.

At the other end—heaven bless the mark !—the genius of pottheen had established his laboratory. On a tremendous fire of turf and furze sat a goodly pot, of comprehension sufficient, perhaps, for thirty gallons of pot-ale. This cauldron was well covered with a wooden lid, which, at its junction to the sides of the vessel, as well as over all its casual crevices, received an earthy impasto of some kind, to make it airtight. Out of the top of the lid issued

5

the worm ; so called in courtesy, only ; for it bore little resemblance to its licensed prototype in loyal distilleries, and was in
shape no logical symbol of the word. Truly, it did not coil ; but
rather ran in and out, crinkum-crankum, in sharp angles, right,
acute, or obtuse, at every turn. Its material was common tin,
daubed most uncouthly with solder—the clumsy production of
some hill-tinker, who was but too well paid for his work by a few
draughts of the first oozing it brought forth. The greater part
of this curious apparatus passed through a large tub of cold
water, called familiarly the cooling-tub, and representing the
condenser of more formal establishments. At length the end protruded, free of all impediment, over another wooden vessel, and
therein deposited, drop by drop, its precious and fully-matured
product ; in fact, the *bona-fide* pottheen, regularly distilled.

About the fire, and at the end of the worm, and from vessel to
vessel of different compass, in which the yielding corn underwent
its different processes of fermentation, previous to a final enclo-
sure in the pot, Jack Mullins now appeared busy, the presiding
and directing spirit of the scene. He moved heavily and silently,
with bent brow and closed lips, only condescending to the various
questions levelled at him, a " Bother—don't be talkin'." Two
or three men were also busy at the vats. An old woman, with
lank, streaming locks, and her neck almost entirely bare, and a
dirty girl, of about fourteen years of age, stood near the worm,
pouring, from time to time, upon it, and into the vessel through
which it passed, their contributions of cold water. Around the
blaze, on straw, lay perhaps a dozen men, old and young, keen observers and anxious expectants. The fire glared on all, throwing
into sympathetic shadow many a wild or sinister eye, and touching with red light the top edges of their shaggy eyebrows, their
prominent cheek-bones, hooked or snub noses, and ample chins.

Howard, continuing his observations, surveyed the height from
which he had fallen. It might be about seven feet ; but he sat
elevated above the floor of the cavern ; and this remark, causing
him to examine the material under him, enabled him to account
for having escaped so well. In truth he had descended, where
he now remained, upon a heap of litter, composed of the residuum
of the pot, and some bundles of straw strewed lightly over, so
that the whole substance was soft and unresisting as any man in
his circumstances could have wished.

He was, however, little pleased on the whole with the scene thus
become revealed by the partial expulsion of the smoke. Mullins's

late hints still rang in his ears ; and, while contemplating the faces
of those round the fire, the unintentional visitant thought he looked on men who would have little hesitation, all circumstances of
prejudice and relative place duly weighed, to assist the master-
ruffian in any designs upon an Englishman and a red-coat. Then he
recollected his untimely absence from his men ; the intelligence
Sullivan had given him ; the disastrous consequences that to them
might ensue : and his cheek and brow flamed with impatience.
While, the next moment, a recurrence to his own immediate
peril corrected, if it did not change, their courageous glow.

The young man who had relieved guard over Howard, well
obeyed the parting orders of Mullins ; for he did not open his
lips to the prisoner, contenting himself with watching his every
motion, and keeping fast hold of the pistol. Utter silence,
therefore, reigned between both, as Howard also strictly
observed his own resolution.

After he had fully investigated every thing and person around
him, and when thought and apprehension found no relief from
curiosity, this blank pause disagreeably affected him. It was un-
certainty and suspense ; fear for others and for himself ; or, even
if he escaped present danger, the unhappy accident might influence his future character and prospects. Under the pressure of
these feelings, Howard most ardently desired the return of
Mullins, in order that his fate might be at once decided.

And in his own due time Mullins at length came. Every thing
about the pot seemed prosperous ; for, with a joyous clatter of
uncouth sounds, the men now gathered near the worm, and, one
by one, held under it the large shell of a turkey-egg, which was
subsequently conveyed to their mouths. Mullins, himself, took
a serious, loving draught, and, refilling his shell, strode towards
Howard, bumper in hand.

"First," he said, as he came up, "since you know more than
you ought about us, taste that."

"Excuse me, Mullins," said Howard, "I should not be able
to drink it."

"Nonsense," resumed Jack—"dhrink the Queen's health,
good loock to her, in the right stuff, that is made out o' love to
her, an' no one else. Dhrink, till you see how you'd like it."

"I cannot, indeed," said Howard, wavering.

"Musha, you'd betther," growled Mullins. Howard drank
some.

"So you won't finish it? Well, what brought you here?"

" Ill luck," answered Howard. "I knew of no such place—had heard of no such place ; but, as I told you, lost my way, and—and—in truth, I tumbled into it."

" An' well you looked, didn't you, flyin' down through an ould hill's-side, among pacable people ? An' this is all thrue ?—no one tould you ?"

" Upon my honor, all true, and no one told me."

" By the vartch o' your oath, now ? Will you sware it ?"

" I am ready, for your satisfaction, to do so."

" Well. Where's our own soggarth, Tim ?" continued Mullins, turning to the young guardsman.

" In the corner, beyant, readin' his breviary," replied Tim.

A loud snore from the corner seemed, however, to belie the latter part of the assertion.

" Och, I hear him," said Mullins. " Run, Peg," he continued, speaking off to the girl, "run to the corner, an' tell Father Tack'em we want him."

The girl obeyed ; and, with some difficulty, called into imperfect existence a little bundle of man, who there lay rolled up among bundles of straw.

" What's the matter, now ?" cried he ; as, badly balancing himself, with the girl's assistance, he endeavored to resume his legs, and then waddle towards Mullins, at a short, dubious pace.

" What's the matter at all, that a poor priest can't read his breviary once a day, without being disturbed by you, you pack of—"

" Don't be talkin'," interrupted Mullins, " but look afore you, an' give him the buke."

" The book !" echoed Father Tack'em—" the book for him ! Why, then, happy death to me, what brings the like of him among us ?"

" You'd better not be talkin', I say, but give him the buke at once," said Mullins, authoritatively ; and he was obeyed. Howard received from Tack'em a clasped volume, " much the worse of the wear," as its proprietor described it ; and, at the dictation of Mullins, swore upon it to the truth of the statement he had already made.

" So far, so good," resumed Mullins ; " an' hould your tongue still, plase your reverence, it's betther fur you. Now, Captain Howard—"

" I only want to ask, is the *shot* come off ?" interrupted Tack'em—" for, happy death to me, I'm thirsty. And," he mumbled to himself, with a momentary expression that showed the wretched man to be not unconscious of the sin and shame of his degradation. "It is the only thing to make me forget—" the rest of his words were muttered too low to be audible even to Howard, beside whom he stood.

"Here, Tim," said Mullins, giving the shell to the young man, and taking the pistol, "go down to the worm, an' get a dhrop for the soggarth."

The shell returned, top-full ; and Tack'em, seizing it eagerly, was about to swallow its contents, when, glancing at Howard, he stopped short and offered him "a taste." The politeness was declined, and Tack'em observed, with fresh assumption of utter flippancy:

"Ah, you havn't the grace to like it yet. But wait a while. I thought like yourself, at first, remembering my poor old Horace's aversion to garlic—which, between ourselves, à-vich, is a wholesome herb after all :" and he repeated the beginning of the ode—

> " Parentis olim si quis impia manu,
> Senile *gutter* fregerit ——"

"Bother," interrupted Mullins, "ould Hurish, whoever he is, an' barrin' he's no friend o' your reverence, could never be an honest man, to talk o' '*gutter*' and the pottheen, in one breath."

"Och ! God help you, you poor ignoramus," replied Tack'em, draining his shell; "what a blessed ignorant crew I have around me ! Do *you* know humanity, à-vich ?" he continued, addressing himself to Howard.

"Nonsense," interposed Mullins, "we all know *that* in our turns, and when we can't help it. Don't be talkin', bud let me do my duty. I was a sayin', à-roon," he went on, turning to Howard, "that all was well enough, so far. Bud, somehow or other, I'm thinkin' you will have to do a thing or two more. 'Tisn't clear to myself, a-gra, but you must kiss the primer agin, in the regard of never sayin' a word to a Christian sowl of your happening to stray down through that hole over your head, or about any one of us, or any thing else you saw while you were stayin' wid us."

Howard, remembering that part of his duty was to render assistance at all times to the civil power of the country in putting down illicit distillation, hesitated at this proposition ; doubtful but he should be guilty of an indirect compromise of principle in concealing his knowledge of the existence and situation of such a

place. He therefore made no immediate answer, and Mullins
went on.

"There's another little matther, too. Some poor gossips of
ours that have to do with this Captain John—God help 'em—
are all this time in the bog, we hear, in regard o' the small mis-
understandin' betwixt you and them. Well, à-vich. You could
just let 'm out, couldn't you?"

"I can engage to do neither of the things you have last mentioned," said Howard, who, assured that concession to the first
would not avail him unless he also agreed to the second, thus
saved his conscience, by boldly resisting both.

"Don't be talkin," rejoined Mullins, "troth you'll be just afther
promisin' us to do what we ax you, an' on the buke, too;" and
his eye glanced to the pistol.

"It is impossible," said Howard, "my honor, my character,
and my duty forbid it. If those unfortunate persons yet remain
within my lines, they must stay there, or else surrender themselves, unconditionally, as our prisoners."

"I don't think you're sarious," resumed Mullins. "Suppose
a body said, you *must* do this."

"I should give the same answer."

"Thouomon dhoul! don't vex me too well. Do you see what
I have in my hand?"

"I see you can murder me, if you like; but you have heard
my answer."

"Stop, you bloodhound, stop!" screamed Tack'em. "Happy
death to me, what would you be about? Don't you know there's
wiser heads than yours settling that matter? Isn't it in the
hands of Father O'Clery by this time? An' who gave you leave
to take the law into your own hands?"

"Bother," said Mullins, "who'll suffer most by lettin' him
go?—who, bud myself, that gets the little bite I ate, an' the
dhrop I taste, by showin' you all how to manage the still through
the counthry? An' wouldn't it be betther to do two things at
once, an' get him to kiss the buke, for all I ax him?"

"You don't understand it," rejoined Tack'em—"you were
never born to understand it—you can do nothin' but pull your
trigger, or keep the stone in your sleeve. Let better people's
business alone, I say, and wait awhile."

Mullins, looking as if, despite previous arrangements, he considered himself called on, in consequence of a lucky accident, to
settle matters his own way, slowly resumed.

"Then, I'll tell you how it 'll be. Let the Sassenach kneel down in his straw, an' do you kneel at his side, plase your rever-ence, an' give him a better preparation nor his mother, poor lady, ever thought he'd get. Just say six Patterin'Aavees, an' let no one be talking. Sure we'll give him a little time to think of it."

"Murderous dog!" exclaimed Howard, with the tremulous energy of a despairing man; "recollect what you are about to do. If I fall in this manner, there's not a pit or nook of your barren hills shall serve to screen you from the consequences. Nor is there a man who now hears me, yet refuses to interfere, but shall become an accessory, equally guilty and punishable with yourself, if, indeed, you dare proceed to an extremity!"

"Don't be talkin'," said Mullins, determinedly, "bud kneel down."

"I'll give you my curse, on my two bended knees, if you touch a hair of his head!" Tack'em cried, with as much energy as his muddled brain would allow; "an' then see how you'll look, going about on a short leg, and your elbow scratching your ear, and your shins making war on each other, while all the world is at peace."

"An' don't *you* be talkin', either," resumed Mullins, who seemed pertinacious in his objection to the prolonged sound of the human voice. "Bud kneel by his side, and hear what he has to tell you, first. An' then say your Patterin'-Aavees."

Evidently in fear for himself, Tack'em at last obeyed. The other men, with the old hag and the girl, gathered round, and Howard, also, mechanically knelt. He was barely conscious, and no more, of the plunging gallop in which he hastened into eternity. He grew, despite of all his resolutions to die bravely, pale as a sheet; cold perspiration rushed down his face; his jaw dropped, and his eyes fixed. Strange notions of strange sounds filled his ears and brain. The roaring of the turf fire, predominantly heard in the dead silence, he confusedly construed into the break of angry waters about his head; and the muttering voice of Tack'em, as he rehearsed his prayers, echoed like the growl of advancing thunder. The last prayer was said—Mullins was extending his arm—when a stone descended from the aperture under which he stood, and, at the same time, Flinn's well-known voice exclaimed, from the roof: "Take that, an' bloody end to you, for a meddling, mur-therin' rap!" Mullins fell, senseless.

"Bounce up, a-vich—you're safe!" said Tack'em, while kneeling

himself, he clasped his hands, and continued, as if finishing a
private prayer that had previously engaged him—"*in secula secu-
lorum—Amen!* Jump, I say—jump!—*O festus dies hominis!
vix sum apud me!*—jump!" but Howard did not rise till after
he had returned ardent thanks for his deliverance ; and he was
still on his knees when Flinn rushed down the ladder, crying out:
" Tundher-un-ouns !—it's the greatest shame ever came on the
counthry !—a burnin' shame ! Och ! Captain, à-vourneen, are
you safe an' sound every inch o' you ? And they were goin' to
trate you in that manner ? Are you in a whole skin, àvich ?"
he continued, raising Howard, and clasping his hands.

" Quite safe, thank you, only a little frightened," said Howard,
with a reassured, though faint smile.

" Oh, the murtherin' thief !—where is he ?" resumed Flinn
—where is he, till I be the death of him ? Get up, you un-
loocky bird"—giving Mullins a kick—" get up, if the brains are
in your head.   Musha, I pray God the stone mayn't have left
'm —get up, an' go on your errand.   Purcell is waiting for you,
an' the farmer's son is there. Get up, an' that you never may !"

" Musha, I meant all for the best—don't be talkin';" muttered Mullins, as, recovering from the stunning blow, he scrambled
on his feet.   " Is Purcell ready ?"

" Yes, you black dog, he is," answered Flinn ; " go your
ways to him, an' tell him you're afther doing all he axed you—
be sure o' that."

" Father Tack'em must come wid me," said Mullins ; " Purcell wants him to make all sure—an' I promised."

" I'll not budge a peg in your company," said Tack'em.
" There's neither luck nor grace at your side."

" For that matter, there's a priest in the house already," observed Flinn, carelessly.

" Is there, honey ?" asked Tack'em, much interested ; " then,
where's my breviary ?"

" An' you'd better go, for another raison," rejoined Flinn.
" There's one abroad that came wid myself to the barn—(only
I left him a little way off, when I saw the hole in the roof, to
make his own way)—that your reverence wouldn't be over-
plaised to see—by the powers, here he comes down the ladder !"
Howard looked, in some alarm, but was greatly relieved to see
the portly person of Father O'Clery in the situation Flinn had
described. The friends, in mutual surprise and pleasure, advanced
to each other.

"Move aside, plase your reverence," continued Flinn
.o Tack'em, as the gentlemen conversed apart—"an stale out
wid Jack as soon as you can—it's the best way for you
both."

Poor Tack'em seemed to agree with the speaker. Folding
round his body, and over the relic of a coat that once had been
black, a loose dark-blue dreadnought, and hiding his bald head
in a slouched hat, while at the same time he tucked his breviary
under his arm, the fallen priest tottered after Mullins towards a
dark corner of the cavern.

But Father O'Clery's quick eye rested on the uncouth figure
while it was in motion, and rapidly advancing, and asking—
" Who's that?" he confronted in terrible severity his lost brother

" Wretched man !"—he then continued, his brilliant black eyes
half hid by the angular depression of eyelid that accompanied his
stern frown—" do I again find you in such a scene, and indeed,
in such a state, as you had solemnly promised never to relapse
into ? Is it thus you are to be trusted ? And has this one
absorbing vice sunk you so very low, that you have no terror,
either on your own account, or on that of the anointed brethren
whose cloth you disgrace, of the shameful death such connections
as these must inevitably end in ?"

" I rejoice, reverend sir," answered Tack'em, while spite of
his efforts to be flippant, his head and eyes drooped, and his tongue
faltered—" I say I rejoice, that you mercifully allot me but that
one unfortunate failing—I like it, sir, I like it—God help me !
And I believe—that is, I am afraid—that while Heaven spares
me a mouth to open, I must be tasting it. Every one has his
fate—I don't mean it heteere—c—doxically, sir—for, through all,
I'm firm in the faith—I'm a sinner, but I believe—but I never-
theless fear, somehow, that we are all born to some misfortune we
can never get over. And, as to the cloth, all I can wish is, that
having once called me into it—many are called, but few are chosen—
and, *nemo mortalium omnibus horis sapit,* as we say in syntax—
having once called me into it, I wish you could call me out of it
again. I am humble enough to admit, I can never wear it well—
and little sorrow would I have to strip it off on any other account.
For, happy death to me, if I get as much by marrying stray
couples, up and down, at the sides of ditches and hedges, and such
places, as would keep a second-hand black coat on my back half
the year round."

" Go, you miserable creature !" rejoined O'Clery—" hide your
5*

head for shame, and, when you get sober, think and repent, if you can. I can only advise and pray for you. Of punishment you have already had your share. A poor exile from the pale of God's Church ; a bad branch of the tree lopped off, and cast aside, I fear, for the burning ! Yet are you obstinate in your sin and scandal ; yet, alas! the name of priest is abused in your person—"

" Aye, troth, sir," interrupped Tack'em, hastily ; " a priest once, a priest for ever—that's the bite on us both ; and the worst is, we can't help it. Good night, brother, and benedicite ;" and he moved towards the ladder.

" And where now ?" asked O'Clery.

" I must go home and read my breviary," answered Tack'em, hobbling up the rugged steps.

" Stop !" cried O'Clery—" Who's that before you ?"

It was Mullins, who, taking advantage of the conference between the two clergymen, contrived to steal up unnoticed until this moment, when his retreating person became visible to O'Clery. As soon as he heard the question directed after him, Jack redoubled his efforts, and removed out of sight every part of his unwieldy person. Tack'em followed as he might, and in silence too, like his leader.

" Here has been infamous work," resumed O'Clery, addressing Flinn and the other men. " Where is the fellow who, as Mr. Howard informs me, meditated a deadly outrage on his person ?"

" Your reverence saw the hinder part of him just now, I believe," answered Flinn.

" I thought so," rejoined O'Clery. " Well, then, my good men, let us settle the business you have invited me here to assist you in : first, Mr. Howard, a word with you." He drew Howard aside, and continued in a low voice : " You are of course as surprised to see me here as I am to see you. I have your story, and now listen to mine. Sitting at Mr. Grace's table, about an hour ago, I learned that some person wished to speak with me, and when I went down, this young man,"—pointing to Flinn— " was in waiting. From a long conversation that ensued between us, I learned that upwards of one hundred stand of arms were ready to be delivered into my possession for you ; and, indeed, other concessions volunteered, which promise to put an end to this petty warfare—on one condition, however, which it is in your power to grant or refuse. But let us continue before the people." Both advanced, and O'Clery went on, aloud :

" I have informed Mr. Howard that you propose, my good people, to give such information as shall lead to the finding of more than a hundred stand of arms, with other things, provided he thinks it safe and prudent to take under his protection the few misguided men—you have told me they are few—now within his lines. And you engage that these men shall approach his soldiers without arms in their hands, leaving them behind, and remaining as hostages until they are, according to true instructions, found on the spot where they have grounded them."

" We just tell you, Father O'Clery, what we were bid to tell you, by some of our gossips that knows more about it. But we'll stand by every word you spake, howsomdever," said Flinn.

" How say you, Mr. Howard ?" asked O'Clery.

" On the terms proposed, I shall venture to protect these men," answered Howard, " but with one exception. Their captain, Doe, must surrender himself unconditionally."

" I fear that will be fatal to the treaty," said O'Clery.

" Not in the laste, your reverence," said Flinn. " Poor people that are badgered into corners in such a manner must look afther themsefs. An' so, if the captain just promises to lend a hand to the rest, he's welcome, an' I hear, to Doe, afther all."

" I promise, then," said Howard, " but good faith must in the very first instance be shown, by giving up the arms."

" We have little to do wid 'em, plase your honor," resumed Flinn ; " only as friends to both sides, an' pacemakers. But I'm tould we needn't go far for the guns an' pistols, anyhow. Arrah, Shawmus," he continued, addressing an old man near him. " wasn't it somewhere here the woman bid us look for 'em ?" And, taking down some bundles of straw, Flinn exhibited a considerable depot of old muskets, fowling-pieces, pistols, great and small, carbines, and blunderbusses.

" All this is very well," said Howard, restraining his pleasure as well as amazement—" and now I have to say that, if these things remain as they are, until morning, when, with some of my men, I can get possession of them ; and if the other concessions and submissions, spoken of by Mr. O'Clery, are made with a good grace, I shall then see about performing my own part of the treaty. But," he continued, after a short pause, and now pressed by a goading recollection—" but, my dear Mr. O'Clery, I fear I have even yet made a childish arrangement. Doe, I can learn, is not in my power."

" Indeed, Mr. Howard ! Do you speak on good authority ?"

"I'm afraid I do. But come, 'tis a point easily ascertained if I were once at my quarters—how shall I safely get there?"

"I will, with pleasure, accompany you, and this young man will guide us," said O'Clery, pointing to Flinn.

"Wid a heart an' a half, your reverence," said Flinn ; "an' don't let the captain be so much down in the mouth about Doc. Whether he's in the bog, or out of it, we'll show him to his honor, captain Howard, some time or other. An' sooner than he thinks, maybe."

"Come on, then ; there's no time to be lost," rejoined Howard ; and he, O'Clery, and Flinn, prepared to leave the cavern by the ladder.

In passing by a recess, which was studiously surrounded with piles of straw, furze, and fern, Howard observed, in deep shadow, the young female and child who had been the first, though unconscious cause of his stumble on such a nest of every kind of disloyalty. She still sat holding the infant to her bosom ; but her voice was hushed, and she only kept that peculiar to and fro motion of the body, by which the women of her country gesticulate a heavy sorrow.

"Who is she?" asked Howard of Flinn as they passed.

"Troth, plase your honor, I dunna," was the reply.

Howard looked round for the figure of the old man, who had accompanied her over the hills ; but, of all those in the place, none resembled his. Father O'Clery, in leading the way, had not noticed the young woman, and Howard now hurried after him up the ladder.

"Let your reverence an' the captain take care o' your heads," said Flinn, as he followed them. "The stones cover the hole all over, an' you'll have to stoop far it a little."

Father O'Clery, from his exploring and unassisted descent, was prepared for this intimation, and cautiously observed it. But Howard, whose entrance had been in an independent way, found much difficulty in lowering his person, neck and knees, as he almost crawled, once again, up to the face of the earth.

The moon had gained her zenith as the party emerged into her reviving beams ; and Howard and Mr. O'Clery both paused an instant to examine, in the broad light, if any appearance of suspicion was attached to the secret entrance they had just cleared. As Flinn truly premised, the large flat stone completely covered the mouth of the excavation ; and, at either side, as also at its elevated end, fern and furze-bush formed such a screen as must

beguile the eye of any uninformed wanderer. After remarking
that the concealment was perfect, the gentlemen, attended by
Flinn, pursued their mountain path to Howard's quarters.

"I must say, Mr. O'Clery," observed Howard, after they had
made some progress downward, "that though other things agitated me more, nothing, through the course of this eventful
evening, so utterly astonished me, as to find a person of your
profession—and such a member of it !—in the place we have
just quitted. I mean·Father Tack'em."

"Poor creature !" said O'Clery, in accents of genuine sorrow ;
"he is, indeed, a source of shame and grief to us. But it will
also be acknowledged how very rarely such unhappy instances
are to be found in our body."

"I know it, sir," Howard returned ; "my only wonder is,
why, when you have ascertained the obstinate unworthiness of
a minister, you do not at once discard him from your brother-
hood. Tack'em, if such be his name, is evidently in priest's
orders still."

"We cannot, canonically, do what you suggest," answered
O'Clery ; "the rule, in such a case, differs in our. separate
Churches. You have heard the poor fellow, himself, say, a
priest once, a priest for ever ; such is our discipline. We deem
that, although we assist in sanctioning the vow by which an
anointed priest dedicates himself to the service of his Master,
we have no power to declare the solemn contract annulled, under
any circumstances. All we can do, in case of irreclaimable error,
is to forbid, to the unworthy priest, the exercise of his priestly
functions, and to deprive him, so far as in us lies, of all lawful
opportunity of assuming them."

"Mean time," asked Howard, "can he assume them, if he
please ?"

"Certainly, and, we say, with as much spiritual efficacy as ever.
For we argue, that the grace, having once adopted its human
conduit, cannot, by any accident that may befall that conduit,
be defiled in its transmission to other human souls. In other
words," continued O'Clery, striking on one of his less serious
tones, "Tack'em—which you have sagaciously surmised not to
be his real name : in fact, 'tis only an expletive of his present
contraband trade—may—(and he does)—join in holy wedlock
scores of runaway couples, who dare not solicit the good offices
of their parish priest, or any of his curates."

CHAPTER X.

Howard had sent word that he should be at Mr. Grace's house at seven o'clock, and he had left his quarters at six, in order to keep his appointment. Seven o'clock came, and Howard did not appear. But it was about this hour that Father O'Clery, while sitting with Mr. Grace and the Protestant clergyman, Mr. Somers (the parish priest had been some time gone), received an invitation to speak with a strange man in the hall. Returning to the company, and generally hinting the result of his conference with Flinn, he was strongly dissuaded by his friends from setting out alone on such an invitation. Mr. Grace urged, that even Father O'Clery's spiritual calling was no certain shield against the displeasure of the deluded people, whom the exhortation of the day might have provoked into hostility towards the preacher. Nor did he suppose an unprecedented case. It had, before now, happened, that a Roman Catholic pastor was visited with the vengeance which a sense of his efficacious interference had aroused.

"And on my conscience, Father O'Clery," continued Mr. Grace, " I know not what to make of Captain John : he will legislate for us all in our turns. I thought my poor old Papist name, Mr. Somers, might have been respected ; but, no later than last night, he sends me a notice to lower my rents, and plead, gratis, for all defendants in the tithe-proctor's court."

" Aye," said Mr. O'Clery, smiling, " and this morning I tore off the chapel-door, before daylight, a paper signed by him, advising the clergyman at whose house I slept, to give over all sermons against his government, as he was pleased to call it ; to take two shillings per annum, for his Christmas and Easter dues ; to marry, at five shillings a pair, and christen at ten pence a head. Then, Father Doyle, in the next parish, has had a visit from him and his men. These are strange times, and Doe a strange fellow. Yet will I hazard the visit this young man invites me to : there is nothing to fear."

He left the house accordingly, and his friends remained anxiously speculating on his return. Mr. Grace, consulting his watch, began to feel additional uneasiness on Howard's account. It was now half-past seven, and no sign of Howard : it was eight,

and yet he came not. Mr. Grace and Mr. Somers grew seriously
alarmed.

To another person, under the same roof, his absence caused
even livelier pain. Mary Grace had, before seven o'clock, retired
to her apartment to make some little preparation for receiving
her lover, as also to discharge some religious observances of the
day. She proceeded half-way in her toilet : the long, fair hair,
was let down, and freshly arranged—a simple flower its only ex-
traneous ornament. Then Mary consulted her glass, with, it
must be admitted, much innocent satisfaction at her appearance.
But, recalling at the moment her neglected duty of Sunday devotion, a reproving blush deepened the healthy bloom of her
young cheek, and, hastily drawing a chair to the fire, she opened
her prayer-book, and strove, with all virtuous seriousness, to
detach her mind from personal vanities, from her lover, and from
every thing distracting and earthly. She scolded herself sharply
for having set about her toilet before discharging her spiritual
duties, and vowed that, to make amends, she would not proceed
in her dressing, would not even glance towards the glass, until
she had reverently performed her devotions.

Just then, the clock struck seven. This was an untoward intrusion : Mary found it the more difficult to banish forthwith
from her mind such speculations as she had penitently sentenced
to temporary exile. Howard was always so punctual to his
appointments—at seven he was to arrive, and it was seven now,
and he would be in the house in a few minutes at furthest. So
that he would have to wait awhile for Mary,—while Mary, being
good-natured and considerate, was loth to keep him waiting.
Her eyes and thoughts wandered as she listened for his knock.
She caught herself inattentive ; scolded herself anew, and again
resumed her devotions.

There were further distractions, and further chidings ; but at
last Mary had finished. As she rose from her knees her feelings
changed first to impatience, then into anxiety, at the prolonged
absence of her lover. He could not have knocked without her
hearing it—even were that possible, Nora, her maid, would have
come to inform her of his arrival. Her heart sank, as a fear of
danger or treachery to Howard crossed her mind, and she sat
down, trembling, her toilet forgotten, her thoughts all in alarm.
We shall here, availing ourselves of the privilege of authorship,
venture to give our readers a glimpse of the maiden and her
bower.

Having doffed her dress, while proceeding with her toilet, she sat in her stays and petticoat, leaning back in her chair, her ancles crossed, one arm hanging by her side, the hand still clasping her prayer-book. Mary had, however, laid her rosary upon the table, taking up in its stead a miniature of her lover, which she now held in her right hand. Her face was, however, unconsciously turned away from the likeness, as, with tears in her soft eyes, she sighed forth her loving and most devout intercessions for his safety. Her slender, but rounded figure, was prettily developed by the undress ; the short petticoat permitted a more than usual exhibition of her plump, but not heavy ancle ; while her polished shoulders and snowy neck must have excited the admiration of such aerial sprites as alone enjoy the freedom we have presumed, for the nonce, to emulate—that of entrance to a young lady's chamber.

Upon the table, immediately beside the dainty red case out of which she had taken the miniature, stood a carved ivory crucifix. At the other side was a tall glass, filled with glowing flowers. Emulative flowers, the creatures of Mary's pencil, adorned the walls of the room, and in the place of honor thereon was her girlish *chef d'œuvre*, a Madonna and child, in crayons. A small, but well-filled book-shelf hung to the right, while before the toilet-mirror lay (as a matter of course, even in Ireland) an album, most elaborately ornamented as to binding.

Immediately behind Mary was her bed, fitly draped in virgin white. The fire blazed strongly upon her as she sat, heightening the color of her cheek, sending soft flashes into her eyes, and toying with the golden cloud of curls around her face and neck. Through her figure, her attitude, her expression, as well as through all her surroundings, there ran a blended character of softness and purity—of innocence and of grace. Her thoughts of her lover were such as angels would not deem unfitting to mingle with the prayers she had just knelt before her God to offer at His feet.

It was some time before Mary remembered her neglected dress. The sound of the clock, striking eight, at last roused her, and she rang for Nora.

Nora entered. A fast-fading maiden of forty was this country Abigail, with strong, staring features, her head surmounted by a stiff-starched, high-cauled cap, pinned under her chin ; and, further, wearing a brown stuff gown, tucked up behind, and leaving her arms bare from the elbows. A blue check apron, a

flaming silk kerchief drawn down between her shoulders, blue
stockings, and sharp-pointed shoes, with large square buckles in
them, completed her attire.

"Not come yet, Nora?" asked her young mistress, whom the very
matter-of-fact presence of the tirewoman seemed to have roused
from her misgivings.

"Not yet, Miss Mary, an' myself thought you would never
ring for me. 'Tis lonely down stairs, for bein' Sunday evenin'
every soul is out, barrin' me. All the servants, I mane, be
coorse. What's wrong wid me, darlin'?" For Mary with a
face of mischievous horror, had recoiled from the proffered cares
of her attendant.

"Why, you dreadful woman!" Mary cried, holding up her
hands, "you have been again indulging in the habit I so often
scolded you for, and which you so often promised me to give over."

Nora, with every appearance of virtuous indignation, protested
that "never a shaugh o' the pipe had herself taken since the
blessed mornin', not six months agone, when Miss Mary forbid
her doin' it." This was, however, a rather loose assertion; for,
in good truth, Nora, after many laudable efforts, had failed in
prevailing on herself to surrender a much-indulged and long-
loved delight. "It rises my poor heart," she would soliloquize,
"better nor anything else in the world. An' sure, there's neither
sin nor shame in givin' into it a little, now an' then, when I have
no work to do, an' nobody the wiser, an' the dours shut to keep
the smoke from upstairs." Nora accordingly sought her own
opportunities for such enjoyment. Nay, the tingle of her mistress's bell had just summoned her out of the centre of a good
cloud that for the previous hour she had been industriously ac-
cumulating.

"I cannot quite believe that, Nora," the young lady said, in
reply to Nora's voluble defence. "Still, I hope you are too
good a Christian to tell me a story—this holy evening too. But
Mr. Howard has not come yet?"

"Musha, no: God presaarve him!" sighed the handmaid.

"Oh, Nora!" cried the girl, involuntary echoing the sigh,
"heaven send that no evil has overtaken him on the road!"

"O, yea. Amin from my heart, girleen," groaned Nora, who,
spite of her addiction to the sin of smoking, was a loving and a
privileged attendant of the mistress she had cared from infancy.
"I'm thinkin' that you love the handsome captain dearly, Miss
Mary, seein' how unasy you are for him."

Miss Mary blushed, but spoke out bravely, like a loving, innocent girl as she was.

"Indeed, Nora, I do love him dearly, dearly!—better," she added, in a lower tone, and with an air of something like self-reprehension, "better than I thought I could ever like anybody again."

"Agin? Musha, good loock to you, girleen. An' how long 'since we liked anybody before! An' we only seventeen now!"

"Oh, Nora! you knew it well," Mary said, softly.

"Avoch! Poor young Kavanagh you're thinkin' of, darlin'?"

"Ah, yes! Poor boy!—Nora do you know there are times when it seems base to me that I could so soon have forgotten—"

"Ullaloo! child. What was that but childer's folly?"

"It *was* childish, I suppose. Yet, perhaps, sweeter for that. It was silly too ;—vain and romantic, I know. Still, Nora—laugh if you will—the recollection of my childish love is very dear to me."

"Lord presaarve me! Love, indeed! Why, sure it's now four years agone. You were then only thirteen, an' he a slip of sixteen or so."

"No more, I believe, was either of us. But—"

"Well, if ever I heard the like! An' to be thinkin of it still! Musha, Miss Mary, 'twas an early notion. Troth, there's many a colleen in the country, as ould as you are this blessed day, that never yet thought of it. An' no wonder! Here's myself that might be your mother—God bless the mark!—an, I'm sure I was a start past eighteen before an idea of it ever crossed me. 'Twas many a long year afther I had my first sweetheart. Thin, there was such a differ betwixt ye in the world, sure I never guessed ye could ever dhrame anything about lovers or the like. Lord save us!"

"But, Nora, I was so young—"

"That you were—over young, alanna."

"I was so proud of—of the boy's fresh and unbounded love. Unbounded it seemed to me : fresh and innocent, it surely was. There was between him and me some distance : that I know. But, after all, my father was not then so rich as he is now, and Harry and his mother were respectable, well to do in the world, and thriving fast to something better. Oh, Nora! I often thought that—that only for that wretch, Purcell—Heaven knows what might have come of what you mock at as childish."

" Well, quarer things have come about, surely. And then our handsome captain—what of him, Miss Mary ?" Nora asked, with a sly smile. Mary colored, and drooped her head. But involuntarily her clasp tightened round the miniature she still held. The tenderness of the grasp said more for the strength of the girl's love, than for that of the romance of childhood. But —it is hard to know a girl's nature.

" Were you ever tould what became of poor Harry, girleen ?"

" Yes. He escaped from the North to America."

" An' the mother died. An' they say—Lord presaarve us ! —that the ould grandfather roves about the country, for mad, just like a ghost, frightenin' the people out of their lives. Though, musha, I don't grudge it to some of them. He came across Purcell once or twice, and, they say, turned him white wid his curses."

" Then he must have cursed deep, indeed," Mary said, with a curl of her pretty lip.

" An' that villain of the world, Miss Mary, that Purcell, to have the impidence to look at you, afther all his black doins, an' wid his upstart consequence that come in such a way !"

" Yes !" the girl cried, with a sudden flush of warm color, and speaking with a generous indignation that was more woman-ly than the false delicacy that to another would have suggested avoidance of such a theme ; " and that while he kept in the shadow of shame and sorrow, the poor creature he had degraded —the poor, unhappy creature he had led astray, I am assured, by giving her his written promise of marriage. Surely, that was enough to make me scorn him, even if there were no other reasons—even if it were possible I could ever love such a man. Thank God !—thank God ! that I am now free from the humil-iating pursuit of such a being. Thank God ! I am now—or shall soon be—protected from it forever, by the brave and hon-orable man I have chosen for my husband." ·

" Musha, yes. An' we hope you'll do your duty by him, Miss Mary."

" That I will—be a good little wife to him, you mean ?" she added, laughing.

" Avoch, no. Only make a Christen o' the Sassenach, Miss Mary. Throth it's your duty, afore God an' us."

" Hold your foolish tongue, Nora—and—Hush !" with a quick start and blush—" there is his knock at last. It is louder than usual—oh ! I hope he is indeed safe with us. There, there, I am very well. Run to the door. Or, stay, I am sure my father will prefer going himself." And Mary, in the prettiest flutter, ran down to the dining-room, where her father and Mr. Somers still sat.

"Mr. Howard, at last, dear father," she said, gaily entering.

Both gentlemen smiled as they looked up at her, so rosy, so eager, so glad, so frank.

"Most likely, Mary," Mr. Grace replied. "Yet we must be sure, before we admit our late visitor. Are the doors and lower windows all barred?"

"Oh, yes! As usual. Do you fear any thing?"

"No; but better leave them so, till we question our friend without. Mr. Grace threw up a window, and called out : "Who's there?"

"A friend to Lieutenant Howard," replied—to Mary's disappointment, and somewhat to her apprehension—a sharp voice from below. "I have a letter from him."

"Is he well, sir?" cried Mary, whose anxiety had brought her to the window, and now impelled her to give utterance to the demand that sprang to her lips.

"He is, quite well. Let me in, madam, I pray, or take this letter. The night is cold, and grows too inclement for tarrying here."

"Throw in the letter, and, if it be from Lieutenant Howard, you will be heartily welcome," said Mr. Grace. "I know, meantime, that you will excuse a precaution which the times render very necessary."

"Here, then. I could quite excuse your caution, if the night were finer." And, with that, the letter dropped into the room.

It was addressed to Mary, who caught it up, and, glancing over the contents, cried, eagerly : "Oh, father, we must instantly pray the gentleman to come in. Mr. Howard writes : 'Be kind to the bearer, for my sake, as he has just rendered me a signal service.' Hasten, dear father, or he will be gone !"

Mr. Grace smilingly complied. He at once went down to admit the stranger. In his absence, Mr. Somers inquired of Mary if any thing disagreeable had happened to keep Howard away. She answered : "No; he only mentioned a necessity for not quitting his present post."

She was yet speaking, when her father returned, saying to Sullivan, who followed : "Indeed, you are welcome, sir –cordially welcome. If you have to travel further, better not speak of it till morning."

"I thank you, Mr. Grace," the young man said, " and accept your hospitality freely as 'tis offered." Here he bowed courteously to the young hostess, to whom Mr. Grace hastened to present him.

" You are welcome, sir," Mary echoed, graciously saluting the visitor.

" Madam, I thank you, also," the young man said, with an earnest glance at her.

" Mr. Howard speaks of a particular service you have just rendered him. Has he, then, been in danger ?" she inquired, in her anxiety drawing close to him.

Sullivan did not immediately reply. As she raised her eyes to his face, she met his fixed upon her with an intensity of expression that for a moment startled, while it half offended her. But, recollecting himself, he added, carelessly : " Bah ! no, Miss Grace. I pointed out to him the best road to his wild quarters, as I met him straying in quest of them. *Voilà tout.*"

" Will you not be seated, sir," the girl said, in a tone and manner of growing embarrassment. Her eyes were, in their turn, riveted upon the stranger with a doubtful, yet eager scrutiny. Her color came and went ; she essayed to speak something more, but her deepening agitation, from whatever cause it sprang, made the words die upon her lips.

" Aye, sir, be seated," Mr. Grace said, " and let us have the pleasure of drinking your health."

" In genuine mountain-dew, I hope ?" the stranger said, and Mary sighed a breath of relief to find his deep gaze diverted from herself. He spoke in a tone of almost condescending pleasantry, and, turning easily away, seated himself at table with a careless grace of manner that went far to still the girl's half-aroused suspicions. She was silently leaving the room, when her father called to her, and, feeling as though under the influence of some wild dream, she returned, and took a chair by him.

" Do not leave us, Mary," Mr. Grace said : " sit by me, child, and we will all presently adjourn to the drawing-room, where you shall give us a song. Yes, sir," to Sullivan, " the right sort, I can assure you. Mr. Somers, there, though, makes it a case of conscience, and has some ' Parliament' to himself."

" I reverence the gentleman's scruples," the young man said, with a covert mockery of voice and glance. Mary sat a little

behind her father, her eyes, as though by some irresistible attraction, watching every movement, every look, every trick of
face or manner in the newcomer.

"Any thing new of Doe, sir?" asked Mr. Grace, presently.

"Why, yes," Sullivan answered; "I heard just now—that
is, your friend Howard told me—he had escaped. Is there no
mention of it in the letter, Miss Grace?"

Mary started, on being thus appealed to. Her voice, too,
was troubled, as she replied, that there was in it no word of
any thing of the kind.

"Ha!" Mr. Somers remarked: "the omission, and your account, seem to hint cause for alarm."

"Bah!" Sullivan said, without raising his eyes from the glass
in which he was now compounding his pottheen punch: "Howard
is too many for him."

"I hope so," cried Mr. Grace. "Welcome, once more, sir.
May we add a name?"

"Now!" Mary's lips all but uttered the word aloud. In her
eagerness she bent forward, and when Sullivan, looking towards
her, met the full gleam of her eyes upon him, he in his turn colored, and was perceptibly—to her, at least, perceptibly—stirred
from his *nonchalance*, real or assumed.

"Surely, Mr. Howard has named me to you?" he asked.

"He has *not*, sir!" and Mary's voice had an unwonted ring
in it.

"That is odd," the young man said, with a smile. "You may
call me Sullivan, Mr. Grace. 'Tis an old name."

"That it is. Mr. Sullivan, your health;" and the old-fashioned
greeting went round. At her father's hearty suggestion, the
young hostess took a wine-glass in her hand to join in the toast.
As she did so, Sullivan rapidly glanced at her. Again she met
his eyes, her hand trembled, her color deepened even to crimson,
she hesitated, and, in addressing him, pronounced the name of
"Sullivan" in a voice so broken as to be scarcely audible. Her
father and the clergyman looked at her with astonishment, then
with pain: they attributed her agitation to alarm on Howard's
account, but feared that to the stranger it might perhaps appear
offensive, a dread in which they were confirmed by seeing that
his emotion, however subdued, was scarce less than that of the
young girl. His eyes were cast down, his lips compressed, his
breast rose and fell, painfully. A rather awkward pause ensued, which Mr. Grace broke by suggesting that they should

proceed to the drawing-room. A suggestion which seemed a welcome relief to all.

Here, while Mary busied herself with drawing down blinds, closing curtains, and the like, Sullivan threw himself into a chair, and, taking up a book of engravings, ostensibly amused himself with its contents. In reality, his dark, flashing eyes, followed Mary in her movements to and fro. And though she carefully avoided glancing towards him, she felt that he was thus watching her. The two elder gentlemen, left to themselves, resumed, in a low key, a conversation which Sullivan's arrival had interrupted.

"I had no idea," Mr. Somers said, "that Purcell had acted so very basely towards the unfortunate young person we spoke of."

At the mention of Purcell's name, Sullivan slightly, though quickly started ; but the movement was so slight as to pass unnoticed by the speakers. He himself continued, to all appearance, absorbed in his book of engravings.

"I tell you fact, Mr. Somers," Grace returned ; "she holds his written promise of marriage."

"I am astonished," the clergyman resumed ; "for in the discharge of what I conceived to be my duty, Purcell being a Protestant, I spoke to him on the subject, and he assured me, with solemn oaths, that he had never entered into any such engagement. In fact," he added, sinking his voice still more, "he swore to me that the connection was not of his own seeking."

"He lied, and was perjured then, like the liar and perjurer he is," the stranger said, deliberately breaking into the discussion.

Mary looked sharply round ; but no extraordinary interest, sufficient to give positive confirmation to her suspicions, was visible in the face or manner of the speaker. Having so spoken, he returned to his examination of the engravings. Mr. Grace eyed him curiously, but said nothing.

"His assertions with respect to her unfortunate young brother appear to have been equally unfounded," Mr. Somers continued, making the remark more general than before.

"Why, what did the fellow say, different from what I have told you ?" asked Grace.

"Every thing different. In particular, he stated that the boy had, joined to his disloyal combinations, provoked the laws of his country, by robberies on the highway."

A more evident agitation was here perceptible to Mary, in the person she read so anxiously. He writhed round in his chair, pressed his hand across his brow, and, as she glided past, she could hear him draw in his breath, and grind his teeth together "Then, you may just term that another slander, false and malignant as the first, Mr. Somers," Grace decided warmly.

Touched and fired, apparently, by the kindly indication, Sullivan, whose identity with the boy, Kavanagh, the reader, as well as Mary Grace, will have already suspected, here flung down his book, and burst out :

"*Sacré sang de Dieu !* A mean villain ! A mean thief, did he say ? a common thief !" and the young man pushed away his chair, and paced angrily about the room.

Mary grew deathly pale ; Grace and the clergyman exchanged glances. In a minute, however, Sullivan was calm, and turned to the rest with a smile on his proud young face.

"A thousand pardons," he apologized, "for speaking so warmly on what little concerns me. Though concern me it does, as such a story must move and concern any one of right feeling, who, like me, might chance to have heard it in all its hideous truth. But this is no theme for the present. You sing, Miss Grace ? I think I heard your father promise us a song from you."

"Well, sir," the host said, "if you are no very fastidious critic, I am sure Mary will be glad to sing to you." The kind old man was puzzled by the mingled vehemence and indolent grace of the stranger's manner, and was glad to get rid of a subject that had called for the recent explosion.

Sullivan bowed, and, leading the hostess to the piano, busied himself with opening it, placing her seat, and looking for her music. Mary was trembling visibly ; her heart had sunk low within her. Yet she seated herself, and mechanically turned over some sheets of music by her side, until Sullivan, stooping over her shoulder, took up a manuscript song she had just put down, and mutely placed it on the stand. The girl's suspicions were now all but certainty. The song was one the words of which had been sent her by her boy-lover, and which he had adopted to her favorite air of "Aileen Aroon." Bowing her head, and without coherent thought, she commenced, with a tremulous hand, the opening symphony.

"Aye, Mary," her father said, when she had played a few notes, "that is a pretty song, and a favorite of mine. Give it us now, my girl."

"Pray do," Sullivan's voice intreated, while he continued to stand at her back. "Pray sing that for us."

Mary, with a strong effort to compose her hand and voice, complied. The song was as follows :—

I.

'Tis not for love of gold I go,
'Tis not for love of fame;
Tho' Fortune should her smile bestow,
And I may win a name,
Aileen;
And I may win a name.
And yet it is for gold I go,
And yet it is for fame;
That they may deck another brow
And bless another name,
Aileen;
And bless another name.

II.

For this, but this, I go. For this
I lose thy love awhile;
And all the soft and quiet bliss
Of thy young, faithful smile,
Aileen;
Of thy young, faithful smile.
And I go to brave a world I hate,
And woo it o'er and o'er,
And tempt a wave, and try a fate,
Upon a stranger shore,
Aileen;
Upon a stranger shore.

III.

Oh! when the bays are all my own,
I know a heart will care!
Oh! when the gold is wooed and won,
I know a brow shall wear,
Aileen;
I know a brow shall wear!
And, when with both returned again,
My native land to see,
I know a smile will meet me then,
And a hand will welcome me,
Aileen;
And a hand will welcome me!

G

How Mary contrived to get through this song, it would be difficult to explain. It had always been a favorite air of her boy-lover ; she had often, in the old days, sung it at his request ; and as, previous to their sad separation, he had cherished the romantic notion of seeking his fortunes in a foreign country, he had written for it words applicable to their situation—the words she had now sung for this stranger. A confused crowd of associations, doubts, and fears, filled her mind, yet she sang it, brokenly indeed, but with peculiar expression ; the very hurry and agitation of her soul lent it strange energy and pathos. She had just ceased to sing, when a hot tear fell upon her neck, and then came another, and another, and another, fast as the big drops from the swollen and sultry cloud. The girl started, shrank, burned, cringed under them. Now, they felt like tricklings of molten lead, parching her skin, and sending a wild glow through her frame ;—now, like the drippings of a thawed icicle, making her blood run chill, and her very bones to shiver. Yielding at last to her feelings, Mary sank back in her chair. But, raising her eyes, she saw reflected in a glass over the piano, the man she had before hesitated to recognize ; his face now relaxed to all its boyish tenderness,—the haughty mouth now quivering in anguished recollection,—the flashing eyes clouded, and sadly bent upon the mirrored image of his early love. Their looks met in the glass. Tried beyond control, the girl could no longer restrain herself. She screamed wildly, and, rising precipitately, rushed, with clasped hands, to her father.

Mr. Grace and Mr. Somers had risen in alarm, and were striving to ascertain the cause of such emotion, when a new sound from without arrested their attention, and diverted it from her. Mary's scream had scarce subsided, when a loud shout arose outside the house, accompanied by the discharge of a gun or pistol.

"Not Captain Doe, I hope !" cried Sullivan, instantly recovering his *nonchalante* manner. Mary, her father, and Mr. Somers stood in mute dismay. Another shout, with exclamations of "John Doe !—John Doe !" broke forth, as though in answer to Sullivan's conjecture.

"By heaven, it is, though !" Sullivan cried, rushing to a window. Ejaculations of apprehension and dismay broke from the others, and Mary, ghastly white, stood with her arms hanging by her sides, leaning mute and terrified against the wall.

At the same moment Nora bounced in. The noise without had

surprised her while enjoying her secret indulgence, and forgetful
of her caution in her fear, she now dashed into the drawing-room
with a short, black pipe spasmodically secured between her jaws,
while, speaking through her teeth she cried out :

"Mistress ! Master ! We're all undone ! Ruined for ever !—
ruined for ever !" Here running to Mr. Grace, she got behind
him, gripped him fast round the waist, and continued : "Mr.
Grace, Mr. Grace, your house is destroyed ! It's all over wid us !"
And totally unconscious of the promulgation of her forbidden
pastime, Nora mechanically emitted a short puff between every
sentence, and, at the end, fell into a hysterical fit of laughing,
crying, and screaming.

The uproar abroad increased ever moment. To the shouts
and exclamations now joined a loud knocking at the front door,
mixed with fiercely imperious cries of " Open ! open !"

"Merciful God ! What will become of us ?" Mary faltered.
shivering from head to foot. Sullivan had left the window, and
now, taking advantage of the general confusion, he sprang to the
side of the terrified girl, and, taking in his one of her nerveless
hands, whispered in a tone altogether different from that in which
he had hitherto spoken :

"Mary ! don't you know me ?"

"I do ! I do !" she answered, trembling even more violently
than before, and drooping her looks before his earnest gaze. "I
knew you almost from the first, Harry Kavanagh !"

"Hush, dear Mary ! But fear not. I am here to protect
you." Then, approaching the bewildered host : " You have arms,
Mr. Grace ?"

"Yes, yes !" the old man returned. " But you know they are
the first things we shall have to give up."

"Give up? No, by heaven, sir ! Let us arm ourselves at
once—you, and I, and the parson there—and we may yet beat
them off. Your arms, sir—quick !" he added, in a tone of something so like command, that Mr. Grace, who was a weak man,
instantly obeyed by leaving the room in search of them.

"My weapons are my words, young gentleman," Mr. Somers
said, in a tone of gentle reproof. "I am a soldier of peace."

"Mine are more to the purpose, sir, on such an emergency as
the present," Sullivan—or, as we may now call him, Kavanagh—
cried with a half sneer. "Soldier, or no soldier, they get a shot
or two from me, the rascals ! Ha ! Mr. Grace, that is something
like," as that gentleman returned with firearms. "Mary, trust in

me, whatever happens," he added, in a whisper, while passing her.

"Stand near us, Mary, and be of good cheer," Mr. Grace said, as he stooped over the chair into which the girl had now sunk, and tenderly laid his hand upon her head.

"Och ! yes, master, we will !" Nora cried, again drawing near him.

"Speak to them first from the window," said Kavanagh.

Mr. Grace flung up the sash, and asked boldly : "What do you want here ?"

"Open your door, and you shall know," two or three rough voices exclaimed together.

"Do you seek arms ?" demanded Kavanagh.

"No ! Who are you that asks that question ?"

"We have no money in the house at present," parleyed Grace.

"Not a rap, good Christhens !" Nora screamed, at his back. "It's all in the bank—all in the bank !"

"We don't want your money," was the contemptuous return.

Here Kavanagh, who, for the last minute, had been anxiously peering out, as if to distinguish a particular object, now, to the surprise of the rest, suddenly dropt on one knee, and leaning his carbine on the edge of the framework, cried, in a suppressed, yet sharp whisper, to some one beneath :

"Mullins ! Mullins !—move an inch aside !" Then to himself : "Ha ! he moves though he does not hear me. Now ! No ! Confound that imbecile ! He covers the scoundrel again ! And, regardless of the astonishment of his companions, he continued kneeling, still on the watch.

Shouts and knocking waxed louder and louder, and Mr. Somers, in his turn, advanced to the window.

"Misguided men," he said, "what brings you here ? Retire, in the name of religion and honesty !"

"Sure we don't want either the money or the lives o' you," answered a voice.

"Though, since the parson is there," added another, less coarse than the last, and evidently feigned, "we shall borrow him for an hour or so. He may be useful."

"Rascal ! villain !" Kavanagh hissed between his teeth, still kneeling and watching.

"My God, Father, what can this mean ?" Mary whispered, her

fears taking a more poignant turn as she listened to this last announcement.

"Och! we're lost!—lost! Our vartue isn't worth a pin!" Nora sobbed, concluding with a gasp, and dancing with her heels in an acme of tribulation, as she gripped her master afresh for protection.

"Open! open! 'tis betther for you, Mr. Grace. Open, or we'll break in!" threatened those below, amid still increasing clamor, and while they battered still more violently at the door. At this moment, Nora, to the surprise of all present, abruptly ceased her lamentations, rapidly quitted the room, and ran down stairs.

"Do you rely on the strength of the hall-door, Mr. Grace?" Kavanagh asked, still kneeling.

"It ought to be able to withstand all the force they can bring against it," answered Grace. "But the back-door is, unfortunately, worse framed for long resistance."

At this point Nora was heard slowly ascending the stairs, with heavy groans, toilsome steps, and strange mutterings. She entered at length, carrying in her arms a tremendous stone, while the short pipe remained wedged in between her teeth. All looked at her in amazement as she continued her laborious way to a window immediately over the hall-door. This she opened, and with much caution deposited her burden on the window-sill outside. Then, squatting down, she watched, with a mixture of the cat and hare in her position and manner, proper time and opportunity for a valiant deed. She had not long to wait. The crowd of assailants all gathered to the hall-door, and commenced a serious attack upon it. Nora pushed her stone. With its deafening fall a loud groan was heard, and then the hurried noise of feet running in confusion from the door. Nora, uttering a hideous giggle, sprang up, and resumed her old post behind her master.

As the crowd decreased, Kavanagh looked out with increased earnestness, and, an instant after, again levelled his piece, and with a sharp "Now!" discharged it. His head and neck were almost at the same time thrust out to mark the effect of his shot. But as quickly he started up with a vehement bitterness of action, and flung the carbine on the floor, with: "No!—curse that angle!—I've missed him! Fire, Mr. Grace. Or, give me the pistol. Yet, no. It is now useless. They flock to the back-yard."

"And over that," cried Mr. Grace, "we have no command from any window in the house."

To the rear of the house, indeed, the besiegers now directed all their efforts, and, enraged apparently by the joint outrages of Nora and Kavanagh, attacked it in good earnest. Amid a continued clatter of kicking, shoving, and knocking, as if with sticks or the butts of guns, one mighty blow was heard, probably the effect of a ponderous stone hurled at the door by the united strength of two or three men. Profound and painful silence reigned above at this intimation of what was coming. A second blow—and the crash of the yielding door followed, mingled with a triumphant yell from the assailants.

"Heaven save us! They are in!" exclaimed Mr. Grace. Mary fell on her knees, and Nora flat upon her face.

"Let me try—let me reason with them first," Mr. Somers cried, as the victorious party were heard rushing up stairs.

"All is vain for the present," Kavanagh said, quietly. Then advancing to the terrified Mary, he whispered, tenderly, but with impressive earnestness: "Again, and in spite of all, be not alarmed. Remain quiet, whatever may happen; trust to me, and fear nothing."

He had scarce done speaking, when at least a dozen men, wearing red waistcoats and having their faces blackened, broke into the room, headed by another, who also wore a red waistcoat, but whose features, instead of being smeared over like the rest of his party, were disguised by a black mask. Around his waist was tied a red sash, in token of authority. All were strongly armed and completely disguised, except the last man who entered, and who, having taken no precaution with his face and person, exhibited to whom it might concern the identity and totality of Jack Mullins.

"John Doe! John Doe!" shouted the leader, as he appeared, and the shout was well echoed. "Speak for me, Mullins," he continued, aside, as this person followed.

"Lawless men!" Mr. Somers exclaimed, approaching them; "what seek you in this unoffending house, and in so ruffianly and savage a manner?"

"First, your arms!" Mullins said, clicking the lock of his blunderbuss, while the others made similar display of their weapons. At a whisper from Kavanagh, the household arms were given up.

"Mullins," resumed the leader, still aside; "get the parson

with us. Tack'em will not be sufficient, as the girl and I differ in religion. 'Twould not be a legal marriage, though the priest might satisfy *her* scruples."

" Well, unfortunate people," good Mr. Somers persisted : " your demand is answered ; why not depart in peace ? You have said you did not want money. What else seek ye ?"

" Why, then, next, by your reverence's lave, no less than yourself," replied Mullins, laying his hand familiarly on the clergyman's shoulder. " Here, men, take the best o' care o' the ministher." And, spite of his expostulations, the good gentleman was immediately guarded by two men.

" Next, my handsome misthress," Mullins went on, approaching the shrinking Mary. " Our captain has a word to whisper wid you."

Nora started up indignant. " Wid me !" she cried ; " wid me, you ugly Christhen ! Never lay a finger on me !" This to Purcell, who had crossed over to where she and her young mistress were.

" Stand out of the way, an' he won't," Mullins said, with a grin.

" I guessed it !" Mary moaned, as Purcell caught her arm to raise her. "All through I guessed it. Father, father, save me !" And, with a desperate spring, she reached and clung to her father's arm.

" My child, my Mary, my only and good child !" the old man said, tremulously. " Men !—if ye are men—spare my innocent child, and you shall have all I am worth !" he added, imploringly, while tears ran down his cheeks.

" Dare not to touch the young girl, if you fear God or man !" added Mr. Somers.

" No harm is intended her," said Mullins, unmoved by these appeals. " Only a pleasant ride in the moonshine, wid all her friends about her. Come, Miss. We are waitin' for you." He seized her arm, and Mary shrieked and struggled in desperation.

Again Kavanagh was beside her ; his low, earnest whisper at her ear. " Dearest Mary," he said, " do not exhaust yourself with useless resistance. Submit for the present. Have you no faith in me ? I tell you, I swear to you on my life, on my soul, you shall not be harmed."

The leader noticed the whisper, though Mary's ear alone could distinguish its import. " Mullins, seize that man," he cried, pointing to Kavanagh.

" Musha, I believe it is the best, for a sartainty," the man assented with matter-of-fact coolness, as he laid hold of Kavanagh. The leader now succeeded in separating from her father the young girl, whom the last-whispered assurance addressed to her seemed to have calmed ; but Mr. Grace broke into passionate cries of :

"My God ! my child ! my daughter ! Is it thus we are parted ?"

"Not at all, Mr. Grace," Mullins said ; "sure you're coming wid us yoursef, sir."

"Let us be off, then," the leader cried, impatiently, as he grasped Mary roughly by the waist. "Are the horses ready ?" to Mullins.

"Yes, all below. Lead on, Captain."

"Come, then !" the captain commanded, as he left the room with his prisoner, who, more dead than alive, had little trouble in obeying Kavanagh's injunction to submit, or seem to submit, passively.

"The minister next !" Mullins said. Mr. Somers was led out.

"Now the ould attorney !" Mr. Grace followed, also guarded.

"Go on !" The rest of the men obeyed his command, and with Kavanagh as his own prisoner, Mullins at last left the apartment.

CHAPTER XI.

ASSUMING our prescriptive privilege of scene-shifters at pleasure, we now return to Lieutenant Howard, and his friend, Father O'Clery.

They were faithfully guided by Flinn to Howard's quarters, where that gentleman found his soldiers in some alarm at the long absence of their officer. A sergeant was in waiting, of whom Howard anxiously inquired concerning the probable escape of Doe. Nothing had been heard of the matter.

"'Tis very strange," said Howard ; "my information was particular, and such as I have no reason to doubt."

"To satisfy you, sir," answered the sergeant, "I can inform you, that, to the centre of the bog, I have myself seen a fire that must have been kindled by no others but Doe and his men. Precaution had been taken to screen it from us by lighting it between some clumps of turf ; but I gained a particular point from which it was visible."

"Then hasten, serjeant—return again to the men, with orders to keep a more watchful eye then ever. For this night let them do good service :—you may mention, that it is likely to-morrow morning early will give them relief." The serjeant touched his cap, and left the cabin.

"I am resolved," continued Howard, turning to O'Clery, "to draw a complete line round the bog at the very first light, and one by one get those poor wretches out, so that their leader may not escape me. And now, Mr. O'Clery, let us do something to rest and refresh you. Our fire is pretty good—be seated—and here is the pottheen. You," he added, addressing Flinn, who all this time had deferentially stood aloof, seemingly unconscious of what was going forward—"you, too, shall warm yourself, and take some refreshment. Come over."

The party were thus disposing themselves to be comfortable, when a woman, rushing by the sentinel at the door, pushed into the cabin, and, with loud screams, cast herself on her knees, then sat back on her heels, and, clapping her hands, cried :

"Your honor an' your worship ! we're all undone ! All ruined ! Oh ! Captain Howard, we're all ruined, murdhered, and kilt dead as herrings ! Ochone ! Ochone !"

It was Nora ; the pipe still between her teeth ; her starched and, heretofore, unwrinkled and spotless cap, now soiled and torn ; her lank hair escaped from underneath it ; one shoe off, and her face a universal convulsion. Howard and Father O'Clery started up, and even Flinn seemed excited and interested.

"What do you mean, Nora ? Is any one ill ? or—dead ? How is Miss Grace ?" asked both gentlemen in a breath.

"Och !—little do I know ! Bud it's all over wid us ! over wid us !"

"Foolish woman! Speak can't you ? What's the matter ?"

"Captain John, a hinnies ma-chree ! Captain John !"

"What of him ? Where is he ?"

"He came to take me off wid him ! Oh !—o—oh ! to take me off wid him !"

"You rave, woman !—She's mad !" said Mr. O'Clery.

"Did you see him ?" Howard cried.

"Saw him an' hard him ! He came to ruin me !—to ruin me !"

"But you have escaped—you are safe !" said Howard, impatiently.

6*

" He has *not* taken you off.—He has *not* ruined you ?"—
echoed Mr. O'Clery, with an odd twinkle of his eye.

" That's nothin' at all !—nothin' at all !" howled Nora.

" What then ?—what has he done ?"

" Run off wid the ministher !—the ministher !"

" Is that all ?" Howard asked, much relieved.

" An' my poor ould masther !"

" Why, you brainless creature !" began Father O'Clery.

" And your lady, then ?" cried Howard white with apprehension.

" An' my poor young misthress ! my poor young misthress !"

" Death, idiot !—why not say that at once !" cried Howard.
When ?—How ?—Whither ? Sentinel !"—he shouted, rushing
to the door. The man entered.

" How long since, Nora ?"

" Avoch, I dunna !—I dunna !"

" Wretched, stupid fool !" cried Howard, stamping his foot—
" sentinel, I say !—has White gone with my last orders ? After
him quickly—fire your piece as a signal—see him—let him coun-
termand my orders—which road, Nora ?—and draw off all the
men instantly—Doe is out—has been to Mr. Grace's—let them
meet me there—quickly. Begone !—Stay ! Which road,
Nora ?"

" Which road, you wretched woman ?"—questioned O'Clery,
losing all patience.

" Avoch, I dunna !—I dunna !"

" Be off then, sentinel ! Mr. O'Clery, let us go to Grace's
house, first—I know you will with me—come !"

" They're after lavin' me !" Nora wailed, still in her first
position, and with uninterrupted clapping of hands. A shot
startled her anew. " Och !" she screamed, " I'm kilt dead !—I'll
be ruined again ! worse an' worse !—worse an' worse ! Captain !
Soggarth ! Captain !"—and the dazed creature ran howling out
of the cabin.

" Troth," said Flinn, thus left alone at the fire, " maybe
this turn 'ud sarve our poor gossips in the bog, without waiting
for the mornin'. It's a bad wind, a-vourneen, that blows nobody
good. If a body could get to spake to them, faith it's likely
enough bud they'd help Mary Grace betther nor the red-coats,
themsefs. We'll try it, anyhow." And after coolly help-
ing himself to a bumper of pottheen, Flinn also left the
cabin.

Meantime, the motley cavalcade continued on its route from Mr. Grace's house.

When Mary, led by the captain, gained the end of the winding approach to her father's residence, she saw, standing under the shade of some old alder-trees, a horse, bridled and saddled, with a pillion behind the saddle, such as is used by the humble class of Irish females. To this pillion her companion unceremoniously raised her. A moment after he was in the saddle before her. Her father was obliged to mount one of his own horses ; Mr. Somers another ; Mullins and his prisoner got on the bare back of a fourth ; and the rest of the party also rode double, and without saddles. When all were in travelling order, the leader ordered four men, thus mounted, to the front. After these, Mr. Grace and Mr. Somers were compelled to fall in. Four other men followed. Then Mary and her companion. Then the remainder of the party. And when Mullins, with his prisoner, Kavanagh, took the lead of all, on an understanding that he was to act as guide, the journey was commenced at a brisk trot.

Avoiding the wild bridle-road which, if pursued, would lead in the direction of Howard's quarters, Mullins guided the party up another narrow and rugged lane, that, at some distance, ran by the front of Mr. Grace's house, and continued beyond it, towards the bare solitudes of the country. Much inconvenience occurred from the deep ruts that, from time out of mind, had indented this way, it being a constant passage for the turf-cars that received their loads among the recesses of the hills around. Large stones also profusely strewed it, with, here and there, pools of water, or patches of miry slough. Neck or nothing, however, the party pushed on ; horses tripping, and stumbling, and falling, and riders cursing, laughing, or crying out, as, with different tempers, they bore their mishaps. The rapid and uncomfortable motion first called Mary out of the torpor into which she had sunk ; and one or two serious stumbles of the horse had the effect of causing her to use some precaution for holding her seat on the pillion. Spite of her loathing for the person whose prisoner she was, the poor girl, having narrowly escaped being flung to the ground, was forced, in self-preservation, to cling to him for support during the remainder of the rough journey on which she had been so rudely forced.

After about half a mile's progress, the way continued over an uninclosed space, by the verge of a descent to the left-hand side, which was less rough than the commencement of the journey.

Taking advantage of this favorable change, the party went on at a gallop. The wind, about the same time, rose high ; and in the rush through it, Mary almost lost her breath and senses, and was again in danger of falling. She rallied herself, however, and tried to collect her thoughts, and even to make observations on what was passing.

Looking before and behind her, she saw herself surrounded by the rude men who had forced her from her home. With much difficulty she was also able to keep her head sufficiently long in an averted position to discover the figures of her father and Mr. Somers. She endeavored to catch their voices,. but the rushing of the wind nearly overmastered even the noise of the horse's feet ; and no other distinct sound reached her. Now and then, indeed, a hoarse laugh, or the burst of many voices, came in some pause or turn of the breeze ; or the distant watch-dog's bark or howl ; or the sudden dash or shriek, heard and lost in the same moment, of some concealed stream, that gave to hill and fell its wild and sleepless plaint. She strove to examine the scenery through which she passed, for the purpose of noting, by old and well-known landmarks, her probable destination. But this effort was also vain. Mary could only apprehend that hill gathered unto hill, and valley running into valley, lay tossed around and beneath her. The black masses varied in shape each time she looked. Even while she looked, line chased away line ; the moonlight faded into shadow, and the shadow became light ; heavy clouds, that for some time had been mustering in the lower part of the sky, mixed and blended with the curving of the mountains ; and all comprehension of form and locality was lost. The very stars, breaking through thin vapor, seemed to run disarranged through their deep blue field of space, and, she thought, glanced in bright terror on her reckless speed.

Another half mile might have been past, when the party emerged on a by-road, that, for the whole distance they had come, ran parallel to that which led to Howard's quarters. The reins were now tightened, and along this road they went with somewhat slackened speed. Some distance on, there was a halt before a wooden barred gate, opening into the back part of the demesne of the principal proprietor of the district. Mullins dismounted to open the gate, and holding it till all had passed, resumed his uncomfortable seat on the bare-backed horse, and followed at a hard trot through a neglected plantation of old trees, and over a narrow path, that was barely visible to any but an habituated eye.

Here the mishaps and distresses of the party were renewed to excess. All over the path, and around in every direction, the roots of the trees, protruded through the spare soil, spread and coiled like serpents ; and rendered slippery by the state of the weather, opposed obstacles, at every step, to the safe progress of the party. Many horses, straying from the path, tripped, fell, and rolled about with their riders. The animal on which Mary sat, though evidently of gentle blood, twice came to his knees. In other respects, also, the way proved difficult and hazardous, from the constant occurrence of branches of trees that shot directly across at the level of the men's breasts or faces. More than once these unseen impediments, giving sudden resistance to a rider, tumbled him to the ground ; and Mary's guide suffered severely from the same cause. The cries and imprecations of the scrambling party added to the wild character of this unusual scene, which was further heightened by the uncertain quivering of the moonbeams through the leafless branches overhead, by the whistling of the night-wind through them, and by their own clatter and groaning, as the grove tossed her arms to the breeze.

At last, this unsafe path was cleared, and through another gate, like the first, badly secured, a second by-road was gained. This kept straight only for a little way, and then suddenly turned to the left, round the hill. Mullins stopped at the beginning of the turn, and, waiting till the leader came up, informed him, that, to their destination, the way by the road was a great round, while, if he chose to walk straight over the hill, he could gain it in about five minutes. The horses, Mullins added, might be sent round under the care of two men. The person to whom Mullins addressed himself yielded, after some consideration, to this arrangement. The whole party dismounted, and, through a gap in the fence of the road, began to ascend the hill, observing the same order in which they had ridden,—Mary, still by the side of the captain, and with the exception of those sent with the horses, the men still divided as at first.

Owing to her feebleness and terror, Mary made but slow progress : her companion remained, however, close at her side. Mullins, taking advantage of this circumstance, used vigorous efforts to outstrip, with his prisoner, the rest of the party. They walked in a very rapid pace against the hill, gained its brow before any of the others, and then ran down its descent, and jumped on a narrow and rough road at the bottom.

"Do you think them two gorçoon will ever find us by the road they took, wid the horses?" asked Mullins, jocosely, as they gained a covered side of the way.

"Hardly," Kavanagh answered. "This is the place, is it not?"

"Thry," replied Mullins. "Just give the least bit of a whistle in the world."

Kavanagh did so, and was immediately answered from a little distance.

"All right!" he cried, in tone of triumph, "all's as it should be. But see! who is this coming up to us on horseback? Stand close."

The horseman was passing them at lightning career, when Kavanagh exclaimed: "Flinn, or the devil, by Saint Dennis! Stop—you rider of the wind," he continued, waving his arm. "Come under the shelve of the hill, here, and in six words tell us what you are about."

"Howard is after you, wid his men, Jack," said Flinn to Mullins, in a rapid whisper, and while he quickly obeyed the directions of Kavanagh. "Bud, the cat gone, the mice may play; an' so I axed them he left behind to help you. An' they will, please God. Keep him in sight, and if he finds you out—"

"Away!" interrupted Kavanagh, "I hear the others coming down after us—enough—go—meet them—steal quietly by this hedge for awhile, and then spur! Move, I say!" Flinn disappeared in a moment.

"His poor reverence, Father Tack'em, that thinks we are so in earnest to-night, ought to be somewhere here too," resumed Mullins, when he and his prisoner were again alone. "Faith," he continued, having peered about him, "I think I see something like himself an' his auld gray mare, standing in the shelter o' the corner, beyand."

Mary and her leader had now won the rugged road on which Mullins and Kavanagh stood, and here she distincly recognized her situation, though she concluded that they had led her to it by an unusual way, or that her speed and agitation had prevented her continions notice of the route. At the hill-side of the bridle-road there ran a fence; but, at the other, the ground was open, stretching, in the moonlight, flat and cheerless, to some distance. Hither she had often walked with Howard; and, in the seques-tered space to the right hand, Mary distinguished five or six gigantic trunks of trees, that had repeatedly attracted the notice of herself and her lover. Perhaps they were the last relic of a plantation attached, a century, if not centuries ago, to some ancient edifice near the spot, but of which all traces were at present lost. To whatever accident they owed their existence in this place, the trunks were very aged ; they should, indeed, be more properly called shells, for they stood completely hollow, though, from the top of each, a few branches still shot, in summer sprinkled with scanty foliage. Mary and Howard had sometimes sauntered into them, by low openings that bore some resemblance to Gothic doorways, of rude and fantastic shape. Struck by the unexpected spaciousness of their interior, they had on one of these occasions amused themselves by calculating that a body of at least twelve men could find shelter in each, while to half the number these primitive receptacles might afford ample accommodation for sitting, standing, or other movements.

Mary was interrupted in her remarks on the place, by the voice of her guide calling " Mullins !"—when they had descended to the road.

" I am here," said Mullins, advancing. " You were very long comin'."

" 'This way—a word," continued the other, beckoning :

" How much further is the retreat you have chosen," he added, aside.

" About half a mile."

" So far still ? Then, fellow, you have misinformed me."

" Thonomon duoul ! No !—to the best o' my knowledge. Sure we'll see it very soon."

" Why not keep our horses and push on with all speed ?"

" Curp-on-duoul !—don't be thick-skulled. Why, I told you that the short cut over this hill was a good mile off o' the road."

" You are sure you have got accommodation for the night in the old building ?"

" Yes—fire an' candle, an' good fern beds, an' the atin' an' drinkin' an' plenty of everything."

" Where is Tack'em to meet us ?"

" Can't you see him yet ? He's snug under the fence, further up."

" Shall we meet our horses soon ?"

" Aye—in a minute."

" Proceed, then." Once more he drew Mary's arm through his, and was slowly following Mullins, when the old man whom Kavanagh had spoken to in the cabin, issued from one of the hollow trees, and, confronting the captain, drew himself up to the full of his unusual height, and, with a shivering and shrill voice, exclaimed : "Let go the colleen's hand !" All paused.

"Death ! Mullins," whispered the captain, "It is that old madman, Kavanagh, and his cursed brawling may spoil all."

"Aye, faith !" observed Mullins, drily enough.

"Stand away, idiot !" resumed the leader, passing, or endeavoring to pass.

"Stand you, where you are, and let her go, I say !" resumed the old man, in a yet shriller tone, to which, through the pausings of the wind, the hills rang—"Let go the hand of Mary Grace ! Free her of a touch she should never feel !—perjurer and informer, let her go !—tyrant of the poor, spoiler of the weak and old, and of the humble fireside—Purcell !—Stephen Purcell !— let go her hand !"

Mary uttered a thrilling scream at these words. Her father and Mr. Somers, with exclamations of surprise, also drew near with their guards, who made no effort to keep them from doing so.

"He is stark mad, and raves wildly, said the captain. "Stand back, old man :—Mullins, remove him."

"He would not lay a hand on me, to harm me," resumed the old man, "though it was to save you, body and soul, from what is prepared for you ! Purcell ! Purcell ! Let the colleen go to her father !"

"Fool !—you call me by a name I know nothing of," answered the leader, still trying to move on.

"Och ! Another lie, black as the thousands you have lived and thriven on !—as the thousands that brought shame, and wreck, and madness on us all !—that lifted the roof from the poor man's cabin, and made his hearth cold as a gravestone ; that took my daughter from me—and my daughter's daughter,—and left my white head houseless, to-night, to meet you by this wild hill, and bid you prepare for a reckoning ! Purcell ! 'tis nigh at hand ! 'tis nigh at hand !" he continued, in a pitch of enthusiasm, as, by a sudden and unexpected movement, he plucked the mask from Purcell's face, and added, " Do you know him yet ? Do you know him for the liar he is, yet ?"

Mary, now fully convinced, struggled hard to escape from Purcell's hold : while Mr. Somers, taking her disengaged hand, cried out, "Ruffian ! dare you attempt such an outrage ? Yield me the young lady's hand this moment—yield it !"

There was an increased struggle, but Purcell at last locked

his hold. Mary just felt herself clasped in her father's arms, when she fainted.

"I yield up her hand, Mr. Somers," said Purcell, after a short pause, "that you may bestow it as I command you. Ye know me, now; 'tis but a little sooner than I purposed, and I care not. Hear me, Mr. Somers—Mr. Grace, hear me—I love Mary, and she shall be mine!"

"Never!" exclaimed Grace.

"Never is a big word," resumed Purcell, with insolence and boldness. "Remember that Mary Grace is in my power, and might, according to any form,—or without any, be mine."

"Never according to any form, though here you shed our blood. We will resist while we have a drop to spill!" answered Grace.

"And I swear by my sacred character," added Mr. Somers, advancing to Mary, and taking her passive hand, "the arm that tears this pure young hand from mine shall first be raised against my life!"

"Hear me, I say, fools! No blood shall be spilt—no force but what is necessary, used—no advantage taken but what is lawful and honorable. The young lady shall be my wife! Mr. Somers, do your office! Mr. Grace, stand by your child! Resistance is vain—I have taken my measures too well. You are here in a solitude where no help can reach you. Look around upon my men—they are armed, and numerous. Do not cross, and, perhaps, provoke me!"

"These men will not assist you in a sacrilege—they dare not!" exclaimed Mr. Somers.

"They will see me through my present purpose, sir. They are my own tenants. I have sworn to them not to touch life or limb, and they have sworn to do anything else I command—have ye not?" continued Purcell, turning to them.

"We have! we have!" shouted his followers.

"But do you not recollect that all this must be useless to you?" rejoined Mr. Somers. "Even supposing that by threatening our lives you can force us into your measure—that you can force me to go through a nominal ceremony—it would still be only nominal."

"Pardon me, Mr. Somers," said Purcell. "I think I am aware of what I do. Your marriage of a Protestant and Roman Catholic is as legal and binding as it could be between two of your own persuasion.

"It is, sir, with a certain proviso," said Mr. Somers; "that is, after publication of banns, or under license, my ministry is legal in both cases; but, without one preparative or the other, the contrary in both."

"By heaven, and I forgot that!" exclaimed Purcell, almost immediately adding, however:

"But come, all is safe yet—Father Tack'em!"

"Happy death to me, here I am, honey," said the degraded man, emerging on his blind grey mare, as the unusually loud summons of Purcell reached him, above all the late conversation.

"And a long ride, and a cold station I have had of it," he continued. "Why, I'm a cripple, sitting there so long."

"Are you ready, good Father," sneered Purcell, "to join in holy wedlock myself and this young lady?"

"God forgive me, that's all my vocation now. Yes, I am ready to tack ye together."

"You surely cannot think, sir," said Mr. Somers, addressing Tack'em, whose person and character he knew, "of proceeding in such a ceremony without due permission and allowance?"

"Why, happy death to me, I came here for that especial purpose. As I said before, 'tis the only sacerdotal function remaining to me—*mea culpa, mea culpa*. I wouldn't, bad as I am, attempt to officiate in any other way than as a miserable couple-beggar. No, I would not. Happy death to me, I would not—no—no! And, indeed, happy death to me, it is glad I am that the name I bore at my ordination is known to few, if to any. I'm Father Tack'em, nothing else, and this name, now my only name, denotes my ministry."

"But, sir," interrupted Mr. Grace, "from all I have heard, you do not attempt to officiate except with the consent of the parties you join in wedlock?"

"Why, honey, it is seldom the consent of parents is sought, where I discharge my mission. Happy death to me, I'm never called on except where there is a runaway affair like this. There is seldom a wedding-supper, and no such condiment as a wedding-cake, when the tipsy Father Tack'em, as I'm called, celebrates the marriage ceremony by the light of the stars."

"Proceed, Father Tack'em!" Purcell exclaimed, assisting the dignitary to dismount.

"Wait a bit, Mr. Purcell, honey."

He waddled close to Mr. Grace.

"I hope you understand me, Mr. Grace. I never seek the

consent of father or mother, sister and brother, and for the best of reasons : because it is ever and always in utter defiance of all such sanction, that I give the marriage benediction. It suffices for me, as in the present case, that the two people I bind together know each other's mind—"

" But if one of them refuses consent ?" Mary eagerly interrupted, who, recovering her senses, had heard the latter part of the debate. " Will you, sir, proceed not only against the will, but to the abhorrence, and certain misery, here and hereafter, of the poor creature before you, and who now joins her supplications to those of her father, praying you, if you believe in God or have a human heart, not to make us both irrecoverably miserable !"

" Eh, honey ?" whined Tack'em, the tears running down his own cheeks.

" I'll quadruple your fee," whispered Purcell.

" No !—nor if you squared it, or if you cubed it, twice over !" squeaked Tack'em, suddenly turning on Purcell with all the fierceness his poor face, voice, and manner were able to express. " Happy death to me, I'll wash my hands of it."

" First, then, give me up the bank-note I feed you with," cried Purcell, advancing angrily.

" What bank-note, a-vich ?"—demurred Tack'em, taking his place in the opposition ranks : that is, between Grace, Mr. Somers, and the old man, who had stood a stern spectator of this scene. " Wait a bit, till I bring you to reason. You see, Mr. Purcell, I was to be paid for each distinct part of my agency in this matter, for the extraordinary trouble as well as for the marriage itself ; well, the last understanding between us, for the whole, was four times the amount of that shabby bit of paper you talk of. Now, let us say that three parts of the gross sum were to come down for the wedding-money. Sure the fourth part, at least, would be little enough for the long ride, and the sitting there beyond, on my old gray mare, for a long hour, like a pelican in the wilderness, or a solitary sparrow on the house-top. What more am I asking from you ? Happy death to me, 'tis a case of conscience, and as clear as day. I'll leave it to your own honest minister, Mr. Somers, here, and let him decide between us."

" Give him back the note, Father Tack'em, and I will make it up to you," said Mr. Grace.

" Will you ?" asked Purcell, assuming, after another short pause, all the ruffian of his character. " And so you, and he,

and all of you, think I am baffled, or to be baffled, amongst
you ? You shall see. I cautioned you not to cross and provoke
me too far, and I promise forbearance only under the belief
that you would not—that you dared not. Now, let us see what
else I can do. Men !" he continued, addressing his followers,
" You are witnesses of the trifling and imposition practised on
me, particularly by this outcast priest, who is a shame to your
religion, and, in this instance, would doubly disgrace it. If you
are faithful to me, or sensible of my past kindness and services,
and alive to those that are to come, you will see me righted—
you will !—I am assured of it. Bind the excommunicated
wretch to his saddle, and lead him after us to a still more
silent and distant place." The men advanced to obey.

"Desperate and unprincipled madmen !" exclaimed Mr.
Somers, stepping before poor Tack'em, who set up a most
pathetic lament, " What are you about to do?—on your own
priest ! I am not one of your persuasion, but I vow to God it
makes my blood run cold ! What !—lay your hands on him !—
on the head that other hands have visited, in another spirit,
and for another purpose ! He is a degraded minister, your
leader says—what have you, or I—and, least of all, what has
he, to do with that ? How can—how dare any of you judge it ?
His Church still allows him the name of Priest, and will you
commit a ruffianly outrage on that name ? Could you ever stand
by to see it done ?"

The men hesitated ; Purcell stamped and raved ; and poor
Tack'em, now crying like a child, took off his broadbrim, and
extending his hand to Mr. Somers, said, piping all the time :
" I give your reverence thanks. I am, as you say, a degraded
priest, and a scandal to my cloth ; but I give thanks, little
worth, for your defence of an erring brother ; and as your best
reward, I promise, happy death to me, from this moment to
watch and pray, and strive and wrestle, that at last I may grow
more worthy of the fellowship I have abandoned."

He was interrupted by Purcell, who, after holding out, in
whispers, abundant reward to his party, and having succeeded
in rallying their bad determination, came on, with loud threats
to Tack'em, and cries of encouragement to them.

" Seize and bind him, I say ! Mary Grace, we once more
proceed together."

" Touch her not !" exclaimed the old man, again unexpectedly
raising his shrill voice. " And you—blind slaves of an accursed

master ! touch not the white hairs of the father, nor the holy head of God's priest ! Too long I have stood here, waitin' to see and to hear somethin' that her tears, and their words, and tears too, might work on him, but did not. Now, there is only time to ask, will ye, afther all has been said, assist Stephen Purcell in his bad scheme ?"

"They will assist me !" shouted Purcell, and was echoed by his party.

"More, then. Are you ready to stand the struggle, and do your best, if he is prevented ?"

"Prevented ! mad and doting wretch ! can *you* prevent it ?" cried Purcell.

"I say, are ye ready ?" resumed the old man.

"We are ready for anything that comes !" they answered.

"Then, Stephen Purcell," continued the aged speaker, "I do not say *I* can prevent you. But—(try to get aside, Mary Grace, with your father, an' the priest, an' the ministher, too—run for the elm-trees, an' stay behind them)—but, Purcell," the old man went on, turning to him after he had spoken the last words, in a hasty whisper, to those by his side, "maybe there's one near you that can and will. Stand out, grandson ! Harry Kavanagh, stand out !"

"Kavanagh ! Kavanagh !" shouted the person who was addressed, springing forward with Mullins from the midst of Purcell's people. "Kavanagh ! Kavanagh !" echoed Mullins. Kavanagh blew a horn that hung under his frock, and, at the sound, an overpowering force, wearing loose blue greatcoats, and strongly armed, rushed from the hollow trees. At the first intimation from the old man, Mr. Somers and Mr. Grace, apprehending the result, had contrived, with Mary and Tack'em, to edge away from the immediate ground of contest. So that when Kavanagh sounded his signal, they were within a short run of the trees, and gained them, just as, to their utter surprise, the ambushed allies issued forth from them.

CHAPTER XII.

"ON, and flash away!—Kavanagh!" continued the summoner, as the men advanced ; he taking, with Mullins, a place at their head.   All repeated his word and cry, and set, with wild shouts upon Purcell's party.

Purcell, at the first signal of attack, had also headed his men, and now made desperate resistance.   He rapidly formed them into a close body, with their backs to the hedge that fenced the hill, and thus awaited the assailants.

On they came, armed with pistols, fowling-pieces, muskets, and bayonets screwed on the ends of poles.   Before the two parties closed, a volley was exchanged between them, from the effects of which two of Kavanagh's people fell, one dead, the other wounded ; while only one man went down on Purcell's side. Amid the smoke and confusion that reigned for a moment after, Purcell judiciously got his men across the fence, over which they knelt, and, reloading their arms, prepared, in this strong position, to continue battle.

"Steal round, with six of the boys, by the slope of the hill, and attack them behind, Mullins," said Kavanagh, when he had observed this movement—"and, of all things, keep your eye on Purcell—meantime we will have another blaze at them, here." Mullins readily obeyed ; and, after a short pause, the other volley was given and returned, Kavanagh still the sufferer, by the loss of two men more, and Purcell, this time, untouched.

"Do that again, my boys!" shouted Purcell, "and the next shot we are safe, and the outlaw our own into the bargain!"

"Are you sure of it?" bellowed Mullins, now within a few yards of Purcell's back, as he and his detachment hurled themselves down the hill on the rear of the whole party.

"Now, every man up the fence!" cheered Kavanagh, pushing, with the rest of his battallion, into Purcell's front.

An appalling struggle followed.   Three of Purcell's faction lay in the trench at the back of the fence ; the rest fled over the hill, hotly pursued.   Kavanagh singled out Purcell.   Both were too close to use their pistols, and could only twist and strain for a fall.   At last Kavanagh slipt, and his antagonist, discharging at him a random shot, jumped over the hedge upon the road. Kavanagh, unarmed, was on his legs in an instant; and, in the next, and when Purcell had scarcely touched the ground outside, he made a desperate spring after, and over him, and landed on the road some yards before his foe, so that Purcell stood between him and the fence, and could not, therefore, readily escape.

Both glared at each other a moment, panting, foaming, and equally excited by effort and aversion. At last Kavanagh exclaimed:

"Do you doubt the word you heard, that you look on me so hard? Villain—accursed villain!—it is Kavanagh!" He covered him with his pistol.

"I see you, and know you well, now," answered Purcell; "but it is so long since we met, no wonder I like to look at you, Kavanagh:" and he moved a little, in order to recover an upright position, which, since his leap, he had not yet resumed, having been surprised by his pursuer in an effort to rise, so that with his body and neck half stooped and wrung round, Purcell, to this moment, returned the gaze and challenge of Kavanagh.

"Stand to me, and yield!" exclaimed Kavanagh, when he saw him move. "Love, alone, could pay you with a poor shot and a moment's pain—I owe you more than that—yield, abhorred wretch! yield!"—advancing as he spoke.

"Thus, then!" cried Purcell, suddenly discharging into Kavanagh's face a small pistol he had hitherto kept concealed. Kavanagh reeled, and fell; mechanically, but impotently, pressing his own trigger as he went down. Purcell was gone.

At this moment the old man, returning with Mullins from the pursuit, saw his grandson stretched, alone, on the ground. With a wild cry he ran, knelt, and raised him in his arms. Blood profusely flowed down Kavanagh's face from a wound in the temple. The old man commenced a heart-rending lament, of which the shrill tones soon had the effect of restoring his grandson to perception.

"Who is this?—where is Purcell?" he said, disengaging himself and standing up. The ball had only grazed his temple, and Kavanagh was no more than stunned, though, from injury done to a branch of the artery, the flow of blood was considerable.

"Curse on the false weapon or false hand that never before failed me!"—he continued—"Come, Mullins—come, grandfather—Mullins, a pistol—let us take different directions—spread out the men. Come !" and the whole party left the scene of contest.

Meanwhile, Mr. and Miss Grace, Mr. Somers, and Tack'em, had, previous to the discharge of a shot, gained the backs of the hollow trees. Of all the group, Tack'em displayed, from the first moment of danger, the greatest degree of cowardice. He fell on his knees, and alternately, in good Latin and bad English, prayed for deliverance. He groaned, he chattered, and sent forth very agonized ejaculations, as the firing and shouting increased. At last a better thought occurred. He looked round, embracing, however, a circuit of observation sufficiently prudential, and his companions could hear him mutter—"Naubocklish !—Naubocklish !—where is the unlucky baste ?—where can she be ?—Naubocklish !"—and they understood that he repeated the name of his gray mare ; which name, translated for the Britannic reader, signifies, " Never mind it." An appellation, by the way, frequently bestowed by Irish sportsmen on their favorite animals of the same species. We recollect a racing-mare of much worth, so called, on the " Curragh of Kildare ;" the Newmarket of the sister island.

But for some time, Naubocklish did not appear. It seemed, however, that Tack'em became aware of her proximity, for after a pause he was heard to add—" That's she—that's she—come, á-chorra, come, á-vourneen," accompanying these coaxing words with his best coaxing tone. Presently his party also became aware of the approach of a horse, indicated by a succession of hysteric snorting, that, if the language of quadrupeds may ever be rendered, loudly proclaimed the excessive astonishment and mortal fear of the said Naubocklish. At length she made her appearance at the side of the hollow trees, occasionally cocking or lowering her ears, standing quiet, or rearing on her hind legs and prancing upward and forward, and to this side and that, her feelings still expressed as has been intimated, and her white, sightless orbs, rolling fearfully in their sockets.

" I'll promise her oats," continued Tack'em, still muttering to himself. He took off his ample hat, and, stretching his neck as far as he dared towards the animal, shuffled his hand in the crown of the beaver, his supplicating and beguiling tones and words rapidly continued. The finesse succeeded. Wheedled out of her fears, the gaunt animal approached, with outstretched nose and neck, in the direction where Tack'em stood ; when she was within arm's length, her master dexterously succeeded in catching

her by the forelock ; after two or three unhappy failures he
next deposited himself on her back, and then, spurring with all
his might, Tack'em and Naubocklish soon disappeared over a
path diverting from the bloody plain. As they receded, her
snorts and his groans were audible through the whole roar of
battle ; and, ere they had become entirely lost in distance,
Tack'em could be seen lying down on her neck, his arms clasped
around it, while, Gilpin-like, his bald head remained uncovered ;
a distinct object even at a great distance, as the moon brilliantly
illuminated its polished surface.

After he had departed, Mr. Grace and his daughter, with their
worthy friend, Mr. Somers, continued in anxious, and by no
means unapprehensive, silence to await the result of the struggle
on the plain. The shots and yells became less and less, as Mullins pursued the defeated party over the hill : and there was
an aching pause left after Purcell and Kavanagh had terminated
their personal encounter. When the cries of the old man arose,
Mr. Somers ventured to look out towards the ground of action,
and so became a witness of the ensuing scene. And, when, in
obedience to Kavanagh's commands, all separated in pursuit of
Purcell, he communicated the state of affairs to Mr. Grace and
Mary.

"Our foes have been routed, and are fled," said Mr. Somers.
"Thanks for this great, though terrible preservation !"

"Oh ! Mr. Somers !" said Grace, "I fear we have only
escaped one bad fate for another—my poor Mary, my child !"
and in an agony of apprehension he strained his daughter to his
breast.

Mr. Somers demanded what he meant.

"You recollect the unfortunate young man, Kavanagh, about
whom we this very evening conversed ? Well, our preserver is
the same person—and—" Grace hesitated, while Mary added,
though barely above a whisper :

"My father fears, Mr. Somers, because—because—this unfortunate young man, Harry Kavanagh, was once attached to me.
And," she added, after a pause, "and I should, in truth, add—
and I to him."

Mr. Somers received this avowal with evident surprise. He
hesitated what to say, and Mary, half ashamed of having said
so much, added falteringly :

"But, Mr. Somers, we were only children. The attachment
was—was a childish one—"

7

"How can we know in what light he looks upon it?" Mr. Grace asked, in a tone of vexation.

"You fear, then, that if his affection for Mary be not forgotten, he will take advantage of the obligation you owe him to renew his attentions!"

"What else can we expect from a desperate man like him? an outlaw, and, evidently, with force at his command?"

"Do not speak so harshly, dear father," pleaded Mary; "I am sure we need not fear anything base or ungenerous from Harry Kavanagh. He had once a gentle, if not a tender heart:"— she checked herself, and an accusing blush spread over her pale cheeks.

"Why cannot we take advantage of his absence, and now, while the way is clear, fly from him?" suggested Mr. Somers.

"If you think we may venture it, come, then—come, Mary, and Heaven guide us!"

"Stay a moment, dear father, and let us rather consider," Mary said, earnestly, and spite of the painful nature of her position, rallying her clear, natural judgment. "Whatever may be Kavanagh's views towards us—whether he means to protect us to our home—or—or—in fact, to make *me* the subject of a fresh claim in his own person—still, we may be assured, he will expect to find us here, and will return to seek us. If we appear to avoid him, after receiving an obligation at his hands, how can we venture to arouse his displeasure? He has many active and desperate men at his side : were he to pursue us, we could not possibly evade him. This very moment even, I fear it would be impossible to proceed far without meeting him or some of his party. Therefore, it appears to me, that however Kavanagh may be inclined to act, there would be no use, and might be danger in doing as you say. And—oh, father!— would it not be at once ungrateful and ungenerous to attribute thus to our deliverer views ignoble and—yes, I dare add—unlike him?"

The poor girl had spoken warmly, but as she finished, her face fell in her hands, and thick sobs broke from her.

Mr. Somers drew his friend aside. "Permit me to ask you —and excuse the abruptness of the question—how far did Miss Grace, at the time she has spoken of, return the affection of this young man?"

"You probe me on a subject," answered Grace, "that this instant occupied, while it distracted my mind. I must candidly

tell you, Mr. Somers—but Mary was then a child—a mere child
—and he was quite a boy also.   Yet I must admit, that, from
my anxious observations of Mary, I though she was foolishly
partial to the lad."

" 'Then excuse another question—Do you think that in her present advocacy of Kavanagh, there is any recollection of the past,
and—any wish to renew it ?"

" God have pity on me if there be !" said Grace vehemently.

" But what do you think, my good friend ?"

" I cannot believe it, yet I fear it," he replied, with increased
d'stress and apprehension.

" Then let us, at any risk, try to escape homeward," urged
Mr. Somers.—"Your father and I, Miss Grace," again turning
to where the weeping girl stood, " have considered the matter we
were speaking about, and it seems best, after all, to remove immediately out of the presence of a desperate man—a man "—he
added with some severity—" of blasted character and ruined prospects."   But all further movement was impeded by the appearance, at the instant they were about to turn towards the hill, of
Kavanagh at one side, and Mullins at the other.   During his
absence, Kavanagh had contrived to wash the blood from his face,
and his cool easy manner was again adopted.

" Stay, Mr. Grace !" he cried, as soon as he saw the party—
" Stop, sir, till I am ready to attend you."   Then turning to
Mullins—" Have you seen him ?"

" No—nor nobody else—this time he's safe," answered Mullins
—"the only thing we found was the horses strayin' by the
wrong road, an' the two grooms looked so quare when we axed
'em !—ho ! ho !"

" He's safe but for a day," resumed Kavanagh—" For that
matter, I might at once order you and these fellows on a pursuit
he could hardly even now escape.   But here we have work yet
to do."

" You have saved us, sir, from outrage and shame," said
Grace addressing Kavanagh, as he rejoined the party.   " We
owe to you the preservation of our honor—of our lives—and we
deeply thank you."

" Do you remember me, Mr. Grace ?" demanded Kavanagh,
abruptly turning his full front to the speaker.

" After the services, you have just conferred on me, sir, I should
be forgetful, indeed, if I did not easily recognize you," replied
Grace, unwilling to admit any acquaintance of more ancient date.

Kavanagh's lips curled with a bitter smile.

"Let me inform you, Mr. Grace," he said, proudly, "that our old friendship might be renewed without odium to your name, station, or fortune. I, too, have grown wealthy since we last met. Not by such means as you suppose, either. I believe," he continued with composure, and as if following a mental calculation while he spoke—"I believe I could, this moment, purchase you, out and out, and then throw all you are worth into the bottom of the sea, and still be a man of weight."

"It is very probable, sir," said Grace, timidly.

"As to the slander I have suffered from foul tongues," Kavanagh ran on, with vivacity, "a tithe of my possessions— possessions honorably won, too, in other lands—were enough to insure eternal silence on that head. You know in your heart, sir, I have never been really guilty of a moral crime or a dis- honorable action even here in my own country. What say you, Mr. Grace, shall we be old friends on the old understanding?"

"It would afford me sincere pleasure, Mr. Kavanagh, to meet you on terms of perfect equality."

"You evade me, sir," the young man cried, with passion, his eye kindling, and his voice rising—"I can fully conceive your meaning. First, you doubt my declarations of ability to establish that character; and then, even supposing all the power on my side, you would prudently step back and watch me setting to work in the endeavor to do so, refusing your countenance, till you had ascertained my success or failure. Oh! brave—I thank you, sir, for your condescension. And so it is, the world round. So are the unfortunate, the wronged, and the oppressed, always sure to be treated. Show me the man of what you call most benevolence and charity amongst you, and I will show you the over-cautious hypocrite, who can wink, or shrug, or whisper, or cast up his eyes, over the lying story that deprives an innocent fellow-creature of rank and estimation; who will never be the first to meet him half way in his solitary struggle towards reinstatement in the world's opinion—if so contemptible a thing were worth the struggle. But, mark you, who will ever be the first—oh! yes, the very first—to hail him with the holiday smile, when he has fought, and won his own battle, and sprung, without a hand, or voice, or wish to assist him, back again to the firm ground he would never have lost, if villany and perjury were not too strong for single, unbefriended innocence!"

Kavanagh strode about in chafing silence: Grace remaining

prudently without speaking. Then, coming to a sudden **stand,** he continued :

"And, so help me God, here I am the most belied and trampled of innocent men. I have not a friend in my native land under the blessed canopy of heaven, wide and beautiful as it spreads above and around us, who would this night lend me a moment's counsel, kindness, or confidence, to save me from the worst fate, here and hereafter. Not one !—to save me from *my own* counsel—and in my state of lonely recollections and temptations—the dark things it urges me to, every hour I thrust it ! Not one to give me the composing shelter of a Christian roof, or to fling me a Christian pillow, that my aching brows might take Christian rest, and waken out of it, with Christian temper, passions, and consolations ! Not one !" The young man resumed his quick walking, every step almost a stamp, while his clenched hand was often raised to his forehead. Again, while he continued in motion :

"This, then, is no country to me !" he broke out ; "I owe it nothing—nothing but my birth, and for that I curse it, and pray that, in utter woe, it may be confounded ! It gave me nothing—nothing but a name—which, in cruelty and wrong, it wrenched from me again—why should I love it ? What are its blue hills and its pleasant fields to me—though, in distant banishment, I have thought of them, till, as the foolish tear filled my eye, their shadowy forms wavered through the sultry horizon, and the fresh noise of their streams and all their old sounds, came on my ear, and were heard in my soul, and at last I wept and sobbed to see them again ! Yet, why should I love it ? Least of all, why should I fear it ? And since it will not cherish or assist me, why should I hesitate to do, in the teeth of its arbitrary prohibition, whatever may, for a moment, assert, satisfy, and revenge me ?"

Mary Grace, who had listened with intense interest to all he said, now could not refrain from breathing one word of appeal, remonstrance, and comfort ; one word ; but its tone and spirit contained a volume of persuasion.

"Oh, Harry !" she softly cried. He stopped, turned, looked trembling upon her ; walked slowly to some distance ; again stopped ; and, after some thought, muttered something to himself in a tone so low as to be inaudible to the others.

"Young man," at this moment said Mr. Somers, "all the gratitude, all the services, we can command, are yours ; and we doubt not but your final disposal of us will still be honorable and just."

Kavanagh returned no answer. To himself he went on, unconscious of having been addressed :

"I know that once she loved me too ;—Mullins !"

"Here," answered the summoned party, walking to his side.

"Did you not say—answer me below your breath—did you
not say that to-morrow night Roving Jack is expected at the
harbor ?"

"Yes ; wid his tight ship. As fast a sailor as ever ran in an
honest hogshead."

. "How soon to weigh again ?"

"How soon? Why the same hour, if he can : just as soon as
the ship's lightened."

"Well—leave me. 'Tis a happy dream," he continued, after
Mullins had strode away : "though country be given up, I should
still have with me the only creature that now makes country
dear. And, perhaps—though my character is altered, and though
men have here stamped a brand on my name, perhaps, even yet,
Mary might remember the past, and love the outlaw."

"He does not answer," whispered Mr. Grace to Mr. Somers,
"but there stands, as if planning some desperate scheme.
Heaven befriend us."

"In truth," answered Mr. Somers, "I do not like his hesitation, and least of all his secret communication with that bravo.
Young man," he continued aloud to Kavanagh, "we have spoken
to you, to offer our thanks and gratitude, and notwithstanding
all you have said, our services, if need be."

Still Kavanagh made no answer ; did not seem, in fact, to
hear. "Yes," resumed Grace, "and to express our full reliance
on your manliness and honor."

"Can we trust you?" asked Mr. Somers, after another silent
pause.

"We can !" Mary interposed warmly.

Kavanagh caught his breath, and with face half turned
towards her, seemed to await her further speech.

"We can !" she repeated fearlessly. "Yes ! alone with him, and
in his power in a desert, I fear not the honor of our deliverer.
Whatever he does—whatever his feelings may lead him to
attempt, he will act with delicacy, and at the proper time and
season. In any views he may have, Harry Kavanagh is not
the man to imitate a villain. Harry Kavanagh is not the man
to blacken a noble action with a bad one !"

The person addressed heard this appeal evidently with deep

feeling. He pulled his hat over his brows, and changed frequently from one foot to another : as his clenched hands hung by his sides, they crushed hard within them the folds of his frock. When Mary had ceased, in the deep silence that followed, the breath was distinctly heard to labor in his throat, rapidly coming and going, as if with alarmed precipitancy it struggled to make way for a burst of combatted resolutions. He beckoned Mullins with two or three impatient motions of his hand. The man came ; when he turned quickly upon him, and, with flashing eyes fixed on his, gasped and gaped in an effort to pronounce a word : the difficulty seemed, by irritating him, to increase his paroxysm of passion. He waved his hand and arm over and over again ; and at last, stamping violently, was able to utter in a choked tone, half scream and half whisper—" Lead on !"

"Whither—whither ?" asked Grace and Mr. Somers, both advancing.

"Oh, Harry !—whither !" echoed Mary, with clasped hands and streaming eyes, confronting him.

"To your father's house !" he exclaimed, in a burst of voice ; " there we can find your proper time and season ! Mullins, get those horses sent round to meet us at the other side of the hill—and do you direct our course—I cannot—I will remain behind—lead on."

———————

CHAPTER XIII.

THE narrative left Howard and Mr. O'Clery setting out, after Nora's intelligence, in great speed to Mr. Grace's house.

They soon gained, by the short path well known to O'Clery, their destination. As the gentlemen hurried along, it occurred to both that much reliance was not to be placed on Nora's dazed information, and, all the way, they had hopes she might have misconceived or exaggerated the real circumstances.

The first thing that raised Nora's credit was the appearance of the little avenue gate, wide open. The friends looked at each other, and pushed hurriedly on to the house. As they approached the door, Howard stumbled over something :—a moment's examination showed them the dead carcass of a fine mastiff watch-dog, which it had been the intruders' first care to dispatch. This was a worse symptom :—a still worse, the hall-door remained unclosed. They entered the house. The hall and staircase were in darkness, and with some difficulty they ascended to the draw-ing-room. Here was a scene of dreary, and, to the spectators. afflicting desolation. Of four lights, two had burned out ; one lay crushed and extinguished on the carpet, and one only lent im-perfect illumination to the apartment. The fire was black : the hospitable hearth chill and cheerless. On a table near it lay, broken and disordered, the little nick-nacks usually adorning it. The chairs were disarranged or overturned, and the carpet soiled and crumpled, in token of the recent intrusion of a vulgar crowd. The window which Grace had thrown up, in order to parley with the assailants, still remained open, and at it, in the faint rays of the moon, sat a little, long-eared, silky lap-dog, Mary's own favorite, piteously howling forth his sense of abandonment and loneliness.

With rapid words of alarm and consternation, the friends ran to the door through which they had entered the room, and called, loudly and anxiously, the names of those they scarce expected to hear them. "Mr. Grace ! my dear friend, Mr. Grace !" cried O'Clery : "Mary ! my darling girl, Mary !" shouted Howard. The empty apartments and staircases feebly answered, like the inarticulate efforts of a child, a shadowy echo of the words spoken ; and deep silence again fell around. The friends snatch-ing the lighted candle, rushed through the other rooms, one by one. At last they gained what they knew to be Mary's chamber. There was her little toilet, surrounded by the books and the drawings :—upon it still lay the crucifix, the glass vase with its delicate flowers, the rosary, the prayer-book, turned down, and Howard's own miniature. As he glanced upon it, a gush of bitter grief blinded his eyes for a moment. He looked towards Mary's bed. It stood, white, pure, and unpressed, as it had been arranged for the night's repose : "O God !" he exclaimed, "and where, instead, is she to lie down to-night !" the thought was madness, and Howard, dropping into a chair, buried his face in his hands—man's bitter, hardwrung tears dropping slowly through his fingers.

Mr. O'Clery, himself deeply afflicted and agitated, strove to administer comfort to the young man, but, for some time, in vain.

"If we had even a trace of the road," said Howard, "if that

accursed woman could inform us which way they went, there might be some hope. As it is, nothing is certain but the ruin of the young lady—and—" he continued wildly—"my ruin also—I will outlive no shame that this outrage must fix on Mary Grace!"

"Hush!" O'Clery said—"here are your soldiers." The rapid and heavy tramp of the men was, indeed, now audible, as they quickly advanced up the approach to the house: "All is not yet lost with help so near us," added O'Clery. "Come, Mr. Howard, man yourself—distribute them over the country by every path and road the ravishers may possibly have taken—and, hark! that bewildered creature comes with them—I hear her shrill cries ringing through the house—come down—let us again speak to her—perhaps she is at last calm enough to collect her senses, and yield us some useful information."

They descended, and, in passing the door of the drawing-room they had first entered, Nora rushed by them, into it, and squatting herself as in the cabin, on the middle of the carpet, set up her old wail, eked out by the incessant clapping of her hands. The little dog, whom the appearance of Howard and O'Clery had for a moment diverted from his howling, now sympathetically chimed in with Nora, and a duet arose from the efforts of both, sufficient to startle the dull ear of the dead.

"'Tis hard to say which is the sillier creature," said O'Clery, as, with Howard, he advanced at Nora's back. "Silence, you obstreperous fool," he continued, addressing her. "Get up and inform us which road these ruffians have taken with your master and your young lady."

But Nora accorded no answer; neither did she suspend her part of the performance.

"Answer us, woman!" cried Howard; "tell us, if you know, which road they first pursued. Answer instantly, or I shall do something unmanly, desperate. Which road, I say?"

"Och! little duv I know. There's no one here! no one here! They're all gone! The hearth is could—could! ochoun! ochoun!" and she suddenly started on her feet, and raced up stairs, before Howard or O'Clery could stop her.

"Gracious God!" exclaimed Howard, in distraction; "the moments lapse in which a well-directed effort might be made. But I'll after her, and try one other experiment," and, separating the sheath of his sword from his belt, Howard bounded after Nora to the top of the house.

7*

" Aha ! that may do—but lay it on lightly, good fellow,"
said O'Clery, following him.

Nora's continued outcry soon led them to her presence. She
had made her way, in utter darkness, to Mary's chamber ; and,
when the friends entered with the candle, they saw her in her
usual position and gesticulation, half way between the bed and
the toilet, while, with tears plentifully rolling down her cheeks,
she went on :

" You're not in your room ! There's no one to read your
prayer-book—an' och ! a-lanna-machree ! you won't put your
darlin' white skin under your own white sheets to-night, an'
sink down among the feathers, like a lily as you are, goin'
asleep on its bed o' daisies ! You won't ! no, you won't ! mille
murthers !"

Somewhat affected by the tears and poetical lament of Nora,
Howard hesitated in the first instance to treat her too roughly.
It was not till, after repeated conjurations, she still obstinately
or heedlessly withheld all rational answer, that she felt the
scabbard gently introducing itself to her broad shoulders. At
the touch she uttered a louder cry than ever, and again succeeded in escaping from her pursuers, first through the chamber-door,
and then down the stairs.

They still followed her. She issued through the hall-door,
and looking around for the huge stone she had lately precipi-
tated from the window overhead, was moving towards it, when
her interminable moan changed into a shrill squeak, and she
hastily ran back to the door. The gentlemen, advancing, discovered the cause of her terror. Beside the stone lay the man
on whom it had fallen, his thigh crushed to pieces. Deprived of
all power to move, and weakened by pain and fear, the wretch
lay stretched on his back ; his features—made more hideous by
the black smearing they had undergone, and which was now half
rubbed off—set in an agony of dread, and his eyes staring
straight upward, with the most ghastly expression. Howard
and O'Clery shuddered at this spectacle, and could not blame
Nora for her cowardice.

The man was sufficiently sensible, however, to comprehend
what was going forward. He had heard the repeated inquiries
made of Nora, and now muttered, as the friends stood over
him :

" Don't kill me—for the love o' God an' the blessed Vargin
Mary, don't kill me entirely, an' I'll tell you where to find 'em."

"Speak, then, and truly," said Howard, "if you hope to live another moment."

The man gave a description of the route he had heard proposed by Mullins, and which was really the course taken. Howard listened eagerly ; ordered two soldiers to garrison the house till his return, and also to remove and tend the wounded man. Then, heading his party, and accompanied by O'Clery, he set off with all speed : Nora still bringing up the rear.

Along the very way they pursued, Purcell, at about the same moment, was hastening, after his escape at the elm-trees, with purpose to call on Howard and his men for assistance ; concluding, from Mullins's treachery, that such was still available. We need not try to picture his feelings at this juncture ; we need not say that all the fiends of hate, disappointment, rage, and bloody impulse possessed him even unto madness. He ran, he panted, he smote his forehead, and called on the earth to swallow, and the hills to slip and crush, his detested and successful enemy. For, at cautious distance, Purcell had stopped to ascertain the effect of his last shot, had seen Kavanagh arise, and heard him order the pursuit. By an unusual, and yet, for pedestrians, a short path, Purcell then fled, bounding forward alone, with the shouts and curses of the pursuers ringing in his ear, the effort for life and vengeance bracing his sinews, and giving all but wings to his terrible speed. He broke through fences, dashed over streams, and trampled down, indifferently, the barren heath and the pregnant furrow ; resembling, with blackest hell in his heart and on his brow, some spirit of the lowest depths, sent forth upon man's slumbering world, to blight, crush, and destroy.

Dripping with wet, his clothes torn and soiled, without a hat, and his face intensely pale and haggard, Purcell, after avoiding the wood, and the road which led to it, found himself free from pursuit, on the open ground which commenced an approach to the first bridle-road that had conducted him from Mr. Grace's house. Over this way he was holding his fierce career, when a man appeared running towards him, in a cross direction. His nerves strung up to the utmost pitch of sensitiveness, Purcell screamed out a challenge to this person, stooping, at the same time, for a large stone that lay before him, as he was now otherwise unarmed. It proved, however, to be one of his own men, flying like himself from the late scene of confusion and blood. Reassured, and, from the presence of one associate, comforted, Purcell dropped the stone from his weakened grasp, and poured forth a torrent of inquiries, imprecations, and vows of revenge. Kavanagh, Mullins, and all, should feel, he said, his arm, in time and turn.

"Come !" he continued, " Howard and the soldiers ! He is saved for me, though they don't think it ! Let us cheer them on ! Let us swear that Kavanagh himself is the man who has forced her away—that we interfered to prevent him—that we were—were—curses ! that they have, by overpowering force, reduced us to this breathless condition ! Come ! Baffled in every way—at every turn—and by that boy ; he that has ever been a stone—a rock on my path ! But we will have it yet ! Come ! The soldiers !"

"The soldiers !" echoed the sharp voice of old Kavanagh, who at that moment started, like a spectre, before him. " Dog of an informer still ! I have traced you as the hound traces his prey—stiff and worn as I am, I have traced you. Now, how do I find you here ? how, but on the ould track ? The soldiers ! What do you want with them ? Will they assist you to bring shame on another white head ? Or, crossed in your own endeavor, do you only go to loose them on the game you have before hunted down ?"

" Stand out of my way, or—I will make you stand out of it !" said Purcell, balefully glaring on the old man.

" Never ! till you unsay that word I heard, and promise at last to spare him ! Haven't you done enough ? Haven't you spent yourself on us all ? Where's my child's child ? Where is my child herself ? Never scowl and gnash your teeth at me, Purcell—where is the comfort you tore, like a villain, from me ? Where the pride and the peace of mind ? Can you make me as I was again ? Can you make me not mad, again ? Oath-breaker and robber ! Stay where you are, and answer !"

" Out of my way, wretch ! or—" Purcell gripped the old man's throat with both his hands. He, however, amid choking breath and utterance, went on :

" Aye ! aye ! do it ! do it ! Keep them round my neck till I fall stark and stiff under your hands ! Kill the old grandfather, that so you may deal on the three generations !"

Purcell persevered in his purpose till the sound of approaching feet were heard, and the man who stood by his side, crying out—" We're taken !" plunged down the slope at the left side, and disappeared. Not till then did he release the old man, and, looking forward, saw, to his great surprise and pleasure, Howard and O'Clery rapidly advancing.

"Hold! hold!" Howard exclaimed as he came up, having heard the cries of old Kavanagh. "What shameful outrage is this?"

"Seize him, Sassenach, seize him! He is the man that this night took off your Mary Grace!"—the old man gasped out, as he rapidly withdrew from the scene.

"Och! saize him! hould him fast! Hang him! Shoot him! Tear him limb from limb!" exhorted Nora, coming in front.

"Soldiers! take him prisoner!" said Howard.

"Stop, sir. You will not surely heed, Captain Howard, the ravings of a madman: all can tell you he is mad. What, Nora, do you not know me? Am I the person this old fool speaks of?" For, we had omitted to mention, Purcell, so soon as he escaped from Kavanagh's men, took care to divest himself of his red waistcoat and sash.

"Och! no! no!" responded Nora.

"You did not, then, see this man at Mr. Grace's?"

"Avoch, no!—Captain John! a-guilla-machree!—Captain John! This is a very dacent gintilmin—if he does his best for us now, I mane," added Nora, in a qualifying tone.

"I will. It is therefore I am here on my way to Captain Howard, with intelligence where to find them."

"On your way *from* them, then?" asked O'Clery.

"Yes, sir,—directly—this moment from them."

"And may I ask how you got among them, Mr. Purcell?"

"Mr. O'Clery—Captain Howard, look at me! You may guess by my appearance and manner what I have suffered and escaped at their hands. I tell you, gentlemen, that—passing the road by chance—by mere chance—I met the whole party—Mr. and Miss Grace—and Mr. Somers—and all—and giving way to my feelings—*you* know how keenly I ought to feel to see Miss Grace in such a situation, Father O'Clery—not considering what I did, I plunged into the midst of them, unarmed; and, after a desperate struggle, am here, scarcely alive to tell you my adventure."

"Were you alone as well as unarmed, sir?" still questioned O'Clery.

"Was I alone, sir? To be sure I was. Who could have been with me? I should be glad to know what you exactly mean, Mr. O'Clery.

"Why I thought that, in the present state of the country, *you* did not usually venture out at night, unattended and unarmed,

sir. But I beg your pardon a moment—Mr. Howard, a word.
By my priesthood," continued O'Clery, aside, "all this is very
mysterious, my young friend. I assume sufficient knowledge of
the human heart to be convinced, from Mr. Purcell's character
—which, moreover, I have good reasons to know—that he is not
the man to do any such exploit as he states himself the hero of.
Nor in my conscience do I believe he encountered, alone and
unarmed, the persons we are at present in pursuit of."

"This then involves the truth of his information as to their
route ?"

"I fear so. And more—do not let him see you startled when
I speak it—Purcell may be the author of this outrage himself !
Stop, for heaven's sake—and let me go on—and his present
appearance before us may be for the purpose of misleading you,
while, in the mean time, his agents shall have secured—"

"I'll run him through the heart !"—Howard broke out.

"Tut !—that would be a bad way of coming at the truth, under
the present circumstances. I wish that old man were here, who
first gave us to understand that Purcell was the true aggressor.
Why should he have his hands on the poor creature, as he came
up ? But, no matter. Suppose, Mr. Howard, you now seem to
place implicit reliance on Purcell—keeping an eye on him, meantime. If he does not immediately lead us on the track—or if, at
all events, it be finally proved he leads us wide of it—then, you
know, he will be in your power still. And, in truth if we now
reject his guidance, the country becomes, a little further on, so
full of cross-roads and difficult ways, that I see not what you
can do."

"And all this time is time wasted !" said Howard, impatiently :
then, turning round—"Mr. Purcell, we place the utmost faith on
your story and your guidance. Pray, have the goodness to fall in
with me, between these men. And now, sir, is your point far off ?"

"Not very far, Captain Howard. I will engage to lead you to
it in a little more than half an hour."

"Haste, then—which way ?"

"For the present straight on," replied Purcell.

"Come, Mr. O'Clery—soldiers, attention !—Double quick time,
and march !"

"Och, no, red-coats !—double quick time, an' run ! run ! run !"
—countermanded Nora, putting herself in motion to join the
main body. But an accident impeded her further career. To
keep clear of the soldiers, and yet trot on at their side, Nora had

deviated a little too much towards the edge of the declivity before described, and in an unlucky moment, slipt at its edge, and, losing her balance, tumbled to the bottom. There, landing on her feet, she stuck fast in a quagmire, from which, in her alarmed, debiliatted state of body, it was impossible to extricate herself.

"An' och !"—Nora cried—"here I am in throuble, an' nobody comin' to me.! Sunk apast my hams in could wather, an' mud, an' all alone ! alone ! It 'ull be the death o' me, an' not a soul near me !—An' my new quilted petticoat, an' my Sunday stockin's ! petticoat an' stockin's ! stockin's an' petticoat !"

And here we must take leave of Nora, sympathizing in her distress indeed, but too much concerned in the distresses of others to be able to lend her immediate assistance, though, no doubt, she escaped, in good time, to live over this eventful night during many a long and prosperous day.

CHAPTER XIV.

MULLINS had led his party, and those they escorted or guarded, through the wood before-mentioned, as part of Purcell's first route, when Kavanagh rode briskly up to him on the road, and said, in a low tone :

"Mullins—Purcell is coming to meet us with Howard and the soldiers. My poor grandfather has just returned from them to inform me."

"Well ?"—asked or answered the imperturbable Mullins.

"Our number is two small to check them, and it may happen we shall have to take care of ourselves."

"An' so we can, wid God's help, and others."

"You think, then, Flinn's new friends will be up ?"

"Never fear :" and both relapsed into silence.·

"He seems to keep his word, though his manner is so suspicious," said Mr. Somers to his friends, while this conversation was going forward in front—"it is certainly our road homeward."

"It is," said Grace, "and now I scarcely doubt but he will, at all events, guide us to our house."

"Do not doubt at all," said Mary.

"Hark!" resumed Somers, "I think I hear the approach of a number of persons over the high ground that leads from your residence to this road."

"If so," said Grace, "we are to be attacked again by Purcell, with a fresh body of men! He has escaped for no other purpose —the villain is too desperate to forego a settled scheme so easily!"—still the advancing footsteps were heard.

"O my God!—who are these!"—exclaimed Mary, once more beginning to tremble.

"No matter—stand close and fear nothing," said Kavanagh, passing her. Again he rode up to Mullins, and whispered, in some anxiety :

"These are the soldiers, Mullins!"

"Well?—Look far through the moonlight, into the hollow, under them, an' thry what else you can see."

"The red waistcoats, I think, by St. Denis!" Kavanagh said, exultingly, while he obeyed the suggestion of Mullins.

"These are not a crowd of common men," Mr. Somers continued to Grace ; "the regular, though rapid tramp of their advance, leads me to believe that they are soldiers."

"They *are* soldiers," exclaimed Grace, joyfully ; "I see the glancing of their caps and plumes over the edge of the height— thank God!"

Howard and his party had now, indeed, just gained a point from which the road became observable. Purcell was the first to point out the opposite phalanx in motion over it.

"There they are!" he exclaimed. "And now it is my time and opportunity to inform your reverend counsellor, Captain Howard, that I fully understood the nature of his doubts and cautions expressed to you, a little while ago, though I waited for this moment to say so."

"Praise to God!" said O'Clery to Howard, in a low voice, "these *are* the friends we seek ; I can distinctly see my dear Mary Grace in the middle of the party."

"I see her too!" exclaimed Howard : "and now an instant's pause, Mr. O'Clery. Your suspicions of Purcell seem to be ill-founded."

"Perhaps, Mr. Howard—but the whole event, and his future conduct, can alone assure me there were no reasons, of any kind, for my caution."

"I beg your pardon, Captain Howard," resumed Purcell, advancing a step towards them. "But I think I may have the benefit of whatever new hints his popish reverence thinks proper to direct to me."

"You are rash, if not intrusive, sir," Howard said, coldly.

"Very likely. This, then, I have to add, that, since I am intrusive, and, since that is the only word for my zealous services, I shall instantly withdraw homeward. You are now in sight of your enemy, Captain Howard, and can no longer require the attendance of an unarmed man like myself, whose strength and spirits are already exhausted. Indeed, recollecting that, for my first opposition and present services, I must become a mark of especial hatred and hostility to those wretches, there seems an additional reason why I should take care of myself."

"Do not let him budge an inch," whispered O'Clery, while, at the same time, he elbowed Howard rather vehemently. "You perceive our friends are returning with a party, towards their own residence, not flying from it, and this looks additionally mysterious."

"Why—what do you really think, Mr. O'Clery?"

"Nothing, specifically. My former grounds of suspicion are certainly altered, but I can't avoid resting on others, though I am not able distinctly to define them. Yet, one question—if this be really the party that perpetrated the outrage—why—I repeat—why, after such a lapse of time, do we meet them moving on the very point they should, of all others, avoid?"

"Good night, then, Captain Howard," resumed Purcell; "I shall, perhaps, find an opportunity to present my greetings to your prime minister also. But, before I go, I too claim the favor of a private word;" and he turned off with Howard; "I know the kind of enemy you have to deal with better than you can possibly know them, and this is my humble but earnest advice and request—prayer, rather—for your own sake, as well as for your friends—do not parley an instant with these ruffians. They are headed by a marked and branded outlaw—you will know him amidst all the others by his haughty air and superior dress. Run that man through the body, or blow his brains out with your own hand! Let it be your very first act! If you hesitate, beware of the consequences—*he* is sworn to do the same by you the moment he sees your face—I have the best private information of the fact; I can show it to you to-morrow morning. Therefore have a care, I say, and remember my caution."

"I shall certainly think about it, sir," said Howard ; "but as to your now leaving us—"

"There are other reasons why you should act prudently," interrupted Purcell, rapidly ; " and as this is no time for squeamishness, I shall just hint them to you. You are betrayed, Captain Howard ! betrayed by the very friends you now purpose to assist ! Listen to me—it would be too long a story, and therefore out of season, to tell you why this is the case, but I can satisfactorily prove it, along with other things, early in the morning. Now, it is sufficient to say, that Grace, aye, and his meek daughter too, have a feeling and interest for the very persons in whose power they are."

" What, sir !" cried Howard, threateningly.

" You may well be astonished, Captain Howard."

" Then, Mr. Purcell," as, calling to mind O'Clery's hints, and contrasting them with the present information, he became first confounded, and next irritated—" then, Mr. Purcell, I insist on your remaining with us till this affair is at an end, for—"

"Excuse me, Captain Howard."

" Excuse me, sir ; it must be so—you have spoken things that require to be explained on the spot—no waiting till morning—no waiting an instant, sir, beyond the opportunity for explanation—I will know what you mean in a few moments—you shall confront my friends, Mr. Purcell, and to them repeat your words, aye, and support them too. Fall in again, sir—serjeant, take care of this gentleman ; and now, forward !"

This, as O'Clery surmised, was more than Purcell had bargained for. In fact, his first burst of rage and revenge had not left him capable of framing a rational scheme. In calling upon Howard, he obeyed the undigested impulse of the moment. But while they came along he had had some time to reflect on the danger he must front in facing Mr. and Miss Grace, and Mr. Somers, after his known agency in the original aggression. Now, cursing himself, that he had at all guided Howard, Purcell's chief anxiety was to withdraw from immediate detection, while, at the same time, endeavoring, by means of incoherent misstatements, that a cooler moment would also have enabled him to reject, to prepare Howard's mind for what was inevitably at hand. In the fever of agonizing passion, of hope, fear, doubt, and dismay, it is not extraordinary that even a clever villain should thus find all his ingenuity prostrated, his cunning and consistency reduced to wild assertion.

But when Howard insisted on his remaining with the party, Purcell experienced the most desperate pang. His heart felt a spasm of despair ; and, with violent energy of manner, he blustered, entreated, and raved by turns, against the order for his detention. This strange behavior but strengthened Howard in his resolve, while he was further assisted by the approving whispers of O'Clery. Finally, when Purcell saw no possibility of escape, he could only return to his former tact, and try, by every species of falsehood, to anticipate the accusations ready to be preferred against him.

" Well, then, Captain Howard," he said, " relying on your watchful protection against the enmity of these men, I have only to press upon you the advice and cautions you have already heard. I repeat, you will find your old friends with new faces ; and, what I have not before stated, you may expect to hear them charge me in the most violent as well as improbable manner, all in defence of the individual I have before pointed out to your vengeance, and because I am, to him and them, an object of common dislike. You do not know," he added, interrupting himself, " you cannot conceive, Englishman and Protestant as you are, to what lengths the papists of this cursed country will go to stick by each other—you cannot imagine what a web of smooth deceit and treachery they can wind round you."

" Give over, sir, it is time," interrupted Howard, indignantly. " We shall soon see all this out. Come, soldiers. But I perceive these people have drawn up across the road, and wait for us."

" They have been so placed for some time," said O'Clery. " You may observe our friends still remain exposed in their centre."

" 'Tis so," said Howard, " we must go to work cautiously, then. Soldiers ! no firing in the first instance. Give them the steel, and let it be your chief object to support me in getting five or six file round the lady and her friends. When we have succeeded so far, press those fellows back, and then do your best. Take as many prisoners, however, as possible. So—forward !"

The whole party were in motion, and about two hundred yards of the sloping ground brought them to the road in front of Kavanagh's men. O'Clery and Purcell remained close in the rear, under the charge of a serjeant and two file.

O'Clery had truly described Kavanagh's position. Miss Grace, her father, and Mr. Somers, were placed in the middle of his line, fully exposed in front, though well guarded behind. At their side and back, about six men, mounted on the horses that had previously served Purcell, kept close together. Kavanagh and Mullins also remained mounted. Across the narrow road, at the right hand and at the left, the remainder of the body formed, three deep, and in good order.

The whole were less than Howard's force, whose spirits increased, as, at the first glance, he ascertained his advantage. But Howard reckoned chances, in complete ignorance of his real situation ; to explain which, we must retrograde for a moment.

After Kavanagh, in consequence of Mullins' hint, had perceived the distant approach of Flinn's reinforcement, he fell back some ten or twenty yards, and halted on the road, a good distance beyond the little valley through which, in silence and caution, his friends pushed their way. This manœuvre was effected for the purpose of inducing Howard to advance upon him, after also passing the valley, and so afford ground to the appearance, in Howard's flank and rear, of the newcomers. Kavanagh's only anxiety now was, lest he should be charged on before the arrival of his reinforcement. He was relieved by the timely and fortunate pause of the military party on the height over the valley. Gaining, therefore, while his men stood still, a point of the road in which he was concealed from the soldiers, he hoisted his handkerchief on a pole, and waved on the body under Flinn's guidance. They saw and understood his signal, and, in a few moments, were up with him, ready to be disposed of as he should direct.

We should observe, that the hollow, through which they defiled, ran at right angles to the road, and continued to run beyond it, at the other side, while the road passed across the inequality by means of a rude bridge, affording vent to a rapid mountain-stream. Along the road were fences of bank, of bush, and interstices of dry wall, formed by flat, slaty stones, laid close upon each other. The clumsy parapets, or boundaries, of the bridge, continued, on both hands, the same line of fence.

When the strange men came up, Kavanagh proceeded, briefly, but clearly, to give Flinn his orders.

"Station your men," he said, "inside the fences to that end of the bridge furthest from where mine stand. Keep them hid there until the soldiers pass you by, and until you hear a volley from us. That moment let them jump upon the road and close on Howard's rear, while we do the same at his front. Then, Flinn, we can disarm the soldiers without another shot. Remember—I will not have a trigger pulled at your side."

Flinn hastened to obey these orders ; and Kavanagh, returning to his own body, continued : " Let every man draw his bullet, keeping a charge of powder only. We need not fear that
Howard will blaze on his friends here ; and there is no use in
wasting lead, when we can have these soldiers just for stretching our hands out. Meantime, attend to what I say. Stand
perfectly quiet till I speak to you. Then fire your blank car-
tridges in their faces, and close in with your prisoners. They
dare not return your fire, but it will frighten them. Then, while
Flinn surprises them at their rear, all you have to do is to assist
in getting up the bran-new muskets and cross-belts. Mind yourselves."

For Howard now quickly advanced, after passing the valley
and bridge, crying out : " Charge ! charge ! but draw no trigger without orders !"

"A word before a blow, Mr. Howard," said Kavanagh, advancing even while he spoke. " What, sir, is this your return
to a man that has served you, and would still do so ?"

" Sullivan, by heaven! Halt, soldiers, and recover arms !"
exclaimed Howard. Then turning to Kavanagh : " Sir, that
you have served me, my gratitude must ever be a witness—you
saved my life. But I have, notwithstanding, to learn how you
would now serve me, when I find that lady in your company."

"And is it then so wonderful that I should set a few of my
poor tenants to rescue your betrothed lady, and her father,
from Captain John ?" asked Kavanagh, with composure.

" Have you, indeed, done me that service ?"

" He has rescued us !—he has ! he has !" cried Mary Grace
and Mr. Somers.

Purcell's voice was here loudly exalted, calling on Howard,
from behind. Howard attended to the summons, as, in great
perplexity, he had just resolved to question Purcell concerning
Kavanagh's assertion, backed as it was by the words of his
friends.

" These are not, then, the people into whose hands you first
traced Mr. Grace and his daughter?" he said, approaching Purcell.

" They are !—they are !—the very same ! Do not heed what
the prisoners now would say, for they *are* prisoners, and speak
under fear, or perhaps as strong a feeling. For, Captain Howard,
what I have all along hesitated through delicacy to state, must
now be plainly told,—before you met Mary Grace, she and this
bravo loved each other !"

"Scoundrel!" cried Howard, "dare you presume to assert such a thing?"

"Ask them both the question, separately. With this caution, that you do not permit them to answer except in a blunt, simple yes or no. By their own words I am ready to abide ; and you, I hope, Captain Howard, in remembrance of the danger I told you to fear from the leader of this infamous outrage."

"Come with me, then, sir, and hear the result. Mr. O'Clery, I cannot consent to your kind and zealous wishes for getting into danger ; I must use some well-meant force to keep you where you are. Sergeant, do your duty—Mr. Purcell, forward!"

They again confronted Kavanagh, and Howard precipitately asked : "What, fellow!—how do you answer to this charge?"

"Let me hear it first, fellow," retorted Kavanagh, indifferently.

"You presumed to pay attentions to Miss Grace?"

"I loved her with all my soul," was the reply.

"Speak, Miss Grace!—Mr. Grace, speak!" Howard cried, in a frenzy.

"It is true," answered Mary, in a tremulous voice.

"'Tis true," echoed Mr. Grace, "but—"

"Silence!" bellowed Purcell. "Pardon me, Captain Howard, but have you not got your answer? Now will you heed whatever evasion they may advance? Listen not to them, I advise again ; they are all leagued against you; they will, as I warned you, endeavor to baffle us; I wonder they have not begun to accuse and falsify me. Be assured, sir, there is but one way to act. Call on these fellows to lay down their arms ; if they do not instantly obey, shoot every man of them on the spot. A moment's delay may be fatal to you; give me a pistol, and I will make sure of the leader ! and oh !" Purcell continued, mentally, "heaven and the devil grant he may follow my advice ; for in the uproar of the fray is Stephen Purcell's chance, if he can ever have any, to close the mouths of every witness against him —father and all, but the girl's self !"

"I know not what to think, or how to act," said Howard after a moment's painful and confused pause. "But"—turning on Kavanagh, pistol in hand—"you are my prisoner !"

"Not yet, Ami !" Kavanagh cried, moving back.

Howard presented his pistol—

"That's the way—fire! fire!" roared Purcell.

"Oh no, no, no! hold, for God's sake! for the sake of justice!" cried Grace, Mary, and Mr. Somers, at once.

" Let me reflect for a moment," resumed Howard, lowering his pistol. " Some one—the servant, Nora—yes! She particularly informed me that the person who took away Miss Grace called himself Captain Doe."

" He did! and that person—" began Grace.

" Silence them, or they will talk us into madness!" interrupted Purcell.

" Silence! silence, I say!" said Howard, obeying, though in his bewilderment he knew not why he did so, the urgency of Purcell.

" I, at least, may speak," said Kavanagh. " He *did* call himself Doe—you hear he did ; and can I, Mr. Howard, be that person? I met you, alone and unprepared for such an attempt, a short time before it was made. More—I was in Mr. Grace's house, and resisted the assailants."

" He was!" interrupted Grace.

" I fired the only shot that was fired—and—I am now glad of it—missed my mark."

" He did, he did!" cried Grace and Mr. Somers.

" And now, when you find your friends with me, and, observe, on the way to their own home—must I not have just rescued them from Captain John?"

" It would appear so, indeed," replied Howard, completely mystified.

" It is not so!" exclaimed Purcell, scarcely knowing what he said, but impelled by a paramount feeling, to contradict Kavanagh.

" True—it is not so!" repeated Kavanagh.

" Then, what am I to think of this monstrous tissue of contrary assertion?" asked Howard, more than ever perplexed and irritated.

" I rescued them—but from the fiend that stands by your side," resumed Kavanagh, not seeming to notice Howard's perturbation.

" A lie! a black lie! Now, Captain Howard, begins the falsehood I anticipated," said Purcell.

" No, no! the truth! the truth! Will you not listen to my assurance?" ejaculated Mary.

" What! this gentleman?" said Howard.

" Yes, that black villain—Purcell!" answered Kavanagh ; " From him who calls himself Doe—he who dares attempt in other people's names what he fears to do in his own."

" Here, corporal, with two men!" exclaimed Howard. " Oh, sir," turning to Purcell, who vainly continued to assert his innocence, " you will excuse any doubt of your honor this may imply. I would only be cautious in my duty. Remove him."

"And now do you know me for the friend I am?" Kavanagh asked, again moving his horse forward.

"I do," answered Howard; "and I beg to stand excused for my mistake. It was, indeed, a mistake, every way. Even when I supposed that Doe was the leader of this violence, I should, if my proper senses had served me, have acquitted you altogether."

Kavanagh smiled, half mockingly.

"Certainly. All was misconception. In the first place, Doe could not have been the man, as he was at a distance, and surrounded by your soldiers, when the thing happened."

"But he escaped!" observed Howard.

"Indeed!" cried Kavanagh, drily.

"You cry 'Indeed!' sir. Now my memory serves, you were the first to tell me he had escaped, long before this unhappy circumstance."

"I might have mistaken. But further, as to your blunder about myself—Captain John, you know, is double my age, and black, and stouter. More like a common ruffian—is he not?"

"Many, nay, yourself told me so," answered Howard.

"I lied, then," said Kavanagh.

"Sir!"

"Though that is no reason," he resumed, speaking quickly, "why you should not now believe me, when, on the word and faith of a true man, I assure you, that Doe is as young as I am—rather like me, too. By St. Denis! like as a twin brother; Mr. Howard, as like me as—MYSELF!"

While speaking these words his hand had been busy unbuttoning the close frock that we have described as fitting tight to his figure. As he ended, laying the reins on his horse's neck, he flung it aside altogether, and displayed an inside dress, consisting of a white vest, or jacket, over which was a red waistcoat, with bunches of green ribbon for shoulder-knots, and a broad green sash round his waist. He also wore a belt, or girdle, in which were seen two cases of pistols.

Howard started back at this startling change of costume, and Grace uttered cries of consternation and despair. Mary, though she too sent forth an exclamation, seemed less alarmed. Purcell, of all the unarmed party, congratulated himself on the circumstance, as, he rapidly argued, it gave him a better opportunity for revenge, by making his deadly foe an object of marked hostility.

As all looked on in silence, Kavanagh, an instant after he had thus avowed himself, turned round to his party, and exclaimed:

"Twelfth subdivision of the flying army of the hills, show your-selves!" and immediately the men all cast off their loose great coats, and exhibited, individually, uncouth imitations of the fan-ciful, but picturesque, uniform of their young leader.

"See how they stare at us," he continued, laughing bitterly.

"Can I believe you?" asked Howard, in unabated surprise. "This armed gang, and their and your strange dress—"

"Serjeant Moonshine!" interrupted Kavanagh, exalting his voice into loud command.

"Here," answered Mullins, striding forward.

"Good. And you, Lieutenant Starlight!" he resumed, in the same tone.

"Here," said Flinn, after a short pause, which was occasioned by his running inside the fence, past Howard and his soldiers, ere he sprang over, and stood by Kavanagh's side.

"And now, my loyal officers and men, what is my own hill-name? Answer!" he still continued.

"John Doe!—John Doe!—John Doe for ever!" they all shouted, until the country rang; Lieutenant Starlight, throwing up his hat while he cheered, and catching it in mid-air, as he jumped buoyantly from the ground.

"If this indeed be true I am heartily sorry for it," said Howard, stepping back towards his soldiers.

"And why so? asked Kavanagh, or Doe, as at pleasure we may call him.

"You have served me--served me at extremity—and eternally. You have saved my life and the honor of my affianced wife. And now, to do my duty by you, which, as the king's officer, I must, will afflict me at the bottom of my soul."

"Your duty, how, ami?" queried the outlaw.

"Unhappy young man!" replied Howard, with the energy of deep feeling; "I must here seize you, to deliver you up to the outraged and impatient justice of your country."

"Two words to that, gallant friend."

"What can you mean? You would not, surely, be so foolishly desperate as to resist my disciplined force with that inferior one?"

"Indeed, I would not," returned Doe.

"And what then?—Mercy, alas! does not rest with me."

"Mercy!—That is a word unknown to my enemies, as they say it is unknown to me. Pshaw!—let us trifle no longer!—Moonshine! men! do your work at every side! Spare present life and blood, but disarm them!"

8

He had scarcely done speaking, when the party which he headed
rushed forward with tremendous cries ; and, as they had been
ordered, discharged a volley into the faces of Howard's soldiers,
Mary, her father, and his reverend friend, still in the thick of the
assaulters.   Almost at the same moment, the ambushed foes in
Howard's rear jumped upon the road at either side, broke through
his ranks, and, more than three to one, grappled with the royal
muskets, simultaneously assisted by Kavanagh's men.   The soldiers,
taken at surprise, and their arms shouldered, made little or no
resistance.   In the midst of the smoke, and flash, and explosion of
the unexpected volley levelled at them, every man in the line found
himself in the sudden grasp of at least three enemies, front and
rear, so that every effort was paralyzed.   Some few shots, indeed,
escaped them ; but this happened while they vainly struggled
against an overwhelming force, and while their pieces, already
seized by tugging hands, were pointed upward.   A few others,
who might have fired straight on, saw Howard's friends immediately before them, and remembered his orders.   In fact, a minute
had not elapsed, until Howard found himself at the head of an
unarmed body, wearing red coats and military caps, indeed, but
deprived of every other badge of warfare, as even their pouches
and belts had been ravished in a twinkling.

Himself, too, did not longer than any of his soldiers retain the
means of defence.   While all was yelling and uproar around him,
Lieutenant Starlight advanced with simply a short stick in his
hand, and—" Captain, honey," he said, " I'm comin' first, to keep
my promise wid you : I tould you in the barn that we'd show you
Doe, some time or other.   Well à-vich, sure, there he is.   An' now,
honor bright; just lend me a loan o' your soord, a moment, an' I'll
take the best care in the world o' you."

Howard only answered by a pass at his antagonist, which Flinn
skilfully parried ; they then set to, nearer to each other, and the
contest ended in Lieutenant Starlight striking the sword out of the
hands of Lieutenant Howard, flourishing it aloft, and then dropping the point.   At the same time Sergeant Moonshine came up,
dismounted, with a sword also girded round his loins, the property, a few moments before, of his more loyal brother, who now
accompanied him, as his prisoner.

Kavanagh, seeing nothing of Purcell, rapidly questioned his
officers concerning him : they could give no satisfactory answer,
and he hastened, after some preliminary orders, to seek him.

" Twelfth and fifteenth divisions of the flying army !" he

exclaimed, in his usual tone of mixed authority and humor—
"form and close your lines ! the soldiers to the rear, doubly
guarded—Lieutenant Howard, in the front, with our friends—
Starlight, look to your man !" And, through the confused crowd
that now were in bustle to obey him, Kavanagh spurred on in
search of Purcell, full of apprehension that he might have escaped.

He found him in good hands, however. In the first moment of
attack, Purcell had fled through the crowd of combatants, and
was running fast from the field, when he stumbled on O'Clery,
who, released by Mullins's capture of the serjeant in whose care
Howard had politely left him, was rushing on in a directly contrary way, to fling himself among the aggressors and exert his
voice for peace. As Purcell and he met, O'Clery, all along influ-
enced by the belief that this man had more to do with the night's
disaster than he chose to acknowledge, unceremoniously seized
him by the collar.   Purcell remonstrated, implored, threatened,
and imprecated, and at last exerted his strength to disengage
himself by trying to bring his captor to the ground. To this arrangement O'Clery demurred, and, as both were powerful men,
a desperate wrestling-match ensued between them, in which they
were seriously engaged at the instant Kavanagh came up, and
which, a second after, terminated by the prostration of Purcell ;
O'Clery falling upon him, and continuing to hold him down by
keeping his hands on his collar and a knee on his breast.

"Bravo, Father O'Clery !" shouted Doe, flinging himself from
his horse ; "I was your debtor before, but this makes me yours
for ever. May I never die in sin, bon Père," he continued,
stooping down with a belt and buckle in his hand, "if there has
been done, this night, a better deed in my honorable service.
But come, take away your knuckles from the wretch's throttle.
The belt is now tight enough. Rise, Purcell, you are *my* prisoner,
and mine only."

"Unhappy young man !" said O'Clery, "it was not for your
hands, or to your judgment, I wished to deliver this person.'"

"Chut ! never spoil a pretty action by a bad compliment.
Come, Purcell, on before me ! You will follow us, I suppose,
Mr. O'Clery ?"

They gained the main body, O'Clery attending in silence, when
Doe called out the names of Starlight and Moonshine. The men
stood by his side ; he whispered them for a moment, and they
precipitately left the road, on horseback, galloping over the
high ground that led to Mr. Grace's house.

"Have mercy on me !" said Purcell, when they had gone.

"I will not kill you *now*," answered Kavanagh.

"Where have you sent those men ?" Purcell resumed, his features displaying the wildest anxiety. Perhaps he had caught a part of Doe's whisper.

"You shall learn," answered Doe. "Have patience a while, Purcell. For, oh ! I had patience with *you*,' a patience of years and of distance—of hope and of despair ! patience, while the brain blazed, and the sick heart was rending itself with agony—while shame, and hate, and the grief that weeps not, were together fastened upon it. Be patient, therefore, in your turn." As he spoke, his face was black as the hatred he expressed, and every fibre of his frame seemed knit.

"His words are terrible ! Be merciful, Kavanagh !" said Grace. Doe took no notice. Mary also appealed to him, and he answered quickly, and with somewhat of reproach :

"I have not harmed *you*, yet, Mary Grace."

"In the name of the religion whose child you ought to be, and whose minister I am, answer *me* !" exclaimed O'Clery, standing out, erect and stern, before Kavanagh : "I fear not your daring and unlawful gang, nor your lonely power among these bare hills and solitudes, and in this dead hour of night. I fear you not, man, though the sword is in your hand, and your foes bound at your feet. Hear my voice ; in the silence of your heart, answer me ! What deed have you done ? what victory gained ? whom have you vanquished, and in whose name, and in what spirit ? Have you stood forth in the land of your birth for its pride or its happiness ? Have you overcome its foes who would give it to the sword, or its chosen soldiers whose power is from the power that hath rule from above, to watch for peace while the husbandman turns the furrow, and while the hand of labor is busy with the culture of the earth ? Crime is unwashed upon the hands of *your* unhappy followers : what crime ? Who are the widows and orphans it has made ? Were the voices that ascended for what it has done the voices of women that were as strangers to you ? Were their wailings in tones and a language strange to your ears, and to the wild echoes that gave back its outcry ? Wretched children of many sorrows and many sins ! have the wives of your bosoms, and the offspring that sat on your knees, never wept or lisped in the same cadence ? Men of blood and of outrage ! what do ye here in unnatural warfare ? While even the birds of prey have cowered in their nests, why are you, alone, disturbers of the sleep of the world, wanderers in darkness, intruders on the deep slumber of the heath and the mountain? Why are ye away from your household hearths? those hearths that are indeed chill and comfortless. But are there none to be comforted around them? Hear you not the cries of many ye have left helpless, rising in vain to you for help? Where are *they?* and what eye and hand is over *them?* Not, perhaps, the eye and hand that, by all breaches of command, heavenly and human, yourselves have averted from them. Sin not, amid all your offences, the sin of wild presumption, to say it! lay not that too flattering unction to your souls! It is declared that the curse descended on the father, shall visit him in his third and fourth generation. And are ye, miserable men, blessed or cursed, while your church proclaims you beyond the pale of her obedient children, while in bitterness only she names your names, and while her voice hath gone forth among the desert places, calling you back, as an angry shepherd, to the flock and fold you have abandoned! Woe to the ear that hath not heard that voice! To the rebel that arms himself for the battle that voice hath not ordained! To the hard-hearted and the hardened! Perishing woe on earth, and the woe of gnashing of teeth in the fire that never quencheth! Hear it from my mouth! Take it from the word of my lips! I speak it to you in your hour of bad triumph, while you are strong in your sin, while your leaders are by your side, and while your captives are delivered for a temptation and for a curse into your hands! I speak it to you while you are as a host, and while I, as a captive also, stand before you! I speak it to you in the solitude where, alone, you have dared to gather together, and where the tongues of the hills and valleys will take it up and repeat it! Woe to the hard of heart, to the deaf and obdurate, to the dweller in his sin! Die, or repent! In hope and in soul, and in the life for ever, die, or cast down the sword!"

This address, excited by the impulse of the moment, and more enthusiastic, perhaps, than the general class of O'Clery's studied exhortations, made an evident impression, which even Doe seemed in no haste to interrupt. On the contrary, he allowed some minutes to elapse in solemn silence, and then said, with much deliberation :

"I have heard you, Father O'Clery, now twice to-day, with all respect due to your character and eloquence. As all my men had not the advantage of your first exhortation, you have, under my sanctioning silence, now enjoyed an opportunity to argue with

them. And I am glad of it, because it will teach them the nature
of the influence under which I, this evening, dispatched an emmis-
sary to you, to treat for a happy, or, at least, peaceful termination
of our sad warfare. Meantime, assure yourself you have done
some good. Lieutenant Howard will, perhaps, take the same
view of the question, when he recollects the last disclosure made
to him, in the place he had the chance to thrust his head into a
few hours ago—in your company, too, Mr. O'Clery. I will not
damp your zeal by asserting that any former conviction, or change
of policy or feeling, assisted your efforts ; enough, that you have
been partially successful, and are likely to be more so. For the
present we rest here. On my own part, however, I beg to vol-
unteer an exhortation in my turn. When my government of these
poor creatures is at an end, spare them. Pity and spare the
starving creature who comes to *you*, Mr. Grace, or to you, Mr.
Somers, for whatever assistance the law's mercy allows against
the law's cruelty. Or to you, Mr. O'Clery, for those comforts or
ceremonies that sanction the interchange of the poor man's affection. Let not justice, humanity, or religion, be held out at a price
too high for the poor man's purchase. Let not mammon sit at
the right hand side of the counsellor or the judge, or kneel down
within the pale of the sanctuary. But of what do I talk ? If
you, sir, and your brethren, cannot of yourselves recollect that,
amid all his trials, his wants, his oppressions, and his crimes, the
wretch looks up to you for the comfort and forbearance you
have been sent to give—if you cannot remember this, why should
I bring it to your mind ? And now, Mr. Howard—"

"For myself I ask not mercy. The chance is yours, bold
outlaw; use it as you will," interrupted Howard.

"I will not deny, Howard," continued Doe, with a sudden
change of manner, "that, for the last month, you pressed me
harder than was courteous on your part. Worse, you checked me
from a vengeance that I had travelled far to take ; you thwarted
me beyond patience ; and I all but swore to have your life."

"If so, why did you save it ?"

"I could not suffer you to fall at the hands of this mean villain," Doe answered, with a contemptuous gesture towards
Purcell.

"He, then, was the prompting assassin ?" Howard asked.

"He was. One of his instruments intended to murder you—
and, you may remember, suffered for it. The other, my non-com-
missioned officer, Mooshine, whom Purcell slightly knew under

another name and character, told me of the plan. I was on the spot
to assist you. You passed me while I hid in that rocky recess
you thought you had fully explored—I saved you! And, *when* I
saved you, I was, perhaps, vain enough to show that I could spare
also."

" When, and how did you break through my lines ?"

" Bah! I was never in them. More than half my men, who
came up at your back just now, were, however; and, for good
reasons, I had it whispered that I headed them. Any other
question ?"

" Yes. Why did you send me this paper ?" said Howard,
presenting the notice he had before unintentionally exhibited to
Graham.

Kavanagh looked at it closely and attentively in the waning
light of the moon, and then answered :

" This is a forged note, signed Doe, commanding you to give up
your pretentions to Miss Grace. I never wrote, dictated, sent,
nor to this moment thought or knew of it. But do not be surprised ; my name is often taken in vain. For that matter, it was
popular among you before I assumed it ; before I was in the
country to do so ; and it will, I am afraid, live after me."

" But, if you did not send this paper, who then ?"

" Just ask yourself who it was that broke into her father's
house to drag her from you, for ever."

" Purcell, again ?"

" Just so," Doe answered, returning it. " And now," he continued, speaking to his party, " Forward !"

" Why, forward ?" said Howard. " Are this young lady and
her father yet your prisoners ?"

" They are yet under my protection, sir," he replied distantly
and haughtily.

" In what view ?—Do you lead them directly home ?"

" They shall pass with me directly by their own house,"
answered Kavanagh.

" By it!—not into it then ?"

" Yes, but not immediately. *Your* house lies a little further
on, in the same direction ?" he added, fixing his eyes ominously
on Purcell. Purcell winced and groaned.

" Doe," resumed Howard, " you should not be a mean, or
heartless, or cruel foe."

" Well, Howard ?—go on. What do you mean ?—we lose too
much time."

"Doe, or Sullivan, or Kavanagh—hero or devil !—Listen to me one moment—answer me one question, if you are a man."

"Out with it. I'll answer."

"Do you love her ?"

"I do."

"What are your views towards Miss Grace ?"

"Pshaw !—move on !—I will guard my own prisoner on foot. Fall back, Lieutenant Howard, from your men, and take your place with mine—draw off the soldiers, first—forward with them—proceed now, Howard. And now, your other prisoners !"

As, in quick obedience to his orders, the party of friends passed Kavanagh, O'Clery, Grace, and Somers, earnestly besought him to declare his intentions. But he only answered that he should do nothing but what a wronged, trampled man might, on his own individual account, dare, and stand accountable for. A few moments, he added, would yield satisfaction to all. Her friends unheeded, Mary again addressed him. But—

"Excuse me, Mary," he said, gravely, almost with sorrow— "we cannot converse at present. In a little time I shall, perhaps, claim that honor. Be of good heart, however. I am, this night, an armed outlaw to avenge a woman's injuries, rather than—but, excuse me—proceed !"

"I will not—cannot leave you behind, and alone with your prisoner," said O'Clery, pausing, while the rest moved forward ; "I wish to walk by your side."

"Begging your reverence's pardon, that would be inconvenient," replied Doe. "Your path is before you, Mr. O'Clery. Take it, or I shall have to call back two of my men."

"If you harm him," rejoined O'Clery, "be accursed and anathema !" and he joined his friends.

Kavanagh remained stationary with Purcell. He looked at him. He looked into his eyes as if they were but the windows of his soul, and that, through them, he could behold the despairing agony which his own heart wildly rejoiced in arousing and contemplating. All grew black and silent around them, as within them. The moon was setting, and the tramp of the receding party grew faint along the high ground that led from the road. Still neither spoke, only Kavanagh looked, and Purcell cringed like a hound. At last his captor burst into a mocking laugh—

"Now, Purcell, you think I will kill you," he said.

"I fear it, Kavanagh ; but, oh, spare me !"

"You are wrong to fear it then. I only wish to feel how my

heart would leap to my throat, and the blood boil to my fingers' ends, when, for the first time, we stood, man to man, and eye to eye, together. Now, Purcell, we follow."

" Be merciful, and I will enrich you !"

" Reptile !—no word !—no breath ! Enrich me !—with the riches you plundered from me ?—my mother ?—my sister ?—my young name ? Silence, Purcell, and on." They followed the party without another word.

CHAPTER XV.

OUR last scene necessarily changes to the grounds before Purcell's house, which lay about three hundred yards from Mr. Grace's residence, nearer to the road that led to and commanded Howard's quarters.

Here Purcell had, from time to time, undertaken considerable improvements, flattering himself that his house surpassed, in every respect, those of the old proprietors in the neighborhood. Such, indeed, was the case. It was a handsome edifice, of modern construction, and he had just planted shrubberies and groves at each side, and against the bosom of a hill that rose at its back, while in front was a spacious lawn, and a sheet of water, which he filled by turning the course of a small mountain stream that was sufficiently near him for the purpose. A high and well-built stone wall inclosed all those improvements.

Outside the wall, and immediately fronting the house, was a rising ground, that afforded a view of the whole, together with the swelling piles of mountain scenery, hurled in disorder around, and shooting up in the distance. In about half an hour after Doe had dispatched them as mentioned in the last chapter, Mullins and Flinn occupied this height. Mullins shouldered a musket, and Flinn flourished Howard's sword, as both paced up and down, like sentinels on post, and in deep and unusual silence.

" Mullins," at last said Flinn, " how very still an' quiet the house an' the place look to-night."

"Aye," his companion replied, continuing to walk about. There was another pause, again broken by Flinn, in a strange whisper: "I never saw it so lonesome an' quiet as it is this night."

8*

"You said that over an' over," observed Mullins.

"I wondher what's keepin' him," resumed Flinn. "An' I wondher, too, why he bids us meet him here, instead o' goin' up to the house."

"Because he took his holy oath," said Mullins, "never to cross the bounds o' the place while they stood in his way to cross 'em."

Again they became silent, till Flinn again rejoined, following Mullins as he strode up and down : "Jack, this seems to please you."

"It *does* plaise me," answered his comrade.

"An' I think we made sure work of it," continued Flinn.

"I think so, too," rejoined the other.

"I set fire to the house in three places."

"And I in twenty. It 'ill be a good blaze."

"I wonder what the captain intends for Purcell ?"

"Toss him in, to be sure, or he's no captain o' mine."

"You're a bloody-minded dog, Moonshine. Tell me this: did you ever fall on a good deed in your life ?"

"I did—on two."

"An' what war they ?"

"I killed a guager."

"Well ?"

"An' I shot an attorney. Don't be talkin'. Here they are."

Kavanagh, with Purcell by his side, and the rest of the party in the same order they had set out, appeared, indeed, approaching the height occupied by Flinn and Mullins.

"Have ye observed my orders well ?" he asked, when they had met. The men answered in the affirmative. He paused an instant; looked towards the house; then consigned Purcell to the care of Mullins, and, approaching Miss Grace, assisted her to descend from her horse. She set her feet on the ground, weak, trembling, and much exhausted.

"Now, and here, Mary Grace, we speak. Give me your hand, and walk forward with me."

"Harry, have pity on me !" said Mary, weeping and clinging to her father, who had also dismounted.

"Spare my child !" Grace exclaimed, detaining her.

"Touch her not—harm her not !" said Mr. Somers and Mr. O'Clery, in a breath.

"Outlaw, touch her not ! Or let it not be while I can look on—kill me, ere you injure her !" cried Howard.

"*Mère de Dieu* !" retorted Kavanagh, in rising passion, " what can you all mean ?   How have I yet harmed the lady ?   How am I disposed to harm her ?   Silence, Howard, till there is reason for your interference.   Mary, will you not advance and speak with me ?" he added, in an altered and melancholy tone.

She hesitated, wept, wrung her hands, and at last walked some paces towards him, and then suddenly dropped on her knees. " Your heart was once generous and noble ; it is yet brave, and ought to be generous !" she said.

" Rise, Mary—this must not be—must not be said—you should not kneel to me !" he cried, hastily, though gently, compelling her to rise.

" Pity a weak and trembling girl !" rejoined Mary, now submitting to be led forward.

" Be calm, for God's sake, and hear me," said Kavanagh, when they had gained a rather distant place : " Mary, you loved me once."

" I did—but—"

" You did, you *did* !" vehemently interrupting her.

" Oh, Kavanagh, that is *not* generous !   You—you speak of a time when we were children together.   A very childish time— I could not *love* then."

" I could, and did.   I loved you with my whole heart, soul, and hope.   A villain cast my hopes to the wind—I left you and my native country, in despair and nominal infamy, and I loved you still.   I settled in a distant land, and, under a changed name, sought knowledge, and wealth, and station—aye, and won them—partly for my revenge, partly for my love of you.   I have come back to my country, and now my revenge is in my grasp— but you, Mary—oh, Mary ! Mary !—you do not love me still."

" Oh, no, no, no !" the girl cried, with bent head, yet in earnest tones. " My heart, my promise, almost my duty, are another's."

" And that other is Howard ?"

" Howard—and no man else.   Now and for ever."

" Swear to me by heaven that you love him."

Mary, urged by her feelings and the situation, wildly gave the oath demanded of her.

He paused ; his eyes fell on the earth : he groaned aloud. Then starting into sudden vehemence, he cried : " Answer me one question, on the pledge of your immortal soul !   If you were freed, without your own concurrence, of these merely prudent engagements, and if you saw and were sure of wealth, rank, and

fair name, to be shared with the object of your earliest love—
with Kavanagh—"

"Never!" she interrupted, wildly, yet with trembling energy ;
"Call them not prudent engagements only—I repeat, in the
divine presence—"

"Stop, Mary, and hear me out! The earth is wide, and upon
her spreading bosom there are hills and pleasant valleys, fairer
and richer than even the hills and valleys of this green land. The
sun shines more kindly upon them ; their airs are softer, their
groves and flowers brighter. Oh, Mary! their solitudes, beyond
the blasting voice of man and man's hatred, breathe out a para-
dise! And with you, as the lady and the queen of their silent
beauty, how happy I could live and die! How happy, after all
I have suffered! and how changed! From what I was, from
what I am! If you hate me now, from what I must ever be. Do
not cast me off, Mary!" he continued, falling in his turn at her
feet. "Save me from this world and the next."

"Rise, oh, rise, Harry—you are not to be lost—God never
made you to be lost, nor to be an outcast from men! Think of
your God, and pray to him for light and patience! I—I will
pray for you on my bended knees, in the morning when I get up,
and in the night before I lie down to sleep—I will pray for you
in tears, in trembling, and in remembrance of the past. But,
Kavanagh, expect no more from Mary Grace. In the divine
presence, I repeat, he is proudly and fondly beloved by Mary,
and no man, and no circumstance, can make him less so!"

"This you swear," said he, suddenly rising.

"I swear it!"

His brow fell blackly. He took her hand, and, walking rapidly, led her back to her father. Then, after a moment's silence,
turning to Purcell, he shrieked out :

"Monster! my destroyer every way! Behold another cup
of earthly happiness—the sweetest, the purest of all—your hand
has dashed from my lips! You sent me—banished me—tore
me from her! You took away the name and the means for
native exertion, and all the opportunity, in and by which I might
have continued present with her, and worthy of her love. You
branded and outlawed me, till she first learned to fear, and
then—abhor me! God, oh God! this is the hardest stroke !"

"Kavanagh, be just—I am not the man that injured you,"
said Purcell.

"Not! must I again repeat how often and how deadly? My poor

mother ! wretch ! my gentle, kind, and good mother ! My blooming, happy, and, till you damned her, my sweet and innocent Cauthleen ! my only sister and my only shame ! Wronged me ! Injured me ! Oh, deep and cool villain !   See these scalding tears, and hear this shivering voice, made childish by a recollection of all your wrongs, and then, fiend as you are, say not that word again !"

He crossed and pressed his extended hands over his face, and the plentiful tears burst, indeed, through the interstices of his fingers.

" Divil a dhrop 'nd come, Starlight, only for this girl wid the white face," said Mullins to Flinn, as they observed the scene. " Myself wondhers what ails him, about her, when 'tis only to give us the word, an' he has her still."

" I wondher, too," answered Flinn.

" I'll jog him on the business, an' get him out o' this soft fit," continued Mullins. He strode to Kavanagh, and whispered ; " Captain, musha, Captain—no more of it now. Only tell us which way to run wid the girl—down to the coast, eh ?"

" Silence, and keep your place !" exclaimed Kavanagh, stamping at him. Mullins withdrew, uttering an " avoch ;" and his captain went on, still addressing Purcell—" Look at these unhappy men, and learn, over and over, how you have cursed me ! I found them, indeed, ripe for my purpose—and some of them stained with crimes that, under me, they should never have committed : my revenge alone could have sought their fellowship. I leagued with them, professedly for their views, but really for my own. But I leagued with them—have led and encouraged them—and stand accountable, before heaven and man, for their late perserverance in outrage. Purcell, Purcell, have you not wronged me ?"

Purcell, starting and clasping his hands, here uttered a loud cry. " Lights in my house ! in every window !" he exclaimed. " What is this ?"

" Lights in your house ? And in hell, tyrant !—a shadow of the flame that shall soon, and for ever, swathe you ! Look again ! 'tis brighter and redder than the midnight blaze that shone over your costly feasts, and on the worms that crawled round to share them !—Look again."

The fierce light grew stronger at all the windows ; then waned, and then flared out again, as it proceeded in its destroying course.

" My house on fire ! my property wrecked ! my papers ! my wealth ! my all !—And was it for this, plunderer and assassin,

—was it for this you led me here ?" he continued, turning in fury on Kavanagh.

"For this ?—Fool, fool, prepare yourself!—if you have ever learned a prayer, repeat it."

Mercy ! I am now below your vengeance !" cried Purcell, suddenly changing his tone and manner. "I am a beggar, and at your feet ! Look on me, I am at your feet !"

"There would I have you be ! By the round world, I have prayed and wept for it! For such a scene and hour I have thirsted, and my tongue hath burned with thirst !—Thus, in my dreams I have seen it, and shrieked and laughed to see it !—Look at your house again !"

While he spoke, the crackling of slates and glass was heard, and, a second after, the flame shot out through the windows and door, clear and straight, like a broadside from some great war-ship. Immediately followed the smoke—the volumes of smoke, massy, thick, and curling, and showing, amid the red light and the murky relief of the hills around, white as a morning vapor that the sun calls from the bottom of the valley. The moon had set, and here and there in the sky black wreaths of clouds moved, swollen and slowly along ; while through them, and between them, the "chaste stars" glimmered wildly on the phenomenon, reduced, by the contrast of lurid light, to the appearance of cold, silvery specks set in a frozen ground of intense blue. The side of every hill and every break, for miles adjacent, caught the sudden glow, removing it fainter and further, into almost desert solitude, till at last it was devoured by remotest darkness. But the rugged features of all the nearer heights became fitfully developed in the blaze, and, grim and haggard, broke out into the night ; nay, at a very considerable distance, high peaks, white in snow, blushed faintly, and without form, like the shadowy indications of grand scenery caught and lost in a dream. The lawn immediately before the house seemed perishing in light, and the sheet of water, flaming like molten ore, reflected and heightened the immediate horrors and magnificence of the scene.

"Now, and at last," continued Kavanagh, "amid this general wreck of your ill-got fortune, bane of my wordly hopes and happiness !—amid—"

"Hold ! hold !" cried Mary, her father, and the two clergymen springing forward, as Kavanagh stood over Purcell, tugging at a pistol that was held in his belt—

"Henry Kavanagh ! stain not your hands with his blood !

Leave him to God and his country ! You said I hated you—I do not—I never did—but now, force me not to abhor !" exclaimed Mary.

"Then, I will not, myself, deal with him," said Kavanagh. "I have never yet coolly shed blood; and the only drop I ever shed was this night, in protecting the life of him who is most dear to you, Mary. But, Starlight !—lead him down amongst you."

"Most unhappy man !" said O'Clery, "you dare not assume the disposal of his life ! In my presence, whose voice is the voice of that religion you are bound to hear and obey—you dare not !" and he stept between Doe and his victim. Mr. Somers also interfered to the same purpose. Kavanagh stood a moment silent, whispered Mullins, and then spoke out.

"I am willing, reverend gentlemen, to be guided by what you say. Only answer me one question. Is it not set down—an eye for an eye, and a life for a life ?"

"It is," they answered; "but the power to exact the penalty lies in the law and authority of the land."

"It is," he continued, not seeming to notice the latter part of the answer: "this man, then, for the life of her who was my mother, and which he has cut short, deserves to lose his own ?"

"For his crimes of this night his life is forfeit, whatever may have been his previous course," they replied. "But, again, we say to you, leave him to pay the forfeit to those who alone can justly claim it, and imbrue not your individual and unpermitted hands in murder."

"He deserves to die ! you have said it. Are there no other voices here to give in a verdict ?"

"He deserves it," answered all of Doe's party, in a deep mutter of many voices—"take his life."

"You have, yourselves, uttered the word, and now you hear its echo," resumed Doe, still speaking to the clergymen. "I have not skill nor time to argue the other question. Enough, if I feel that the permission was spoken to all mankind, as well as to a few; and to you or me, as well as to any others—to the injured, if to any; to the heart made desolate, and to the survivor left alone. Therefore, my officers, away with him !" he continued, in a sudden change of voice, as Mullins and Flinn, by an unobserved manœuvre, and in obedience to his former whisper, had fastened their talons in Purcell, and were dragging him along—"Take him to his own threshold—there—put him out of pain—shoot him—and then—"

He was interrupted by cries of intercession from the clergymen, who hastened after the men, from Mary, her father, and
Howard; and by despairing appeals from Purcell, whose arms
had escaped from the belt.

"Come wid us out of his way—he's always dangerous in a
passion," croaked Mullins, tugging him off.

"Kavanagh, have mercy on me!—Captain Howard!—Mr.
O'Clery!—Miss Grace!—speak for me!—a word!—a single
word!" the wretch continued.

"Come, don't give us any more o' your nonsense; come, we'll
be kind to you," Mullins continued. By this time, O'Clery had
reached them, and, with his clenched hand, knocked down Flinn.
Purcell, a little relieved, struggled some steps with Mullins towards the edge of the abrupt height on which they were situated. Here both fell, and ere O'Clery could further interfere,
they rolled down the side of the steep, grappled in each other,
and straining and foaming at every turn over. They were stopt
by the high wall that arose immediately at the bottom. Half a
dozen men rushed after them, intercepting O'Clery; but, ere any
could reach the spot, the report of a pistol, followed by a groan,
was heard.

In a moment the men re-emerged from the hollow, bearing
Purcell by his arms, legs, and feet between them. His face was
sprinkled with blood; his eyes projected, without winking, from
their sockets; despair seemed to have fastened on all his features,
and yet the remnant of a hideous smile was about his mouth.

"Why does he smile?—where is Moonshine?" asked Kavanagh. "Who fired the shot?" he continued, when the men did
not instantly answer. It was Purcell, who, in the struggle at
the bottom of the wall, had snatched a pistol from Mullins's
girdle, and, with the muzzle at his breast, literally shot him
through the heart.

"Poor Jack is gone from us," the men answered at last.
"What are we to do with Purcell?"

"Flinn will tell you. Lead him off!—let me not again look
on him. He makes the flesh of a man creep and run cold!"
cried Kavanagh. They instantly bore away their prisoner, Flinn
leading them: and Purcell, stupified, and still wearing his fearful smile, now said not a word.

"Your hand, again, Mary Grace, resumed Kavanagh, when
they had left the height, "and be quick—be quick! Why do
you draw back and shiver? Mine is not yet blotched. Howard!

—men, let him advance ! here—take her—she is yours—you will be kind to her, for her own sake, for my sake, Howard— I saved your life—you are free. In the morning send your soldiers to the barn, and they shall there find their arms, along with those you saw, and others—now they are free also."

"Still generous, though utterly lost !" cried Mary—"Kavanagh ! call back that dreadful command !"

"Noble, though unfortunate man ! leave him, as all of us exhort you, to the laws he has this night outraged—give up your desperate courses, and if my friendship—" Howard was going on when Doe broke in with—

"Peace ! I give them up, because I had intended it. Miserable and misguided creatures ! return even to the oppression you would vainly oppose, and to the hard lot that, embittered as it is by utter poverty and cruel neglect, you can never hope thus to improve. Traitors I will not call ye ; but men of many crimes ye are, even as a higher voice has said it. Forgive me the bad example I set—reform, repent, and be industrious. This gallant and honorable officer, and all the gentlemen that hear me, will, if you deserve it, be to you the friends they kindly wished to be to me."

"We will ! But what is your own fate ?" asked Howard.

"No matter what. Better, perhaps, than I merit. To-morrow night I sail from my native land, to resume, in a distant one, other acquaintances and another station. But hark to that !" he exclaimed, pointing to the house.

A sudden explosion of fire-arms reached them. Almost at the same moment, the roof of Purcell's house fell in, and one tremendous spire of flame darted to the heavens, illuminating for a few seconds more fiercely than ever, all contiguous objects, and even the remotest distances. Then succeeded the vomiting and expanding smoke, and the red fragments of burnt timber that the exploding air impelled upward. Then almost utter darkness wrapped once more the hills, the fields, and the blotted sky. But, ere thickest shadow had veiled the countenances of all near him, Howard, for the first time, brought to mind, while looking on Kavanagh, the features of the young man who had so much interested him in the tent, on the evening of the pattern.

While all paused in consternation, Doe continued : "'Tis over ! Mother and Sister, you are revenged ! Yet, now I hear that sound, and see that sight in more sorrow than my first yearnings promised—Who comes ?" interrupting himself, as the faint but wild cry of a woman was heard; immediately after, Cauthleen tottered forward, and sank at his feet, exclaiming :

"Brother, spare me, 'tis poor Cauthleen."

"Spare you, my poor girl, spare you !" he repeated. "Rise, come to your brother's heart. You have a brother still ! I did not think to see you so soon, Cauthleen," he continued, pressing his flushed cheek to her pale one ; "but—but—oh, Cauthleen ! Sister !" The young man bowed and wept on her neck.

"I always loved you, Harry—and—I—hoped—I—" she could not, amid sobbings and chokings, utter the words, till she sank, fainting, in his arms.

"The health has faded from your cheek, my girl," he resumed, "and you are worn and wasted—a shadow of my once beautiful Cauthleen! 'tis over! Looking around : "Farewell all and everything, but this poor bruised flower, which, to raise up and nurse, and call back to bloom, must now be my life's only care and occupation ! Farewell, country ! my native hills—my hearth made desolate—my lost love ! Mary, I ask not now to touch your hand with mine—farewell !"

He bore his insensible sister on his arm down the hill, and was followed by all his party : Mr. Grace, Mary, Howard, their reverend friends, and the disarmed soldiers remaining behind. Never again were the outcast brother and sister heard of in the land of their birth, their sorrows, and their crimes.